THE WIDOWS' GUIDE TO MURDER

AMANDA ASHBY

Storm

Ebook ISBN: 978-1-80508-794-6
Paperback ISBN: 978-1-80508-796-0

Cover design: Emily Courdelle
Cover images: Shutterstock

Published by Storm Publishing.
For further information, visit:
www.stormpublishing.co

ALSO BY AMANDA ASHBY

The Widows' Guide to Backstabbing

Domestic thrillers

The Stepmother

The Ex-Wife

I Will Find You

Remember Me?

Romance – adult

Once in a Blue Moon

What Were You Thinking, Paige Taylor?

Falling for the Best Man

Dating the Wrong Mr. Right

You Had Me at Halo

Romance – young adult

How to Kiss Your Enemy

How to Kiss Your Crush

How to Kiss a Bad Boy

The Heartbreak Cure

The Wedding Planner's Baby

Middle Grade – paranormal adventures

Midnight Reynolds and the Phantom Circus

Midnight Reynolds and the Agency of Spectral Protection

Midnight Reynolds and the Spectral Transformer

Wishful Thinking

Under a Spell

Out of Sight

Young Adult – paranormal adventures

Demonosity

Fairy Bad Day

Zombie Queen of Newbury High

ONE

'Take this book and go and read it to them.'

'Read it out loud?' Ginny Cole's jaw dropped. She wasn't someone who stated the obvious but surely there had been a misunderstanding.

'Do I really need to answer that? This is a *library*, after all.' Louisa Farnsworth raised an arched eyebrow. She was probably in her mid-forties with a straight nose, very blonde hair and a curvy figure that was currently wrapped in a fitted black dress.

Ginny suspected the dress was from some expensive label she'd never heard of. Her own outfit was the same white linen shirt and navy trousers that had been selected for comfort and practicality. She'd built up her wardrobe ever since her marriage to Eric, thirty-five years ago, when she'd taken over the job of running his surgery. She'd only been twenty-five at the time and had quickly learnt no one was looking at her. She was good at being in the background, making sure things ran smoothly. 'But I'm not familiar with the story.' Ginny clutched the picture book her new manager had thrust at her.

A group of mothers had gathered in the dark corner of the gloomy library. Some were in chairs, while others leaned against well-worn cushions as they tried to contain small, screaming children.

'They're a bunch of two-year-olds. They don't know it either. I'm not sure why you're looking so surprised. You did apply to work in a library.' Louisa flipped open the grey leather-bound diary she'd been holding, as if to confirm Ginny was in fact the correct person. Then she let out a disappointed sigh and closed the diary.

Ginny tried not to wilt under the unspoken jab at her character.

It was true she'd applied to become the part-time librarian in the small Lancashire village of Little Shaw, tucked deep in the Rossendale Valley and surrounded by moors. She'd only moved there from Bristol two weeks ago, and honestly hadn't expected to get the position at the community-run library, which had been taken over by the parish after funding cuts had threatened to see it close. But after a short interview with the chairperson, Marigold Bentley, on Friday, she'd been offered the job on the spot.

There had been no mention of story time, or Louisa Farnsworth for that matter. And it was clear that Marigold hadn't told Louisa much about Ginny either. Had the library manager been expecting someone younger? Less drab? Better at spontaneously reading picture books to children?

'It's my first day. I thought there would be an orientation before we started.' She hated how meek she sounded.

A lifetime of practice would do that to a person.

'Books. Toilets. Issue counter.' Louisa jabbed a perfectly manicured fingernail in different directions around the room, like a traffic warden tired of doing the same job again and again. 'Consider yourself orientated. Now, go and read the book. And once you've finished, I'll show you how to use the computer. You *can* use a computer, can't you?'

'Yes.' Ginny tightened her grip on the well-worn book cover and tried not to notice how much her hands were shaking.

Maybe Nancy had been right.

Her sister-in-law kept telling Ginny that Eric wouldn't judge her for selling the quaint semi-detached house that they'd bought for their retirement. But eight months after his unexpected death, Ginny had been determined to continue with the plans they'd made together. What she hadn't expected was the drop in her income, or the need to get a part-time job so late in life.

Or the horrible void that clung to her like a shadow.

'Hmmmm.' Louisa sniffed, then turned on her high heels and swept back across the library, ignoring several people as she went.

'How much longer?' one of the mothers asked, desperately gripping a small girl who was doing some kind of strange body contortion. 'It was meant to start ten minutes ago.'

'Sorry. It's my first day,' Ginny said, as another child made a dive for her ankles. She managed to keep her balance, but only just.

'Nelson. None of that,' the child's mother scolded but made no effort to collect him. 'Miss is going to read you a book, aren't you, miss?'

'Y-yes. I guess I am.' Ginny studied the tiny seat that was waiting for her. It was made for a young child, which meant it was also made for a young bottom and knees, and not the slightly arthritic joints of a sixty-year-old widow who had been comfort-eating a few too many Bakewell tarts ever since the funeral.

She eased herself down, and gamely looked at the cover. *Rabbit and Bear Learn to Sing.* Well, that didn't sound too dreadful. Feeling buoyed, she turned the page to a lovely water-colour picture of a rabbit and a bear sitting in the middle of a field of spring flowers. Unfortunately, someone had used a

Sharpie to draw in whiskers, vampire teeth and what Ginny could only presume were toilets.

It was going to be a long morning.

By three in the afternoon, Ginny realised that the horrific story time had been one of the highlights. Which wasn't to say it had gone well. Disaster would be closer to the truth. Her voice was too soft to be heard, and she didn't have the natural pacing or intonation that a good narrator needed. Eric had always been better at that sort of thing.

He'd done a lot of amateur dramatics while studying medicine and she sometimes thought that's what had given him his wonderful bedside manner. Of course, if Eric was alive, she wouldn't have moved to Little Shaw on her own. Or needed to start a new career at this time in her life.

In her defence, she'd only applied for the job because she thought she *would* be suited to it. She loved reading, was quiet by nature, and had spent plenty of time at the Clifton library. Not to mention the appeal of the Little Shaw library, set as it was in an old parish school made of rough-weathered stone, with a small park to one side of it, complete with a fountain.

But the inside had proved to be dreary, with dull lighting and mismatched furniture that had been kicked, bumped and scratched one too many times. Ginny longed to brighten it with fresh flowers and some cheerful cushions. And to get rid of all the dust that coated so many of the surfaces.

'Are you listening to me?' Louisa hovered over Ginny's shoulder, barking instructions on how to use the catalogue. She pushed aside her mental redecorating and nodded.

'Yes, you're showing me how to sign up a new member.' At least in this she felt more comfortable. The system was less complicated than the one they'd used at the surgery, and Ginny diligently kept her notebook by her side, writing everything down as Louisa powered through how to navigate the various screens. A training manual would have been useful, but five hours with Louisa had already taught Ginny not to ask too many questions.

'Good, and now we will—' Louisa broke off with a snarl and stalked to the front of the library, where a woman in her mid-seventies was standing. 'Esme Wicks, you are barred from here. Barred, do you hear me?'

'I think everyone can hear you.' Esme had a startling silvery bowl-cut, and a wide smile that seemed to grow as she patted the lumpy bag hanging from her shoulder. 'Though you might want to keep your voice down. I heard the manager's a real dragon.'

Louisa's dark eyes narrowed, and her shoulders stiffened. 'How dare you. I've already reported you to the police. Don't think I won't do it again.'

'Oh... this will be fun.' A man who had been studying the nearby book display of new releases grinned. 'It's been at least three days since their last fight.'

'Last fight?' Ginny's brows knitted together. 'What's happening?'

'Esme was banned two months ago because she hasn't paid her library fines. However, she says she should never have been charged because the DVD had the wrong disc in it, therefore it's like a double jeopardy.'

'And who's to blame the poor love? You don't pay good money to see Richard Armitage in *North and South* only to end up with Jeremy ruddy Clarkson,' a second person joined in. 'So now Esme's running a one-woman protest outside. On account of her civil liberties. But Louisa Farnsworth doesn't give two hoots about civil liberties and refuses to let her step foot across the door until the fine is paid. Won't even give her an OAP discount. Rude, if you ask me.'

As if on cue Esme lowered the bag to the ground and a

skinny black cat emerged. Its golden eyes narrowed, and it stared at Louisa as it stalked towards a display of knitting books.

'Don't you dare,' she warned. But the cat just let out a low hiss and stretched out its long body. Then it jumped, sending the books flying in all directions.

'Now that right there is a power move. That stray cat has been hanging around for weeks and seems to like tormenting Louisa just as much as Esme does.' The man at the book display let out a low whistle.

'Get out, you old witch, and take your blasted cat with you.'

'Not my cat. And not my path that it just crossed. Guess that's seven years' bad luck for you.' Esme beamed and disappeared outside.

'That's for breaking mirrors!' Louisa shouted as she cornered the cat and shepherded the small thing out of the door. Then her icy glare swept across the many customers who had been following her progress. 'Is there anyone who wants to join Esme out there? Just say the word.'

It had the effect of silencing the room and the two customers who'd been giving Ginny a running commentary scuttled away.

'Is everything okay?' Ginny asked, once Louisa had returned to the counter.

'I swear if I see that filthy animal one more time, I'm going to scream. Someone must be feeding the dratted thing.'

'If it's a stray, shouldn't we take it to the vet and see if it has been microchipped?'

'See if it's been microchipped?' Disdain dripped from Louisa's words like icicles. 'We're not paid to run a charity service. Which is why *now* is a good time to go over our late fees. They are non-negotiable. Everything must be paid in full. No exceptions. Just because we're community run, doesn't mean we don't need the money.'

Ginny opened her mouth to protest. She'd worked with

enough distressed patients over the years to know just how tight money could be, and what a strain it could cause for them and their families. But Louisa shot her a quelling glare.

'Right. We don't waive fines. So, how do we take the payments?'

'We have cash and card. But *no* cheques.' Louisa detailed the process in a rapid-fire monologue, only stopping when her phone buzzed. She snatched it up and answered, without missing a beat. 'What?'

There was silence as whoever was on the end was talking to her. Louisa's face darkened and Ginny immediately felt sorry for the caller.

'Ridiculous. You must be able to fit me in. I can't walk around with a missing acrylic nail. It's clearly shoddy work.' The library manager waved her hand around and Ginny could see that one of the blood-red nails from this morning was indeed now missing. There were several more seconds of silence before Louisa jabbed her phone. Her large diamond wedding ring glittered in the afternoon sun.

'Incompetent people. I need to go there now. One of the volunteers can work on the desk while I'm gone, and you can clean up the reading corner and get it ready for the knitting group. They are allowed tea and coffee but do not on *any* account give them biscuits. Once that's finished, you can shelve. Start in the seven hundreds.'

It was all said in a way that suggested Ginny should know what any of it meant. Without waiting for a reply, Louisa stalked away, leaving Ginny with the sinking feeling that she'd made a terrible mistake.

By the end of the day Ginny's feet ached and there was a dull thud between her brows where a headache was forming. But it lessened as she stepped out into the late September afternoon.

Even in autumn, the village of Little Shaw really was delightful. It had once been home to several small mills, during the Industrial Revolution, though none as large as those in the surrounding towns, which perhaps explained the lower population.

A narrow stream ran through the centre, while an arched stone bridge connected both sides together. As she crossed, willow trees groaned and swayed in the breeze, the leaves now turned a gleaming bronze.

There was an ancient stone church at one end of the lane, and looking back across the stream was a seventeenth-century pub called The Lost Goat. Several people were huddled around the outdoor tables, braving the cooling temperatures. Ginny knew the chalkboard had a daily witticism written up. Today it read: *I can't fix the weather, but I can fix a drink.*

The high street was further along, and consisted of a collection of shops, including a post office, an old-fashioned grocery store, and even a quintessential haberdashery, which looked like the Bennet sisters might step out of at any time. A cobblestone street snaked up the side of the valley to more cobbled streets and sloping terrace houses, but Ginny turned right and continued along the level road leading out of the village, turning left at a small junction. It was a pleasant walk and ten minutes later she had reached her new home.

It was a tidy semi-detached property built with the same matte yellow stone that typified the area. According to the estate agent, it had always been known as Middle Cottage. Probably for the same reason that someone had called the road Ten Mile Lane, despite it only being a mile long.

The bricks had been restored, windows replaced, and the front door was a cheery pastel pink, which – Ginny didn't dare admit to anyone – was one of the reasons she had fallen in love with it when they'd viewed it last year. Eric had been more transfixed by the lovely garden at the back. There was enough room at the front for her car, and to house her pots of lavender and herbs, but she had plans to add a bench seat and plant some bulbs. Though that was for another day. Right then, all she wanted was a cup of tea.

She took off her white sneakers, which were now covered in damp leaves, and left them under the small bench by the front door to clean later.

'Oh, love. You wouldn't believe the day I've had. Let me just put on the kettle and I'll tell you all about it.'

There was no answer as Ginny stepped into her slippers and headed to the kitchen at the back of the house. It didn't shock her as much now. In fact, it would be more shocking if Eric *had* answered, since she didn't particularly believe in the afterlife. Yet she couldn't break the habit of talking to him.

Still, it wasn't like it was hurting anyone.

Tea in hand, she went through to the front sitting room. The removal company had managed to fit in the sofa they'd bought together just after they were married. The soft pink and green Sanderson roses were faded and it was in need of recovering but she couldn't bring herself to do it, in the same way she couldn't leave it behind. Besides, it matched the pale Turkish rug and the low wooden coffee table.

She looked over to the blue wingback chair in the corner and started filling Eric in on her first day. It only ended when her phone rang, and Nancy's name flashed up on the screen. Ginny sighed. Part of her wanted to ignore it, but her sister-in-law would just keep trying.

'So, tell me how it went,' Nancy demanded as way of greeting.

'It was fine. Everyone was very friendly and welcoming.'

'Virginia Cole, I've known you for over half your life. I can tell when you're lying. What really happened?'

Ginny closed her eyes. This was the other reason why she'd

hoped to avoid the call. But she had to get it over with at some stage.

'The manager seemed to think I'd worked in a library before, so there wasn't much training. It probably doesn't help that I haven't had to start a new job in such a long time. I'm very rusty, and I do hate not knowing how everything works and where the paperclips should live.'

'You're the least rusty person I know. At least where work is concerned. Was she younger than you? Maybe she was intimidated by your experience or age?'

'No, that definitely wasn't the issue.' Ginny recalled Louisa's snappish manner and derogatory glances. 'She's very glamorous and doesn't seem to have much patience. I'm not sure she even likes people.'

'And she works in a village library? Sounds like an odd fit. Anyway, tell me what else you've been up to. Have you met any of the neighbours? Invited them in for a cup of tea?'

'I've been busy getting everything unpacked, and then I had to get ready for the job interview. Which did involve meeting people. Well, *a* person. And, of course, now I'm working five days a week I'll talk to all sorts of folk.'

'Yes, but you can't just talk to them in that polite way of yours, and then lock yourself up in the house. What's the point of starting a new life if it looks exactly like your old life?'

Ginny tried not to look at all her furniture. Or her comfortable slippers and favourite teacup that she was currently clutching. She knew Nancy was right. It was like Ginny constantly had a glass wall between her and the rest of the world. And that no matter how hard she tried, she couldn't cross back over to the other side.

She was saved from answering by the sound of Nancy's husband calling out in the distance, telling her that Emily had arrived. 'I'd better let you go. But give my love to Ian, Em and the two wee ones, and I'll call you soon.'

Nancy sighed. 'I'm sorry if I sounded harsh, but Eric would hate you sitting there each night, stuck somewhere between the living and the dead.'

'I know,' she replied, in an over-bright voice, and then finished the call.

It was several minutes before Ginny could look over at the empty wingback chair. But when she did, she managed to control herself.

At 6 p.m. she turned on the news so they could both catch up, before reaching for the crossword book.

She'd first met Eric thirty-five years ago when they'd both been on a bus tour in South America. It had been the most daring thing Ginny had ever done and ended up being the best. Not only had she fallen in love with the shy but brilliant doctor, but they'd been able to share the extraordinary experience together. There had been no internet, or television, and so they'd fallen into the habit of doing one crossword puzzle a night. They'd married just weeks after returning to London.

'Right, here we go. What is a six-letter word that means to start a new life?'

Was the crossword book judging her? Had it somehow heard Nancy on the phone and changed the question, just to make a point? Irritation skittered through her, then she did what she'd never done before: she ripped out the whole page and crumpled it into a small ball before throwing it across the room. There. See? She could do new things very well indeed when she tried.

Feeling better, she flipped to the next page. 'Okay, let's try this one instead...'

TWO

By the next morning the headache had gone, and Ginny carried her breakfast to the narrow conservatory built in the side return and looked out to the garden. It was a lovely conversion that really made the most of the morning sun. She'd managed to fit in two wicker chairs and had filled the ledge with some of her houseplants. She'd always been an early riser and even though she wasn't due at the library until ten o'clock, she was already washed and dressed.

Old habits really did die hard. Which, of course, according to Nancy, was the whole problem. Still, things could be worse. She spread last year's marmalade onto her dry toast but before she could take a bite there was a soft thump.

She peered around the room, but nothing was out of place. A wave of melancholy went through her. Was this the worst part of being alone? That nothing was ever out of place anymore? With a sigh, she took a bite, and—

Scratch.
Scratch.
Scratch.

It seemed to be coming from the French door that led to the garden. She put down her plate and stepped outside.

Next door's damson tree was half leaning against the wall, its poor branches struggling under the weight of too much unpicked fruit. Another gust of wind blew, but the scrape of leaves along the old bricks wasn't much above a whisper.

Still, while she was out there, she could gather the windfalls that lay on the ground. She'd long made jams and marmalades from the fruit trees that Eric loved to grow.

He would have hated to see the heavily laden branches on the other side of the fence. 'Needs to be harvested and thinned,' is what he would've said. She hadn't met her new neighbour yet, but judging by the state of the hedgerow at the front of their house, they didn't have much time for gardening.

A sudden creak of a back door made her stiffen, and she peered through a gap in the fence to where a man had stepped out onto the poorly maintained patio. His head was bowed over a phone, and he was wearing brown trousers and a black leather jacket.

Nancy's remonstrations ran through her mind. And while Ginny didn't feel up to inviting him over for a cup of tea, she could offer to help with his fruit tree. In return she would happily give him some damson gin, once it was ready.

'Hello, I'm your new neighbour, Ginny. I'd like to talk to you about the tree,' she said in her best bright voice. The man looked up. He was probably mid-thirties, but his scowl made him seem older – and grumpier. Her bravado drained away. 'Or I could come over tomorrow? It's just there's a lot of fruit on it, and—'

'I'm not interested,' he snapped, and stalked back inside his house.

Not sure what else to do, Ginny finished gathering the fruit and retreated to the kitchen. At least Nancy couldn't say she hadn't tried. She carefully sorted and washed the fruit, and once it was done—

Scratch.

She turned to discover a black cat standing on the kitchen table, one claw slowing dragging across the wood. Is that what the noise had been?

It had large yellow eyes that seemed to say, *Finally.* Then, without waiting for a response, it walked the length of the table and licked a paw. Ginny wasn't a cat expert, but it did resemble the one that Esme Wicks had released into the library. None of which explained what it was doing here. Or how it had got inside. Then she saw a recipe book lying on the floor, spine cracked wide. She picked it up, remembering what the cat had done to the book display.

'I take it this was your handiwork?'

Again, the cat didn't answer.

'I'm sorry about yesterday. Louisa shouldn't have yelled at you. But I can't have a cat either. Eric is allergic—' She broke off. Yet another thing she hadn't adjusted to yet.

The cat let out a thin wail. While its fur wasn't matted, it was very skinny. She did have a tin of tuna in the cupboard. Should she give it some? But if she did, it might expect more.

The cat seemed to notice her internal debate and nudged her hand with its nose.

'Fine. Let's get you fed, and we'll cross the next bridge when we come to it.'

While the cat ate, Ginny looked up the local vet and rang the number. But it was too early to be open, so she left a message.

By the time she put her phone down, the cat had devoured everything. It then climbed onto the table and curled up on the crossword book.

Ginny glanced at the old farmhouse clock on the wall. If she left now she could put up a notice at the corner shop and buy some proper food before she started work. There was a notice-board at the library as well, but she didn't feel up to asking Louisa about using it.

The cottage didn't have a cat door so she left the kitchen window slightly open, apologising to Eric as she did so, since he could never leave the house without making sure everything was properly locked.

Her car was parked down the small drive at the side of the cottage, but it was silly to take it out when it was such a lovely day, so she shrugged on her coat and headed into Little Shaw proper.

The shop was made from the same local stone as the library. Above it hung the name 'Collin's Grocery Store' in gold lettering while out front, instead of the traditional baskets of fruit and vegetables, were pails of early autumn hydrangeas, cosmos and dahlias.

Inside was equally charming, with a long wooden table running down the middle of the shop, flanked by a mismatched collection of Welsh dressers and wooden shelves on the side walls, full of heavenly loaves of bread, tubs of apples and large platters of pastries.

In the corner were several small round tables for eating at, but the only customers were a group of women, all around her age. One was pouring out cups of tea but stopped to unashamedly study Ginny.

Did they know she'd driven to Todmorden to do her grocery shop at the large chain supermarket, all because she was familiar with the brands and the layout of the aisles? Maybe Nancy had been right about her making more of an effort?

Ginny peered around for a noticeboard, but on not finding one, she walked over to the counter.

'Alyson's out the back. A delivery just arrived,' the woman with the teapot told her. She had shoulder-length silver hair and a long face with bright blue eyes. 'Hard to say how long it will take.'

'Oh. Maybe I'll try again on my way home from work—?'

'Damn. Does that mean you're going back in?' a second woman with thick curly hair wanted to know.

'What do you mean?'

'Ignore them, they're just being silly,' the third one said in a warm voice. She knitted as she spoke, the needles clacking softly in time with her words.

'Silly? Well, I must say I do resent that. The last person who worked with Louisa Farnsworth only survived a day. And the one before that didn't even get through the first hour,' the one with the curly hair protested.

'It's a bet, you see.' The silver-haired woman retrieved what appeared to be a Snickers bar and handed it to her friend. 'I prefer cold hard cash, but Hen' – she nodded at the knitter – 'won't let us gamble anymore. Not since the strip-poker incident.'

Strip poker? Ginny blinked. Was she joking?

'We're not usually so judgy,' Hen assured her, still knitting away. 'But Louisa is an acquired taste. Like Marmite. I'm sure she has a good heart, deep down.'

'Deep, *deep* down. I'm JM.' The silver-haired woman held out a hand. 'And you're the new owner of Middle Cottage.'

'Yes, Ginny Cole,' she said, trying not to act surprised. While she'd never lived in such a small village before, she had heard enough about them. And so many of the elderly clients at the surgery had been lonely and tried to make up for it by gossiping as they sat in the waiting room. But it was still strange to think people had seen her and spoken about her. 'It's nice to meet you all.'

'You, too. I'm Tuppence,' the one with the curls chimed in. 'We would've said hello yesterday, but Louisa only lets us in on

Fridays for book group. Says we're a disruptive influence, which is nonsense.'

'We heard you lost your husband and since we're all widows, we wanted you to know you're not alone.' Hen gave her a welcoming smile and finally put down her needles.

Oh. Ginny's chest tightened, as a familiar onslaught of feelings flooded her. But the three women didn't try to fill the space, either not noticing, or not finding it unusual. It finally passed and for the first time Ginny saw that along with teacups and plates of cakes, they all had notebooks spread out across the table.

Another wave of emotions went through her. This time panic. Were the three women in some kind of bereavement group? More importantly, were they trying to get her to join? She swallowed.

Nancy had tried to convince Ginny to go along to a local group in Bristol, but she'd not been able to bring herself to do it. It was hard enough to discuss Eric's... *passing*... with herself, let alone with a group of strangers.

'Thank you,' she managed. 'B-but I don't think I'd be very good at talking about my feelings—'

'Feelings?' JM raised an eyebrow and then let out a bark of laughter. 'Oh, you thought we were in some kind of club for widows? Let us assure you we're not.'

'Goodness, no,' Tuppence agreed. 'I mean, we do talk about our other halves, of course. It would be hard not to. Taron died ten years ago, and I still miss him. But he'd no doubt strangle me if he thought I was moping around after such a long time. "Tuppence," he'd say, "you're an artist, so go and make art and stop with this silliness."'

'Taron always did love to live in the moment.' Hen patted Tuppence's arm and gave her a supportive smile. Then a shadow crossed her face. 'Unlike my Adam, who was more cautious. Explained why he became an accountant, I suppose. He died twenty years ago, so I've had the most practice.'

'And I've had the least. It's been seven years since Rebecca died,' JM added, her voice matter of fact. 'That's when I met these two. They noticed that I'd left the house wearing my slippers, and after that, decided to take me under their wings. But they never made me talk about anything I didn't want to. They just made sure I was okay. Real friends don't let you walk down the street in your pyjamas.'

'Unless you want to,' Hen clarified. 'We're not here to judge.'

'As for the notebooks, we're trying to figure out what our new community group should be. It's very important to have a project.' Hen picked up a flower-covered pad and waved it in the air.

Ginny was starting to wish she'd never walked into the quaint shop.

She didn't want to think about widowhood or projects, or life without Eric. All she wanted was to get through the day without crying.

She was saved from answering by the appearance of the shopkeeper returning from the back room. She was probably in her late thirties with messy brown hair dragged back off her face. There were dark shadows under her eyes and a general air of weariness to her. This must be Alyson.

Pleased for an excuse to break away from the three women and their conversations of how to survive widowhood, Ginny excused herself and stepped over to the counter.

'Can I help?' Alyson asked, not sounding very enthusiastic.

'I hope so. A black cat turned up this morning and I think I recognise it from the library. I wondered if you have somewhere for me to put this notice up' – she waved a hastily hand-written note at Alyson – 'or know if anyone has lost a cat.'

'Definitely a stray,' JM called out from behind her. 'If

anyone was missing their cat, there would have been a front-page article in the local newspaper.'

'We don't get a lot of excitement around here,' Hen added.

'Oh. I see.' Ginny swallowed, not quite sure what to do next. 'Well, do you have any cat food? Just until I've spoken to the vet. They might have heard something.'

'Over there. It's organic.' Alyson pointed to a wooden shelf. Ginny went and stocked up on several jars, trying not to look at the eye-watering price. Even though she had enough money to cover most of her living expenses, she still needed to be careful. But there wasn't much she could do now except take it up to the counter.

'Goodbye, it was nice to meet you all,' Ginny said, once she'd paid and transferred everything into her shopping bag.

'You, too,' JM said, as the three women suddenly stood and gathered up their belongings.

JM was very tall and slim in a pair of wide-legged trousers and a crisp blue shirt that made her look like Marlene Dietrich. Tuppence, who was a good deal shorter, had on denim overalls that were liberally covered in paint splatters and had been paired with pink gumboots. And then there was Hen, whose floral Liberty blouse was half covered by a thick, hand-knitted Aran cardigan and teamed with a long denim skirt.

But despite their differences, they all had something interesting about them. *Unlike me.* Ginny looked down at her old navy coat, suddenly grateful it was hiding the plain black trousers and patterned blouse that she'd always worn every Tuesday. Then again, it wasn't like her out-of-style coat was much better.

Sighing, she gave them a quick wave goodbye and walked outside.

The three women followed her out, chatting amongst themselves as they went. Maybe they were going to an exercise class or some other activity together? She'd noticed several flyers around the village, advertising things like yoga, Pilates and something called Powerhoop, all taking place in the church hall. But, instead of turning down the cobbled laneway that led in that direction, they continued behind her as she crossed the old bridge.

She turned again and JM gave her a cheery wave. 'Don't mind us. We just wanted to see how you get on in your second day.'

Ginny wasn't sure how to reply to the comment, so kept walking until the library came into sight.

It had once been a school and, unlike the weavers' cottages with their large windows, there were only two small, high-set windows that flanked the old door, making it difficult to see in – and no doubt difficult for the poor Victorian children to see out.

Which might explain why there were several people all on the tips of their toes, trying to do just that. As to *what* they were looking at, Ginny had no idea.

'Trust William to be there. He's so nosy,' Tuppence said, as they caught up to her. 'I'm surprised he didn't drag over the bench seat so he could get a better view. Oh, wait... he's doing it now.'

'He never was the sharpest tool in the box,' JM agreed, as Ginny checked her watch. The library should have opened half an hour ago, so why were all these people outside?

Esme Wicks, who had been arguing with Louisa yesterday, ambled over.

'What's going on, Esme?' Hen asked.

'I'll tell you what's going on. Mrs High and Mighty is refusing to open. She thinks we can't see her, but we know she's in there. The office light is on and that car of hers is parked out the back.' The last part was said in a raised voice, as if the sound would carry through the stone wall to the back of the library, and into the small office.

'Why wouldn't she let anyone in?' Ginny asked. Louisa

hadn't mentioned a late start. Then again, she hadn't mentioned much.

'Let me count the reasons,' a voice called out, which was met with a chorus of agreement. 'Louisa Farnsworth is cruel. Last week she told me that she wasn't getting in the latest Lee Child despite the fact there are thirty people who've requested it. But I know they are in that back office of hers. Loads of them. She just didn't want to share.'

'Too lazy to put covers on them and enter them onto the catalogue.'

'Maybe that's what she's doing now, and she's forgotten the time?' a meek man suggested.

'Yeah, right.' Esme let out a snort before turning to Ginny. 'You can tell her that she can't keep us out. It's our civil liberties.'

'But aren't you banned?'

'That is correct. But it's still my civil liberties to be able to see that door unlocked so that I can be banned from going in. Otherwise, what's the point?'

'You'd better use the spare key,' another voice interjected.

'What spare key?' Ginny's gaze went from person to person, feeling like a very slow learner.

'It's hidden.' JM pointed to an ornamental rock in the narrow garden bed under the window. Someone was currently standing on it to try and get extra height for looking inside, but they hastily stepped to one side.

'There's a spare key to the library and *everyone* knows about it?' Ginny rubbed her brow. The hope that today would be better was fading fast.

'Of course. It's for an emergency. It's very important to have a back-up plan,' Tuppence assured her.

'So, if everyone knows about it, why hasn't anyone used it yet?'

Her question had the effect of causing the entire crowd to

take a hasty step away from the window, as if they'd just received an electric shock.

'The last time William did that he wasn't allowed to borrow magazines for three weeks. No warning or anything,' Esme said, before turning to glare at a portly man in his eighties. 'And you would *think* that due to his experience, he would join me in my protest. Solidarity.'

William wrinkled his nose. 'You know I'm with you in spirit, but it's bad for my health if I don't read the daily newspapers. I can't afford to get on her bad side again. None of us can.'

'Hmmm.' Esme made a non-committal noise, as all eyes turned back to Ginny. Clearly none of them wanted to risk Louisa Farnsworth's wrath.

After yesterday, Ginny couldn't blame them. Still, she hadn't been on Louisa's good side yet, so she supposed it couldn't get worse. 'I'll do it.' She rolled the stone to one side to reveal an old-fashioned brass key pressed into the soil. Everyone seemed to be holding their breath as she picked it up, and then cautiously followed behind her, pantomime style.

The key went easily into the lock, and she pushed the door open.

She couldn't remember seeing an alarm system yesterday but checked the wall while listening for the beep, beep, beep to let her know if one had been set. There was nothing apart from the excited gasps of her rear-guard.

One of them started to follow, but Ginny shook her head. Whatever was going on, she couldn't imagine Louisa wanting the library open for business until she'd okayed it.

'Would you all mind waiting out here?'

There were a couple of protests, but they grudgingly stepped back and she snibbed the door before venturing in. It was dark, thanks to the small windows, and she groped her way to the bank of light switches. What she really needed was a torch. Then she recalled that there was one on her phone.

She fumbled around in her large bag, trying to find it underneath the cat food, the lunch she'd made herself, the two notebooks, a paperback to read, and a flask of tea. Her fingers finally located it just as her foot crunched on something hard, and she lurched forward. With one hand still in her bag, she stumbled into the counter. Pain radiated through her hip and the bag slipped off her shoulder, spilling the contents onto the counter and floor.

Letting out a soft groan, she waited until the first wave of adrenaline passed through her before assessing the damage. She patted her hip, which didn't seem like it had come off worse for wear, and then looked down to see what the culprit had been.

It was a set of keys with a large letter L on them, making it easy to guess they belonged to Louisa. On the counter was an expensive-looking leather jacket and a tiny handbag. Had Louisa not noticed her keys had fallen onto the floor?

Ginny retrieved them, along with two jars of cat food that had rolled away, and then gathered up the rest of the contents of her bag and once again hitched it over her shoulder. Then she used the torch on her phone to reach the light switches. They slowly flickered to life, breaking through the dimness as she walked past the rows of books and out to the office.

'Louisa?' Her voice echoed in the empty space, making Ginny feel like she was trespassing somewhere she shouldn't be. 'It's me. Virginia Cole. The new library assistant.'

There was no answer as she reached the door, which was shut. Of course it was. She swallowed and knocked three times, but there was still no answer.

Maybe Louisa was catching up on work emails and had forgotten the time? If so, Ginny couldn't imagine her being happy at the interruption. She glanced back to where several faces were pressed against the window outside, watching her intently.

They must be standing on the bench, which she couldn't

help but think was dangerous. However, they seemed more interested in her progress than in any health and safety concerns. JM gave her an encouraging thumbs-up.

Since when had this become her life?

At the surgery she'd always been so in control. And even though each day had brought new challenges, the overall running of the place had been as smooth as clockwork, with no real surprises.

She'd only worked at the library for one day and already felt off-kilter.

Still, there wasn't much else she could do. Eric used to tease her that she was a person who finished what they started. And he was right. So, even if she was about to be fired, at least she would've seen it through.

She turned the handle and stepped inside.

The lights were on, the low hum of the computer suggesting it was in sleep mode. The tall shelves were lined with new books, and a stepladder was lying on the ground. And there, in the middle of the floor, was Louisa Farnsworth, half covered in a pile of books, the pages spread out like birds ready to take flight.

The Lee Childs everyone had been waiting for.

Louisa was wearing a scarlet dress, and her head was twisted to one side at an unnatural angle, while her blonde hair spread out around her. Ginny's mind tried to piece it together. The ladder, the books and the swelling around her neck. Had she fallen while taking books from the shelf? It certainly appeared that way, and while Ginny knew that a broken neck wasn't necessarily fatal, any kind of head trauma was dangerous.

Louisa's right hand was thrown across her chest. Four of her fingernails were the same blood-red as yesterday, but the fifth was still missing.

Ginny couldn't help noticing that the dull stub of a nail

underneath was striated with horizontal white lines. Had the marks come from the nail being ripped off?

She caught herself. *Now's hardly the time.*

Instead, Ginny dropped to her knees. There was no blood visible, but the blueish tinge on Louisa's skin was not good, nor was the blank stare. Ginny wasn't a nurse but had always kept her first-aid skills up to date and had lived with Eric for enough years to know the basics. She didn't dare touch Louisa's neck, so she picked up her limp wrist of the other hand, without the missing nail, and felt for a pulse. But it was as she'd feared.

Louisa Farnsworth was dead.

THREE

'Mrs Cole, I believe you're the one who found the body.'

Ginny closed the magazine to find a young PC hovering over her. Well, she said young, but these days she found it increasingly difficult to tell if someone was fourteen or thirty. But she had seemed nice enough since her arrival twenty minutes ago, along with a second officer, who was currently outside the library, maintaining what Ginny could only imagine was aggressive crowd control. At least there were no more faces peering in through the window.

Since then, the PC had spent her time with the paramedics who had appeared not long after. And so, unsure of what else to do, Ginny had called Marigold Bentley, at the parish council, and left a detailed message before sitting down at the long reading table to wait.

'That's correct. But please call me Ginny – everyone does,' she said, her heart tapping out a boom, boom, boom in her ear.

For most of her life, Ginny had been an ardent rule follower and had a secret fear of being arrested and thrown in prison. It had even come up in a crossword puzzle once: capiophobia. And Eric had often teased her about how far out of her way she went to make sure no security guards thought she was shoplifting.

'I think they know you're innocent by the fact you haven't actually taken anything,' he would whisper, and kiss her on the cheek. Except he wasn't here now. Ginny swallowed and tried not to look at her shaking hands.

'I'm PC Anita Singh,' she said in a Scottish accent, and sat down. Up close, Anita was tiny, with dark eyes and lovely long lashes. 'How are you feeling? It must have been quite a shock for you to find the deceased like that.'

Ginny closed her eyes.

There was none of the aching grief that had accompanied her since Eric's death. But she'd only known Louisa for a day and wasn't sure she even liked her. No. That wasn't fair. No matter what Louisa had been like at work, she must have had a family and people who loved her. People who would now be struggling, just as Ginny had been. *Still was.*

'I'm okay,' she said, not wanting to admit that talking to the police was harder than finding Louisa's body. 'What did the paramedics say about her death?'

'It's a suspected heart attack. One of them recognised her and said she'd been admitted to hospital several times because of an irregular heart thing.'

'Arrhythmia?' Ginny said, from habit. It would explain the collapse, and why she had been clutching her chest.

'Yes, that's the one,' Anita agreed, after glancing at her notepad. 'I need to ask you a few questions if that's okay. It's better to do it now, while things are still fresh in your mind.'

'Please go ahead.'

'Thank you.' She flipped to a new page and asked a few basic details to confirm Louisa's identity and Ginny's relationship to her. At the mention it was only Ginny's second day at the library, she raised a brow. 'Probably not what you expected. Is there anyone you can call?'

'I've left a message with the parish chairperson.'

'Excellent. So, can you tell me everything that happened leading up to when you found the deceased?'

'I'll do my best.' Ginny calmly recounted the discussion with the crowd of people outside the building, up until the moment she entered the small back office where Louisa had died.

Once she'd finished, the PC put down her pen. 'And was the front door definitely locked?'

'That's correct. Though apparently the spare key's hidden under a rock, which means—'

'—anyone could have come in at any time,' the PC finished off. 'What is it with these small towns?'

'It did seem a bit odd. There isn't an alarm system. But I checked the windows and they were all closed.'

'Did anyone else come in with you?'

'No. I snibbed the door shut after me, just in case.'

'Good thinking. Was there anything to make you think another person had been here? Or if anything was missing?'

Ginny closed her eyes. Was there? It was hard to recall, and she wasn't familiar enough with the place to say. 'I don't think so.'

'And what about yesterday? Did Louisa complain of any chest pain, or seem to be unwell?'

'Not to me. She was annoyed about an acrylic fingernail and left early to try and get it repaired. Obviously she wasn't successful, but I suppose that's neither here nor there.'

Anita looked up, her mouth set in a curious line. 'Why do you say that?'

'Well... because the nail was still missing when I found her,' Ginny said, suddenly feeling very silly. Why had she even mentioned the phone argument with the nail salon yesterday? Was it because of those strange bands on the exposed nail?

Eric had talked about them in the past, and so while she'd

been waiting, she'd decided to look them up on her phone. They were called Mees' lines, apparently, and could be a symptom of kidney failure.

Or arsenic poisoning.

Of course, Eric also talked about the dangers of people thinking they were a medical expert based on a two-minute internet search.

'That's a specific thing to notice.' Anita scanned back through her notes. 'Was it because it was on Louisa's left hand, where you checked for the pulse?'

Heat rose up her cheeks. 'N-no. The missing nail was on the right hand. The index finger.'

Anita's dark eyes fixed on her. 'Ginny, is there anything else you want to tell me?'

Was there?

What if it was nothing and she was just sticking her nose in where it didn't belong? If only Eric was there. He was so much better at this than she was. Not to mention he was qualified to answer. Besides, if it was poison, surely the toxicology report would pick it up? They didn't need her to tell them their job.

What should I do, love?

As usual, Eric didn't answer. But if he had, she knew what he would most likely say.

That unless there was a reason to do a toxicology report, the body might very well be sent directly to the funeral home. Especially if there had been a pre-existing heart condition. Better too much information than not enough.

'It's probably nothing, but there were marks on the fingernail that made me wonder if she'd been... well... poisoned.'

At the mention of poison, the young PC's mouth opened, but before she could speak, the paramedics reappeared from the back office, pushing the trolley that contained Louisa's covered body.

'Wait,' PC Singh told them abruptly, then turned to Ginny.

'Excuse me. I need to talk to them.' Then without another word, she hurried away, leaving Ginny once again at the reading table, suddenly feeling very foolish.

The next hour passed in a blur as more police arrived, along with the coroner. Marigold Bentley turned up as the police cordoned off the back room, and Louisa's personal possessions had been gathered. Somewhere along the way Ginny's prints were taken as part of the investigation, before she'd been returned to the long table and the unread magazine.

She was just checking the time when Marigold strode over to her, expression grim.

She was probably ten years younger than Ginny and looked like she'd just climbed out of a Land Rover with her fitted jeans, sturdy boots and green quilted hunting jacket. Her brown hair curled under at the shoulders as if it had been recently blow-dried, and she was wearing pearl earrings and a three-strand necklace.

'Oh, my dear. What a terrible thing to happen. How are you holding up? The lovely PC said you've been marvellous.'

'I'm not sure about that.' Ginny stood, her legs cramped from too much inactivity. 'Have they told you anything?'

'No. But I did overhear the coroner saying they'd found lesions on the body consistent with arsenic poisoning. From what I can gather, it's being treated as a homicide,' Marigold admitted, and Ginny's throat tightened, wishing she'd been mistaken.

'What will happen now?'

'James Wallace should be here soon. He's a detective inspector and is very thorough at his job.' Marigold closed her eyes, suddenly looking drained. Of course, she would be. After all, it was a small village, and as the chairperson of the parish council, she must have known Louisa well.

'Sorry, I should have asked how you are feeling. Were you close?'

'I won't lie. We've had our moments. But we're such a tight community and any unexpected death is shocking. But the fact it might be murder...'

'It's like something from a book,' Ginny agreed. 'What about her family? I know she wore a wedding ring. Did she have children?'

'No. She only married five years ago, and neither of them had children from their previous relationships,' Marigold said, before her eyes filled with worry. 'Oh, Bernard. That poor man. What terrible news for him to receive.'

'Indeed.' Ginny knew only too well what that single moment was like. The one that turned everything into a 'before' and an 'after'. 'Are you sure I can't do anything for you? A cup of tea? Or make any calls?'

'It's okay. But thank you for asking.' Marigold looked at her. 'You're very calm under pressure. Does it come from running your husband's surgery for such a long time?'

'I suppose so.' Ginny was used to being told how practical and sensible she was. And while she knew it was true, it never felt like a compliment. 'What will happen to the library? Do you have anyone who could take over?'

'I've just spoken with one of our previous volunteers, Harold Rowe, and he's agreed to step into the role until we find a replacement. He's a retired archivist who took care of our local history collection. When the previous manager moved to Scotland, Harold applied for the position. But, while his qualifications were excellent, there were concerns about his people skills and, ultimately, Louisa was the successful candidate.'

'That's very fortunate,' she replied, trying not to judge either Louisa or Harold's people skills.

Something crossed Marigold's face. 'Well, yes. Though in full transparency, after Louisa's appointment, Harold resigned as a volunteer, accusing her of miscataloguing several local biographies. Things got a little bit heated... It's because he is a stickler for rules. But his heart is in the right place.'

Ginny hid a smile. Eric always hated that expression. After all, if someone's heart wasn't in the right place, then the concept of being 'good' or 'bad' would be the least of their problems. 'I'm sure the community will be pleased he's agreed to help. Have the police said when we can re-open?'

'They're waiting for the SOCO agents to arrive and gather forensic evidence. It will depend how long that takes.'

'Sorry to interrupt, Mrs Bentley.' A police officer walked over. 'We have a few more questions for you. But, Mrs Cole, you are free to go. If you would like, I can give you a lift home.'

'I think that would be wise,' Marigold agreed. 'There are a lot of people out there, which might be overwhelming. I love our community, but they do like to know everything as it happens. And thanks again for being such a trooper. I'll call as soon as we can re-open.'

'Let me know if there is anything I can help with,' Ginny said, before following the officer outside.

Police had taped off the road, but a large crowd had gathered on the other side, looking at her with interest. Ginny was pleased not to face them, and gratefully climbed into the back of the police car. The short trip was made in silence, and it was a relief when she was finally home with the front door shut firmly behind her.

'Oh, Eric, today was truly dreadful. Can you believe that new manager of mine is dead? And I was the one to find her.' She put on her slippers and headed towards the kitchen, letting the familiar routine soothe her scattered emotions. 'I felt so useless. What they really needed was you, not—'

Meow.

The cat jumped down from the table and stretched out his limbs before sleepily cocking his head at the empty food bowl on the floor. Poor thing. She quickly fed him and checked her messages to see if anyone had answered the lost cat notice.

They hadn't.

'Try not to fret. I'm sure there's a good reason why we haven't heard back yet.'

The cat continued eating then padded into the hallway and curled up on the bottom stair, as if he'd always lived there.

If only she had that kind of confidence – to feel comfortable in new places, and with new situations. Sighing, Ginny carried a cup of tea into the sitting room and put on the radio. She didn't want to think about dead bodies, poison or police interviews. Instead, she turned to the empty chair in the corner of the room until the terrible sensation of being overwhelmed began to dissipate.

'I wish you were here, my love.'

FOUR

Ginny woke with a start as something heavy landed on her foot. It was accompanied by a plaintive *meow* as sharp claws tugged at the blanket at the bottom of the bed.

'I take it you want me to get up.' She tried to shake off the brain fog from the previous night. She hadn't slept well since Eric's death, but last night had been particularly bad, and dreams of his funeral had been interlaced with visions of Louisa's lifeless body.

The cat walked up to her hand and nudged it. His fur was soft and even though she could feel the bones down his spine from lack of food, he still felt warm as he purred in response.

In the kitchen he took on the tragic air of a starved creature as she filled up his food bowl, then flicked on the kettle. Out of habit, she studied the paper calendar on the wall to check her appointments for the day, but the only thing marked into the little square was *Work. 10–5.*

The kettle boiled at the same time as the phone rang and she looked longingly at the empty teacup. She didn't recognise the number, but years of being married to a doctor made it impossible for her to ignore a call, no matter how much she might want to.

'Hi, this is Pippa, from Carlyle Vet Clinic,' a chirpy voice said on the other end. 'You rang yesterday about a stray cat.'

'That's correct. I was hoping you might know who the owner is.' Ginny gave a full description, while the cat began to clean its hind leg. Once she was finished, Pippa's voice had lost some of its cheer.

'Oh... so it's definitely a black male?'

'That's correct. Does that mean you know who he belongs to?'

There was a long pause. 'In a manner of speaking. His name is Tyson, and while he isn't microchipped, we think he belonged to a couple of farm workers. However, they were recently evicted from their rental property and have left the area.'

'That's shocking. No wonder he's so hungry. I can't believe they left him behind.'

'It happens a lot,' Pippa explained. 'We've had several calls about him over the last few weeks, but no one's been able to catch him. Seems he's quite aggressive.'

Ginny glanced over to where the cat was now rolling on his back, his paw lazily stretched up in the air. He didn't seem aggressive. Then she remembered the way he'd hissed at Louisa.

'What do you advise I do with him? Is there a shelter nearby that can rehouse him?'

'Yes, there's one at Walton-on-Marsh. But I'll be honest with you, when it comes to rehousing, black cats can be tricky. And because he's an older boy, with potential behavioural patterns—' She broke off, as if trying to select her next words. 'I don't want to give you a false impression of what might happen.'

The cat would be put down.

Ginny tried to imagine driving Tyson to the animal shelter, all the while knowing what his fate would be.

'What if *I* wanted to keep him? Is that possible?'

'Absolutely.' Pippa's cheerful tone came back. 'You will have to bring him here to get microchipped, and it would be best if we checked him over to make sure he doesn't have injuries. Especially if he's been living rough. But I could fit you in on Saturday morning.'

'Thank you.' Ginny booked the appointment and added it to the wall calendar after she had hung up. Then she turned to the cat, who was now studying her with interest.

Did he know he'd been abandoned?

'I'm sorry that happened to you, Tyson.'

The cat hissed, and Ginny crouched down to look at him. That was the first time he had been aggressive, apart from to Louisa.

'What is it? You don't want to stay here? Or is it your name, T—' The cat hissed again. Well, that answered that. Though she suspected it wasn't the name itself, but about whatever experience had accompanied it. 'We can get you a new name. What about Blackie?'

The cat gave her an unblinking stare which seemed to convey the sentiment of *Really? Is that the best you can do?*

He had a point, and so Ginny looked around the room in search of inspiration before her gaze settled on the bookshelf in the corner. It was filled with Eric's books, including a collection of short stories by Edgar Allan Poe.

'I'm almost certain he wrote a story about a black cat.' She took it from the shelf and flicked through it. 'Ah, yes, here it is. His name is Pluto. What do you think?'

The cat turned his head away and yawned. Clearly, Ginny had to up her game.

'What about Raven? That's one of Poe's best-known poems. Not that I want to encourage you to catch birds, but it does sound dashing.' Still the cat didn't respond, and Ginny closed the book and slipped it back on the shelf.

'Sorry, Edgar Allan Poe, we have a tough nut to crack. Maybe we'll have better luck with the dictionary?' She reached for the large Oxford edition as a soft black paw landed on her wrist. Then he nudged at the spine of the Poe collection she'd just put back.

'Are you telling me you *did* like one of those names? Pluto? Raven?' she asked, but the cat merely continued to claw at it. She thought of the upended recipe book and the crossword book that was now covered in black fur. 'Is this destruction of books going to become a habit?'

She took the book out and pushed it over to the cat. He promptly sat on it. She supposed that answered her question.

'I can't call you Edgar Allan Poe,' she joked, only for the cat to blink three times in a row. 'Wait, what are you saying? You do like that name? It's quite a mouthful. What about Edgar?'

His purr was a long rumble and Ginny broke into a soft, spontaneous laugh. 'Edgar Cole it is. I'll let the vet know when we go for your appointment on Saturday. And I suppose I'd better get some supplies for you.'

However, Edgar had lost interest and wandered to the back door, waiting for it to magically open. Ginny let him out and then made a list of all the things she would need to buy for her new roommate, including getting a cat door installed.

She was just shrugging on her jacket when her phone rang. It was Nancy.

They'd spoken last night, and after the news about her day, it had taken all of Ginny's energy to convince her sister-in-law and brother-in-law not to make the long drive north. It had been a thoughtful gesture, but Ian hated driving at night, and she'd only worry about them.

'How are you? I hope you managed to get some sleep,' Nancy said.

'I promise that I'm okay, so try not to worry.'

'How can I not? I feel so guilty. This is all my fault.'

'Your fault?' Ginny furrowed her brows together.

'I should never have let you move up there. I knew it was a bad idea for you to be so far away. All on your own. It was very wrong of me.'

'You could hardly have known that I would find—' She broke off. 'Well, it's not something anyone could have predicted. And there's only one person who should be blamed, and that's whoever poisoned her.'

'It's still hard to believe. Have you had any updates on it? I couldn't find anything new online.'

'The police haven't been in touch, which I suppose means they don't have any more questions.'

'I'm pleased to hear it, because Ian and I think you should come to Bristol for a few days.'

Oh. She hadn't expected that. 'That's very kind, but I can't. The library is closed today but should be opening again soon. I'll need to be close by.'

'Opening again soon?' Nancy's voice went up a notch, a tone usually only reserved for when Ian changed the car oil while wearing a white shirt. 'That's ridiculous. They'll need at least two weeks for things to calm down and get the blood out of the carpet.'

'I don't think the community who use the library will see it that way. And there was no blood,' Ginny reminded her, pragmatically.

'I was being figurative. How can you be so calm at the idea of going back into a place where someone was *murdered*. And don't talk to me about the surgery and patients dying, because it's not the same thing.'

No. Indeed it wasn't.

'I don't mean it will be easy, but I promised Marigold. She's under a huge amount of stress. And we both know how few jobs there are for sixty-year-old women living in a small village.'

'Which is yet another reason to move back. Bristol is so

much bigger and with your reputation, you'll be flooded with offers. And you'd be closer to everyone who loves you.'

Except the one person Ginny loved the most was no longer there.

She was silent as she turned to face the window. Edgar was sitting underneath the overhanging branches of the damson tree, completely focused on tracking the shadows as they danced against the wall.

'There's another reason why it's not great timing. I seem to have acquired a stray cat.'

'First a murder and now a cat?' Nancy, who had only ever owned dogs, put equal emphasis on both words, as if unsure which was worse.

'The two things aren't related,' she said, before remembering the cat's dislike of Louisa. 'Well, I don't think they are. He followed me home. The vet surgery said he's a stray and on account of his age, he wouldn't have much hope of getting rehoused. And he does seem very sweet. Speaking of which, I was just heading out to get supplies for him.'

'You know, you can walk and talk on your phone,' Nancy reminded her, though it was only part of a long-running joke because Ginny had always refused to take calls while she was on the bus or out and about. It also meant that Nancy had decided not to push Ginny any further. At least for now.

Which was good, because Ginny still couldn't explain why she didn't want to go back to her old life, even though she wasn't sure how to create her new one. At least driving to the pet shop would save her from having to think of the answer.

Two hours later, Ginny unloaded her small silver Ford Ka and carried her purchases into the house. How could one cat need so many things? She'd ended up making the ten-mile trip to the large pet store in Rochdale, where they'd advised her on everything from special feeding bowls and a carrier cage, through to a very ugly cat tower, that Ginny instantly hated. She'd also bought a cat door that could be installed into her conservatory once she booked a handyman.

Ginny put away her purchases, then carried the cat tower up to the spare bedroom so she didn't have to look at it. Edgar roused himself enough to sniff several of the boxes before sitting in front of his food bowl, like a statue performer patiently waiting to earn money.

'It's half full.' She ignored his request and wiped down the bench. Her bag was still sitting there from yesterday... and so was her flask and lunch box.

Letting out a groan, she began to unpack it. 'This is what happens when my routine gets thrown.'

Edgar continued to sit by his bowl, unmoved. But Ginny, who'd spent the last eight months talking to Eric, took it in good stead.

Should she introduce the pair of them, or would that be strange?

She emptied the flask, threw away yesterday's uneaten sandwich, and retrieved her notebooks and the battered copy of *Three Men in a Boat* that she'd been rereading, and—

A grey leather diary?

The last item wasn't what she'd been expecting. She examined it. The leather was soft under her fingers, and she turned it over in her hands. It was familiar, but why was it in her bag? There was no lock on it, and on the inside was a row of brass rings so that the pages could be replaced each year. Except, whoever owned it had removed all the paper, leaving it empty.

The only thing she could find was a cream-coloured envelope poking out from the inner pocket. She eased it out and inspected it. The card was heavy, and a crest was embossed on the flap. Ginny slipped it open. There was no letter inside it but across the front, in scrawling cursive, was the name *Louisa Farnsworth*.

Of course. That's why it was familiar. Louisa had carried it around with her for most of the day.

But why was it in Ginny's bag? She hadn't even used it since yesterday morning at the library. *Unless...* She remembered the darkness of the library as she stumbled over the keys on the floor and dropped her bag. Had she accidently gathered it up at the same time?

It was the only explanation that made sense, though it also meant the police would need it as part of their enquiry. Her chest tightened with the all-too-familiar panic of doing the wrong thing. She would have to let them know.

The number PC Singh had given her went through to a centralised message system and, not wanting to give the police more work than they already had, she decided to take it down herself.

Edgar let out an irritated meow so Ginny shook out a few dried biscuits before heading out.

Unlike the rest of the village, the police station was a plain, single-storey brick bungalow. There were several news crews camped on the other side of the street and a queue of people snaked around the corner. Ginny, who hadn't stopped to consider it might be busy, came to a halt just as two women walked out of the station door. One she recognised as Esme Wicks, while the other was so similar in appearance that she must be related.

At the sight of Ginny, the two women with their matching bowl-cuts headed over.

'Don't tell me you're back for more questioning?' Esme said, before nodding to the woman next to her. 'This is my twin sister, Elsie. Else, this is the new librarian, Ginny Cole. You know, the one who found the body.'

Elsie's eyes brightened. 'Lucky thing. I wish I'd been there, but I had to finish a wedding dress.'

'She's a seamstress. But agreed to come in with me to make sure I didn't experience any harassment, on account of being Louisa Farnsworth's arch nemesis.'

Ginny, unsure how to reply, gave her a polite smile. 'I hope it went well.'

'Eh... it was a bit underwhelming if I'm honest. They didn't even offer me a cup of tea. Said they were too busy. Probably because of this lot.' She jerked a contemptuous thumb over her shoulder at the line of people. 'Bunch of time wasters is what they are.' Esme's voice rose like a Shakespearean actor and several heads swivelled in their direction.

'Are they not waiting to be interviewed?'

'Nah. They're just concerned citizens who refuse to call the hotline. I think they want to get on the television.'

Her sister, Elsie, nodded towards the journalists. 'Or waiting until it's turned into a Netflix show. I wonder who will play you, Esme?'

'I suspect it would have to be Judi Dench. I think she'd capture my determination to stand up for my civil liberties.'

'So they don't know anything about the murder?' Ginny asked, before the two sisters could continue their casting session.

'I wouldn't think so. Take Ethan over there.' She nodded towards a young guy in his early twenties who was in the queue. 'He's convinced we have a serial killer on the loose.'

'I tell you that my theory is solid!' he called back to her. 'Sybil Wiggs, first killed in 1312. Then another murder here in 1859. It's clearly a pattern.'

'I hope for my sake you're wrong.' Elsie glared at him. 'I'll be out of business if any more of my clients pop their clogs before settling their bills. This is the third one in as many months if you can believe it.'

Esme sniffed. 'Louisa owed her eighty pounds for rehemming some dining-room curtains. Horrible job it was, too. Isn't that right, Else?'

'Aye.' Elsie nodded as a bus rumbled towards them. 'Esme, we need to catch this one. You know that young John will only wait five minutes for us.'

'Not like the old days. Anyway, duck. I'll see you tomorrow when the library reopens,' she said, then chuckled as Ginny frowned. 'They finished with it this morning. No doubt you'll hear from Marigold soon. Oh, and don't bother lining up with this lot. Just go straight in. Like me, you're a legitimate witness.'

Without another word, they slowly trundled towards the bus stop, debating between George Clooney and Brad Pitt for the leading men.

Once they were gone, Ginny chewed her lip as she studied the long queue. It didn't seem right to walk straight through the front door while they were patiently waiting. Then again, she didn't want to report a supernatural serial killer, and would much prefer to get the whole ordeal over and done with.

Decision made, she walked to the door of the station. Several people from the queue watched her with interest, but seemed happy enough to let her pass, and she stepped inside.

The reception area was grim, with well-worn linoleum floors and uncomfortable-looking plastic chairs hugging the walls. A woman in her thirties was sitting at the counter, her mouth in a flat line.

'If you're here about a theory, you'll have to wait out there.' She jabbed a finger at the door.

'I'd like to talk to PC Singh. I work at the library and spoke to her yesterday. She told me to get in touch if I remembered anything else.'

The woman's humour improved. 'Oh, sorry. You wouldn't

believe how many people we've had trying to come in today. PC Singh isn't here right now. Can I take a message?'

'I actually want to give her something.' Ginny retrieved the grey diary and brought it over to the desk. 'This belonged to Louisa Farnsworth. Somehow it got into my bag yesterday, and I only just found it. I thought it might be important.'

'I see,' the woman said, as a door crashed open from the bowels of the office.

A man stalked past, a phone clamped to his ear and an air of irritation trailing behind him like a cape. 'I don't care if you need to stay up all night. I want the results yesterday,' he barked, and finished the call.

The receptionist didn't seem concerned by the interruption and just gave Ginny a smile. 'Here's DI Wallace. He might be able to help.'

The man muttered something under his breath before turning towards them, which allowed her to see his features for the first time.

It was her rude neighbour. The one with the damson tree.

She swallowed as his dark brown eyes narrowed. Then he swore again and rolled his neck. It was unclear whether he recognised her since he didn't say anything.

'Hello, I'm Ginny Cole. We met the other day. I live in Middle Cottage.' She held out her hand, which he ignored. For someone so young, he was very grumpy, and strangely it helped calm her frayed nerves. She pushed forward the diary. 'I found Louisa Farnsworth's diary in my bag.'

'You found evidence in your handbag?' He raised an impassive eyebrow.

'I dropped it when I opened the library yesterday, and everything fell out on the counter. It was an honest mistake,' she said, knowing how proud Eric would be of her for standing up for herself instead of assuming it was a hanging offence.

He didn't answer, instead retrieving a pair of plastic gloves from a box on the reception desk and slipping them on before opening it up.

His mouth twitched as he stared at the brass ring binders. 'It's empty.'

'Well, yes, but there's an envelope in there with Louisa's name on it, so it could be important. And, of course, you might find prints on it.'

'You mean apart from yours?' He shut the diary and handed it to the receptionist. 'Give this to Anita when she returns. I'm going to the morgue.' Then he stalked away, leaving Ginny and the receptionist on their own.

Well, that was her told.

'Try not to take it personally.' The woman at the desk smiled at Ginny. 'Detective Wallace's bark is worse than his bite. Now, could I just double check your details, and then I'll make sure to pass this onto PC Singh.'

It didn't take long, and Ginny had just stepped back into her own house when Marigold rang to let her know the library could open tomorrow, just as Esme had predicted. Still, at least if Ginny was at work, she would be able to forget she'd made such a ninny of herself. And that they'd solve the case quickly and she could forget it ever happened.

FIVE

By the following morning it was clear that while Ginny didn't want to think about the murder again, the residents of Little Shaw were made of sterner stuff, and their conversations drifted up and down the high street as she walked to work.

She arrived an hour early, hoping it would prevent her from being thrust into reading children a story before she had even put her handbag down. She was nothing if not optimistic.

Thankfully, Harold Rowe didn't have any interest in making her read picture books to a live audience. Instead, he stood just inside the library door, his arms folded across his chest.

He was in his mid-seventies, with a round face, red cheeks and grey eyes that gave the impression he didn't suffer fools gladly. Or at all. Added to that he was wearing a perfectly ironed, crisp, blue shirt, a Harris tweed jacket and polished leather brogues – the antithesis of Louisa's body-hugging dress and blood-red nails.

It was easy to see why they'd clashed.

'I've been studying your application, and it appears you've

never worked in a library before,' he said, making no effort to move.

'Yes.'

'Hmmmm.' He rubbed his well-shaved chin. 'It also appears that you only started work the day before Louisa Farnsworth met her... unfortunate fate. Which I assume means you don't know the standard practices and procedures.'

'Again, that's correct,' Ginny said, not sure where he was going with his questioning. After all, when she'd applied for the job, it was as an assistant with the agreement that her lack of experience wouldn't be a hindrance. 'Though if you would like to train me, I'd be most grateful. I like knowing how to do things correctly.'

'I suppose that's something.' He walked to the counter, motioning her to follow. There was an old ring binder sitting there, which still had a layer of dust on the cover. 'While I was last here, I took the liberty of creating a comprehensive training document which, judging by the state of it, has not been used by anyone. Then again Louisa wasn't known for her love of learning. I would appreciate it if you could read it and take the contents seriously.'

'Of course,' Ginny readily agreed. 'And what about my day-to-day tasks? Is there anything you would like me to do? Should I shadow you?'

'Good god, no.' He shuddered, as if she'd just offered him a piece of food that had fallen onto the floor. 'I have spent the last six years watching this small but wonderful collection be drowned in what can only be described as a blood bath. Which is why I agreed to come back and help. My focus is on restoring the archives and hoping that dreadful woman didn't really go through with her threat to burn the old Ordnance Survey maps and a second-edition William Baxter.'

'Surely you can't be serious?'

'There's *nothing* I wouldn't put past Louisa Farnsworth. As

Henrich Heine said, "Wherever they burn books they will also, in the end, burn human beings".' He quoted the phrase before seeming to remember what had happened, and cleared his throat. 'But, while I'm out at the back working on the collection, I require you to manage the day-to-day running of the place. *And* stop the well-meaning volunteers from doing anything dreadful, or getting into any fights.'

Ginny blinked. She'd only met one other volunteer so far. A quiet ex-nurse who didn't seem capable of fighting with anyone, or anything.

There was a light tapping from the front door and Harold made a huffing noise. 'That will be some of them now. I believe Cleo and Andrea are rostered for this morning. Try to discourage them from talking. There will be enough gossip going around after what happened without them adding to it.'

Without another word, he thrust the binder at her and disappeared into the small office where Louisa had taken her last breath. The fact he found that preferable to talking to a volunteer wasn't something Ginny wanted to delve into. And with that thought she went to open the front door.

'To think there was a real-life murder in Little Shaw. Is that really where you found her?' Andrea leafed through a pile of magazines that had been returned, checking for damage. But she kept stopping her task every few minutes to ask more questions.

'I'm afraid so.' Ginny printed out the list of reservation requests, pleased she was starting to navigate the computer system on her own.

'And is it true that she'd been strangled, but that the police are trying to cover that up?' A customer leaned over the counter, eyes wide.

'Not that I'm aware of,' Ginny said, and excused herself to

start collecting the books on the list. She saw Andrea and the customer exchange looks, and then continue to speculate on how Louisa might have been strangled.

It had been like that all morning, and while Ginny had done her best to discourage the gossip, she hadn't been successful.

Still, both Cleo and Andrea had been very patient as they showed Ginny the system, and even though Harold hadn't reappeared from the back office, the training manual was excellent and filled with the kind of meticulous details she preferred. The folder itself had the name of a conference stamped on the inside, much like the many that Eric had collected over the years.

However, Harold had carefully glued over the original cover and replaced it with:

LITTLE SHAW LIBRARY
Policies, Procedures, Training, Health and Safety,
Readers' Advisory and Miscellaneous.
Created by Harold Rowe 2017
Can all new staff please read thoroughly and complete the
handout sheet at the end as well as initial the first page to
confirm you have undergone this comprehensive training?

Underneath it, someone had simply written, *No thanks.* There were also several scribbled lines on it, as if someone had been testing to see if a pen worked. And the corners of the paper were frayed, where the glue hadn't held.

Ginny had the feeling that Harold Rowe liked books better than people.

After she'd finished collecting the reservations she spent the next half-hour going over the section on lost books, before heading back to the counter. Andrea was on her lunch break and Cleo was cleaning a cooking book that had come back covered in a fine layer of grease. At the sight of Ginny, she made a clucking noise.

'To think it's like our very own Agatha Christie story, and you were the one to figure out it was poison.'

'I didn't figure it out,' Ginny protested. She was almost getting used to people breaking into a discussion with her. 'And the coroner's report hasn't come back, so we don't know for certain.'

'Yes, but Marilyn's daughter, who dates Hairy Ralph, said it definitely is,' Cleo said, as a woman in a green cardigan staggered up to the counter with an armful of books. 'Here, leave this one to me. It's only Rose, and she's a busybody. You don't want to have to deal with all her impertinent questions.' Cleo moved off with a tut.

'She's one to talk,' came a low voice. A teenage boy appeared by Ginny's side. He was probably about eighteen, with a pale face and dark hair, though most of it was hidden underneath the grey hoodie pulled up over his head. He seemed to notice her confusion and pointed to the large printed-out rota pinned to the wall.

'I'm Connor.'

'I'm Ginny,' she said, trying to hide her surprise. The three volunteers she'd met so far were retired women, so when she'd seen Connor's name, she'd assumed it would belong to an elderly gentleman whose wife had signed him up to get him out of the house. 'I'm afraid everything's a bit upside-down today. I take it you've heard about Louisa?'

'Hard to miss. This place is usually dead on a Thursday afternoon. I guess dark tourism is alive and well in Little Shaw.'

'Dark tourism?' Ginny raised an eyebrow.

'You know – people wanting to check out death and murder. Like the Pendle Witch tours or having a drink in one of the pubs that Jack the Ripper went to. You wait. I bet the parish council will start making T-shirts, maps and phone apps.'

'Don't be so ridiculous, Connor,' Cleo snapped, not bothering to turn around. 'And now you're finally here, you can go and do some shelving.'

He ignored the comment, but did give Ginny a slight nod of his head. 'Anything particular you want me to do? Since, contrary to popular belief, Cleo *isn't* actually the boss.'

'Oh.' Ginny swallowed as Cleo's shoulders stiffened in response. When Harold had instructed her to stop the volunteers from fighting, she had assumed he was exaggerating. Clearly not. 'How long have you been volunteering?'

'You mean volun*told*ing,' he muttered, before pushing back his hoodie to reveal straight brown hair that hung down to his shoulders. 'I've been here three months, ever since a *thing* that happened, and Wallace and Mrs Farnsworth decided I could either do this or get charged with vandalism. Still not sure I made the right call.'

'Are you saying DI Wallace ordered you to work here?' Ginny tried to imagine the grumpy man she'd met doing something like that. It did seem to fit with his draconian temperament.

'Pretty much. Not that I'm allowed to serve at the counter in case I scare the customers... or steal the money. I'm stuck doing the shelving.' The admission was accompanied by a glare, as if daring Ginny to challenge it.

'Maybe you could show me how it works? It's only my second day here and I'm trying to learn as much as possible.'

'Sure. Whatever.' Connor collected a trolley of recently returned books and moved over to the fiction area. As he worked, he also took out several books that had been wrongly shelved before carrying on. Ginny, who had earlier watched Andrea casually pushing a P G Wodehouse in front of a H G Wells, was impressed, but before she could say anything, Cleo appeared, eyes gleaming with curiosity.

'PC Singh would like a word with you. I asked her what it was about, but she refused to tell me.'

'Can't think why,' Connor grunted, which earned him a sharp glance.

'Thanks for getting me.' Ginny steered Cleo away before they could start bickering again. 'Will you be all right on your own until Andrea is back from her break?'

'I suppose I'll have to be, since Harold Rowe is about as much use as a chocolate teapot. I still can't believe he came back here. After the last argument he and Louisa had, he swore he'd never cross this threshold again. If you ask me, they were as bad as each other.'

Ginny didn't reply as she hurried back to the counter, where PC Singh was resolutely turned away from the several library-goers trying to catch her attention. Her shoulders dropped in relief when Ginny joined her.

'Thanks for seeing me. If you have five minutes, I'd like to talk. Preferably somewhere without an audience.'

'Of course.' Ginny gestured to the staffroom out the back, hoping her panic didn't show on her face. Andrea was just returning from lunch, which meant the room would be empty.

Once they were inside, Anita's face softened. 'Sorry I missed you at the station yesterday. I heard the Guvnor was very blunt.'

'He didn't seem thrilled to see me.'

'He's an excellent detective. Just a little stressed right now. We're very understaffed. But I wanted to say thank you. And for Tuesday.' She lowered her voice. 'I've been working towards my National Investigators' Exam and would have hated if this had slipped under the radar.'

'I'm pleased I could help. Have there been any updates?'

'I'm afraid I can't tell you anything.' Anita grimaced, as if she was fighting her instincts. 'Other than to say we have several lines of enquiry. But I did want to give you my personal number in case you need to get in touch again.'

It was the same generic card for the station that she'd handed out before, but this time with a mobile phone number scrawled on the back. Ginny tucked it into her pocket just as Anita's phone rang. The PC answered it and her shoulders suddenly stiffened.

'Of course. I'll meet you at Collin's Grocery Store. I'm five minutes away.' Anita finished the call and they both returned to the main part of the library, where she bid the PC goodbye.

A scraping sound caught her ear, and she turned just as a woman with thick, curly hair and pink gumboots crawled out from underneath one of the shelves.

Tuppence?

Frowning, she headed for the shelves, but before she could get closer, the other woman scurried away. Usually, she would think it was odd behaviour, but after their conversation the other morning, it seemed very much in keeping with her personality. Then she remembered Louisa had banned the three widows from entering, apart from Fridays. Was that why Tuppence had been hiding? Was she worried that rule might still hold? If Harold ever came out of the back office, Ginny would ask him if they could lift the ban. And for poor Esme as well.

At the counter Cleo and Andrea were having a loud conversation about why the police had come back. They both smiled at her expectantly but, since the PC hadn't told Ginny anything, she just shrugged.

It was met with twin frowns of disappointment, but she was saved from further probing by the clunk, clunk, clunk of the return chute door being opened, followed by the thud of books tumbling into the cart underneath.

Pleased for the distraction, she neatly piled them, ready to be returned through the computer system.

At the bottom of the pile was a small pink envelope addressed to *Ginny Cole – new librarian.*

Cleo had mentioned that people sometimes returned personal items such as bookmarks, shopping lists or even their own books. But this was clearly meant for her.

Inside was a single sheet of paper. It was scented, with a border of flowers running around it, like something she'd used back when people wrote letters and thank-you notes. She unfolded it.

We need to talk, but there are too many eyes on us.
Meet us at TLG at 5 p.m.
All will be revealed.

Ginny rubbed her eyes and then read it again.

'Everything okay, Mrs Cole?' Connor reappeared with an empty trolley.

'I'm not sure. I just received a note. But I can't make it out. I think it's some kind of joke.' Ginny passed him the piece of paper.

Connor scanned it then nodded to the DVD stand, where a tall woman was standing. She had on an oversized jacket and large hat, but her straight hair was visible. It was JM. A moment later she'd pulled the hat down over her eyes and marched out of the door, almost knocking over a bunch of school children.

'It's from the three widows that hang out together. They want you to meet them at The Lost Goat at five.'

'Why wouldn't they ask me directly?' Ginny wrinkled her nose, though at least the TLG made sense as an acronym for the old pub she kept walking past.

'Because they're unhinged,' was the blunt reply. But when Ginny didn't respond, Connor seemed to understand she required more of an explanation: 'They were part of the Neighbourhood Watch but were kicked out for causing too much trouble. They even broke into someone's home because they thought it was on fire. Turns out it was just a candle. And *I'm* the one who gets in trouble for a little bit of tagging. Everyone in the village calls them "the widows without a cause".'

At the last part Ginny flinched.

When she'd met the three women, she'd been overwhelmed at their frank conversation about their dead partners, but that didn't mean they deserved to be teased for trying to move on with their lives. After all, isn't that what she was trying to do? Find out who she was without Eric?

But it still didn't explain what they wanted to talk to her about.

Was it to join this new group of theirs? The one they said they'd been working on over a cup of tea? Or was it for the same reason that everyone else had wanted to speak with her today? Louisa's murder.

Suddenly, Ginny felt tired. But just like she couldn't ignore a ringing phone, she couldn't bring herself to decline their invitation. Still, at least it would give her a reason to finally visit the pub.

SIX

The Lost Goat was busy by the time Ginny had ushered the last of the library-goers out of the door, gone through the cashing-up procedure, locked the money in the safe and said goodnight to Harold Rowe, who was still surrounded by piles of books in the small office.

There was no sign of the widows at the wooden tables overlooking the canal, but the chalkboard had been changed and now read: *Trust me, you are a great dancer. Vodka x*

Reluctantly smiling, she stepped inside.

The walls were a dark emerald green with equally dark framed prints, but the lights were bright and bounced off the gleaming counter to give the place a well-loved feeling. It was busy and the low hum of chatter let her know people were still talking about the murder.

The three widows were in the far corner, along with Alyson from the grocery store. JM stood and gestured her over, a bit like an air-traffic controller. 'You made it. Excellent.'

'We weren't sure if you'd be able to break the code or not,' Tuppence added.

'I got you a Pinot Gris.' Hen put down her ever-present

knitting needles and held up a wine glass. 'But if you would prefer a cup of tea or some water, we can change it.'

'Um, thank you.' Ginny found herself nodding to all three statements before sitting down. She wasn't much of a drinker but took the glass all the same.

'You remember Hen's daughter, Alyson, don't you?' JM said.

'Of course.' Ginny smiled. She hadn't realised the tired woman from behind the shop counter was related to the placid Hen, but, looking closely, she could see they shared the same almond-shaped eyes, and jawline. 'I did mean to go back into the store yesterday to take down the notice about the missing cat.'

'You found the owner?' Alyson toyed with an empty glass. She looked even more exhausted, and there was a haunted expression in her eyes.

'No. Turns out he was abandoned, so I've decided to keep him. Which was the other reason I meant to go into the store. I need to find a local handyman to install a cat door.'

'You couldn't do better than Mitch Reeves. He works here but does odd jobs on the side.' Hen peered around the bar, before shrugging. 'He must have slipped out. But he's very good. I'll give you his details. I'm sure he'll fit you in.'

'Thank you—'

Ginny was cut off by the appearance of a short man in his fifties. His face set into an angry grimace as he folded his arms and, up close, it was clear he hadn't slept. His eyes were rimmed red, his chin was covered in stubble, and there were several stains down the crumpled shirt that was straining under his rounded belly.

'Oh, you're here.' It was Alyson who spoke first, her thin face drained of colour. 'I've been trying to call you. I want to—'

'I don't care what *you* want, Alyson. How dare you call me, and don't think I didn't see you drive by the house this morning.

The police are on to you, and the sooner they lock you up, the better. In the meantime, you had better stay away from me or I'll see Wallace about it. Do you hear me?' Spittle flew out of the man's mouth and his cheeks turned a mottled purple colour.

'I think the whole place can hear you, Bernard,' JM said in a cool voice, and Ginny caught her breath.

Bernard?

This was Louisa's husband. Suddenly his dishevelled appearance made sense. Though it was hard to understand why he was so angry at Alyson, whose mouth was quivering, tears glistening on her damp lashes.

'Good. Because I'm just saying what they all think.' He waved his arms in the air, but JM just glared at him.

'Oh, really? Well, may I remind you that it's illegal to defame someone in the pub during happy hour. So, maybe *we* should be the ones who go to the police.'

'Defame her? She poisoned my wife. I know she did. After all, the bread came from her shop. Doesn't take a rocket scientist to figure out who laced it with arsenic.'

Several people around them gasped and Ginny's mouth went dry. PC Singh had been called to the grocery store that afternoon. Is that where the poison had come from?

'Nonsense,' JM retorted but Bernard didn't seem to hear her as he waved his arm in the air.

'And now she's hiding behind her crazy friends. Well, it won't work,' he roared. 'She's a murderer.'

The whole pub turned silent as the words hung in the air, and Bernard's red face shone with rage as he locked his gaze on Alyson. It seemed to be her undoing – Hen's daughter let out a muffled sob and hunched forward in her chair, her arms wrapped tightly around her chest. Next to her Hen's brow tightened with worry.

'You take that back.' JM got to her feet, towering over

Bernard. She took a step closer just as another man elbowed his way through the gathering crowd.

'Whoa, what's going on?' the newcomer demanded.

'It's Edward Tait,' Tuppence whispered to Ginny as JM squared up to the other man.

'Let's see, not content with accusing our friend of a crime, your client is now trying to intimidate us. Which we both know is grounds for me to take legal action of my own. Harassing a witness, and—'

Bernard made a snarling noise and lunged forward.

'Christ, JM.' The man stepped in front of Bernard and blocked his path. 'The poor bastard's grieving. He doesn't know what he's saying. And can I remind you that you're *not* actually a lawyer.'

'No, you may not. Now, unless you want a repeat of the May Day parade, take him home so he can sleep it off. Or we can always wait for Rita to throw him out.' JM gestured in the direction of the bar, where a middle-aged woman with soft brown curls and navy eyes had just appeared, holding a crate of tonic water. 'And do not let him go around making any more false accusations.'

'False?' Bernard screeched before Edward crammed a hand over his mouth and dragged him away from the table and out of the door.

Once they were gone, Alyson let out a low sob and Hen put a protective arm around her. 'There, there. Try not to take it personally. Edward might be a toad, but he did have a point. Bernard's grieving, which means he isn't thinking straight. You just need to give him time.'

'W-what's the use? He hates me.' Alyson sobbed, her dark eyes red and swollen. 'He thinks I killed her.'

'Nonsense. He's just being silly.' Hen patted her daughter's arm. 'It was always going to be a difficult moment. Though why he thought he could start screaming at you while JM was sitting at the table is beyond me.'

'JM did half a law degree in the seventies and has been running rings around Edward Tait ever since,' Tuppence explained with pride. 'He considers her his biggest competition.'

'Edward is a very irritating little man. And so is Bernard for that matter.' JM gave a dismissive wave of her hand, but was cut off by Alyson, who abruptly stood up, her chair scraping against the floor as she fumbled for her coat.

'Sorry, Mum. I think I need to be alone.'

'Alone? No, love. Let me come with you.' Hen rose, forgetting about the large knitting bag that had been sitting in her lap. It fell to the floor, sending several brightly coloured balls of wool unravelling out like a bowl of spaghetti, while a collection of tiny baby bonnets landed in a soft heap.

JM retrieved the bonnets and chased down the numerous balls of wool. She returned with them in her arms and dumped them onto the table where they formed a messy heap.

'Please, I'm okay.' Alyson shook her head and stumbled out through the crowded pub, ignoring the looks of interest as she went.

'Let her have a good cry. Hopefully she'll wear herself out and fall asleep. Goodness knows she needs it.' Tuppence guided Hen back into her seat, and she immediately began to separate the tangled wool with an ease that could only have come from years of practice.

Ginny reached for one of the loose threads of wool and followed Hen's lead of gently loosening it from the main tangle, before trying to roll it back up. The action was soothing but nothing to stop her from feeling like she'd wandered onto the set of a soap opera.

'But what if Bernard goes to the cottage and screams at her?' Hen fretted, before seeming to notice that JM was attempting to roll up one of the balls but had instead turned it into a complicated version of cat's cradle. Hen deftly released JM's fingers, before coaxing the strand into a neat roll, the worry never leaving her eyes. 'I knew she should never have married that man.'

Married?

The ball of wool Ginny had been working on dropped into her lap. As in *married*? It seemed incredible. How could Hen's timid daughter, Alyson, have once been married to Bernard? To the same man as Louisa Farnsworth?

She recalled Marigold telling her that Louisa was Bernard's second wife... but if she'd had to guess at what his first wife had been like, well... she wouldn't have picked Alyson. And—

She let out a low gasp as she suddenly understood why Bernard had accused Alyson of killing Louisa. Not merely because she worked at the store where the poisoned bread might have been sold, but because she'd once been married to him. Was that why they'd invited her to the pub? Because Ginny had found the body. Yet, what could she tell them that wasn't already circulating around the village?

A brave person would just ask them, but she'd never been able to put herself forward like that. Nor had she been able to just get up and leave mid-conversation, no matter how much she wanted to.

Forgetting her plan to not drink, Ginny took a sip of her wine. It did nothing to unscramble her racing thoughts, but the crisp sweetness did send a buzz of warmth through her.

She looked up just as the three women she was sitting with exchanged a glance and then, as if a silent consensus had been reached, Hen let out a sigh and put away the last of the wool.

'I suppose you're wondering why we asked you here?'

'Well, yes,' Ginny admitted, still not sure how to just ask. She cautiously peered up at Hen. 'Is it about Louisa's death?'

Hen's mouth trembled and she nodded. 'It's all such a

mess… and now Bernard's going around saying all kinds of terrible things. I'm just so worried about what will happen if the police find the letter.'

Letter?

Ginny took another gulp of wine. This time longer, but it did nothing to help her make sense of why these three women were staring at her so intensely. An uneasy feeling crawled along her skin.

'Hen, I think you should start at the beginning. It might help Ginny understand why we need her help,' JM advised.

'You're right. My mind is all over the place.' Hen dabbed her eyes before sucking in a deep breath. 'I was very young when I had Alyson, and her father wasn't a good man. Didn't stay around long enough for me to tell him I was pregnant. So, for a long time it was just the two of us. Then I met Adam. We married not long after Alyson's fifth birthday, and she loved him as much as I did. She took his death very badly. The way she saw it, her real father deserted her… and now, so had Adam.'

'The poor thing.' Ginny forgot about the wine, or even that she was sitting with three strangers. All she could think about was Alyson, and the haunted expression in her eyes.

Hen took a shuddering breath. 'It was terrible. Alyson was only eighteen and she became a recluse. She wouldn't speak to anyone and barely left the cottage. But finally, when she turned twenty-three, she got a job working for Bernard… and it seemed she was going to be okay. Then they started dating. He was thirty-five years old. I-I guess she was looking for a father figure.'

Ginny closed her eyes. Even though the twelve-year age gap didn't need to mean anything, it was hard to imagine the vulnerable young Alyson with a much older Bernard.

'The marriage lasted for ten years,' JM continued. 'Alyson thought they were happy. Then he suddenly bought a flash new car and got hair transplants, and before she could say "clichéd midlife crisis", he filed for divorce and married Louisa.'

Tuppence sighed. 'JM and I don't have children, so we've always treated Alyson as ours, and it's been hard watching her suffer. Even though the wedding was four years ago, the poor thing hasn't taken it very well – Alyson, that is. Refused to even go back to her maiden name, which means we have two Mrs Farnsworths in the village... or, we did have until Tuesday.'

'How dreadful.' Ginny tried to imagine Alyson and Bernard together as a couple. Or Louisa and Bernard for that matter. 'But surely Bernard doesn't really think Alyson killed Louisa?'

There was silence and once again the three women exchanged a glance. Hen fiddled with her knitting and Tuppence shifted in her chair, but JM rolled her shoulders back and spoke.

'She's always believed he would come back to her, you see. And over the years there have been a few... incidents. But eight months ago, it all came to a head and Alyson got into a terrible fight with Louisa. There was a restraining order and everything.'

'It's not something she's proud of,' Hen quickly added. 'I suppose you could say it was the tipping point, and we finally convinced her to get counselling. There's a lovely chap in Rochdale who did wonders for Mary Reynolds and her fear of flying.'

'He did ever such a good job. She went all the way to New York without a hitch,' Tuppence added, before JM gave her a sharp look. 'Er... not that it signifies. Point is that Alyson's sessions seemed to be helping. We thought she'd turned a corner. But then the chap got the notion in his head for Alyson to write a letter to Louisa and tell her exactly how she felt.'

'It was meant to be cathartic. A way to release five years of rage.' JM took over, like an athlete who'd been handed a relay baton. 'Though I find breaking things more useful. Nothing like a little bit of glass smashing to get rid of your worries. Anyway, the idea was to get everything out of her system and then burn it. But, for some reason, she put it in an envelope with Louisa's name on it.'

'And I stupidly posted it.' Hen let out a low wail. 'I was vacuuming the house and thought it would be nice to give her room a freshen up. When I saw the envelope, I added it to my pile to take to the post office. I didn't even realise it didn't have an address on it. After I discovered what I'd done, I went back, hoping it would still be behind the counter. But Errol being Errol, saw the name and personally delivered it to Louisa on his way home.'

'Poor Hen still feels horribly guilty about it,' Tuppence added, as if the other woman wasn't sitting there. 'And any good the letter writing might have done Alyson was gone. She's been making herself sick about it for the last two months. Of course, we told her not to panic. After all, it's nothing Louisa didn't already know. And what could she really do?'

'But now Louisa's dead, we're worried what will happen if the police find the letter. What if they think that—' Hen broke off and choked back a soft cry.

'Hush, we won't let that happen.' Tuppence squeezed Hen's hand then turned to Ginny. 'We think Louisa hid it some-where in the library.'

So *that* was why they'd asked her to the pub.

Ginny's stomach tightened as she thought of the empty envelope she'd found in the diary and given to the police. Could it have been the same one? Had Louisa kept it for two months?

'Are you sure Errol gave Louisa the letter?'

'Oh, yes. He delivered it straight to her. And there's no chance she'd have thrown it away. My bet is that she was waiting to use it, if Alyson tried to go near them again,' said Tuppence.

'But if the police find it, there's no way they won't assume it's a motive. Plus, with the other run-ins they've had, the restraining order... and if it's true that the poison was in the sourdough bread that was sold at the store... it's a lot of evidence.' JM toyed with her empty glass.

'What about the police? If Alyson went to them and explained the situation, they would understand. She could get her therapist to vouch for her,' Ginny suggested, but at the mention of the police, JM's face darkened.

'DI Wallace has taken a personal dislike to us thanks to a few completely unrelated incidents that aren't worth going into. If we went to him, it might make matters worse. *That*'s why we need to find the letter. No letter, no motive.'

Ginny wasn't sure that was true but could sympathise with Alyson's suffering. And after her own run-in with DI Wallace, it wasn't difficult to understand their concerns. 'How do you know the police haven't found it already?'

'Because if they had, Alyson would already be at the police station,' JM said in a tight voice. 'And we can't let that happen. You saw what a mess she is. That's why we've been searching for most of yesterday and today. We tried Bernard's house last night but couldn't find anything.'

'You searched Bernard's house?' Ginny was distracted as she recalled all the police tape that had been around the library. She couldn't imagine it had been any different at Bernard and Louisa's house. 'But when? How?'

'We broke in, of course. Last night. We knew Bernard was staying with Edward Tait, and the police had left for the evening. Tuppence is a whizz at picking locks,' Hen explained, giving her friend an appreciative smile.

'It's true. There are some very good YouTube videos, and it's surprisingly easy once you get the hang of it. No one suspects little old ladies. Well... apart from Wallace.' Tuppence grimaced. 'But I digress – the letter wasn't in the house.'

'We think it was either in the grey diary that she always carried with her, or somewhere else in the library,' JM said.

'That's why I was in there today searching for it, but then

that PC came in, and I had to abort the operation. So, we realised we need someone on the inside,' Tuppence finished off, and they all turned to her.

Ginny flinched under the weight of their collective gaze. They wanted her to help locate the poisonous letter that might implicate Alyson in a murder, which they suspected was in Louisa's grey diary.

The same grey diary I handed into the police.

Oh dear. She picked up her wine glass and drained it, trying to block out her thudding pulse. Why hadn't she just gone straight home to Eric, like she usually did, instead of coming here? Why had she taken the job at the library? Or moved to Little Shaw in the first place?

But before she could answer these myriad internal questions, the woman from the bar appeared at the table, holding a wire tray filled with empty glasses.

'Sorry it's taken me so long to get this table cleared. Between Bernard's outburst and no staff, it's turning out to be quite the night,' she said, in a thick London accent. 'But assure Alyson it won't happen again. I told Edward that I'll give Bernard a pass because he's grieving, but next time he wants to kick up a stink in my pub, he'll be out on his ear. Innocent until proved guilty, right?'

'Thank you, that's ever so good of you. I'll let Alyson know.' Hen managed a watery smile, which the woman shrugged it off, as if uncomfortable at receiving praise, and instead shifted her gaze to Ginny.

'Nice to see you here. I was wondering when you would get up the courage to join us. I'm Rita.'

Ginny's cheeks heated as she recalled how many times she'd walked past the pub, too shy to go in on her own.

Hen squeezed her hand. 'Don't worry, she's teasing you. Rita's a widow, like us, so she understands.'

The landlady nodded. 'I lost my Kevin four years ago and

know how easy it can be to sit dwelling in the past, instead of getting on with the business of living. Though I can't imagine it helped much when you found your new manager dead. Not the usual way to start a new job.'

'No indeed,' Ginny said, not wanting to think about Louisa's lifeless corpse again. Or Bernard's furious expression as he'd screamed at Alyson.

Rita seemed to pick up on that and gave her a friendly smile. 'Still, what's done is done. And it's good to see you out and about.'

'Thank you for the welcome. It's a lovely pub.'

'Not when I first took over. It had been let go and the bar was only propped up by the old fellas who came in. Not that my changes have put them off.' She nodded to a row of men, some of whom Ginny had seen in the library earlier on. 'At least now we get others as well, including the tourists. I like to think it's good for me and good for the village.'

'A rising tide lifts all boats,' Hen quoted in the gentle way that Ginny was starting to suspect was part of her personality. 'But don't forget about our next book club. We're reading *Cold Comfort Farm*. I dropped a copy off for you last week.'

'I know. You're a doll, and I swear I'll try and get it read this time,' Rita said, before the sound of broken glass rang out. She closed her eyes briefly, as if trying to find her zen centre. 'I'd better go. Some of us have to earn a dishonourable living. But, Ginny, it's nice to meet you. Don't be a stranger.'

Ginny promised she wouldn't, before turning to find Hen, Tuppence and JM staring at her. She was going to have to tell them the truth.

'About the diary...'

'You know where it is?' They all leaned forward.

'It's a long story, but it ended up in my bag. I only discovered it yesterday and took it straight down to the station. I thought they would want it as evidence.'

'Who did you give it to?'

'DI Wallace.' Ginny studied her fingers. Handing it in had been the right thing to do, but she hated disappointing people. 'He didn't seem that interested because none of the pages were there.'

'It was empty?' Tuppence gasped.

'Not quite.' Her throat tightened and she couldn't bring herself to look up at them. 'There was an envelope, with Louisa's name handwritten on the front. It was cream-coloured, with a crest stamped on the flap.'

'Oh, no.' Hen put down her knitting and her lower lip trembled. 'That sounds like Alyson's stationery. What if it's the same one? If only we could've seen it.'

'Actually, you can. I took some photos.' Ginny retrieved her phone and scrolled through the photo file, then realised they were all staring at her. 'I did it out of habit. At the surgery, where I used to work, it was very important to document everything.'

There were four photos in all, and she passed her phone around.

Hen looked up from the screen. The heavy lines around her mouth had already faded, and her eyes were shining. 'That's not Alyson's handwriting.' Then her elation faded. 'But it does look like the envelopes she uses. In fact, I'm certain of it. I don't understand.'

'Seems clear enough to me.' JM drained her glass. 'Someone is trying to pin this on Alyson by using her stationery. That's why they put the arsenic in the sourdough – because they knew that Louisa had a standing order at the store. One loaf of potato and rosemary every week.'

'Are you sure?'

'Yes. She loved the stuff and got in a dreadful rage when it was sold out last year. That's when she started ordering it instead. I told Alyson not to keep her as a customer after the restraining order business, but would she listen?'

Ginny closed her eyes, thinking of what she'd read. The Mees' lines built up over time, which meant Louisa must have been ingesting low doses of the poison for several weeks, or even months. Then, combined with her arrythmia, someone could have been hoping she would have gone into cardiac arrest, and it would look natural.

She opened her eyes and stared at the three women at the table. 'But to poison Louisa in such a way... and to set Alyson up... it seems very extreme.'

'Which is exactly why they did it,' Tuppence declared, her eyes wide with horror. 'They thought no one would question it... and if they did discover the poison, it would look like Alyson did it, given the history between them. Oh, they're good. Very good indeed.'

'Nonsense. They're not *that* good, since we're already on to them,' JM reminded her, and then gave Ginny a reassuring look. 'We're ex-Neighbourhood Watch so we have a nose for this kind of thing.'

'Whoever is behind it has got it in for my poor girl. A-and for Louisa, obviously. Oh, dear, this is such a muddle, and I'm terrified that no one will believe Alyson is innocent.' Hen's voice began to tremble, and her shoulders fell. 'We need to find the letter.'

They all fell into silence, and Ginny bowed her head as her own past pushed its way into her mind.

Her father had died when Ginny was six, leaving her once gentle mother deep in grief, and – what Ginny now suspected – the throes of undiagnosed depression. It led to a chaotic eight months where her mother had swung between going out for nights on end, through to refusing to leave the house. Along the way there had been many visits from well-meaning social workers, several arrests for shoplifting and disturbing the peace, and eventually a prison sentence. Ginny had gone to live with an aunt, and while her mother had eventually joined her, she'd never been the same. All because no one had stepped up to help, or to understand what was really going on.

She was jolted from the memory by the grating screech of a chair being pushed back, as JM wordlessly stood up and walked over to the bar, the throng of drinkers instantly parting to let her through. She returned several minutes later holding a tray with four short glasses on it. They were filled with a glistening amber liquid.

'We need Drambuie.' She handed out the drinks.

Ginny couldn't remember the last time she'd had spirits, but the thick, syrupy aroma tingled in her nose, and she found herself following the other three women's example and lifting it up to her lips. Sweet honey and orange with a hint of oak filled her, burning her throat and heating her veins. It helped push away the memories of her mother, and of Louisa's dead body, leaving her light and relaxed.

'Most of this village think that the three of us are crazy old women who have nothing better to do than run around and cause trouble.' JM put down her glass, and Ginny swallowed, thinking of what Connor had told her.

Widows without a cause.

'I don't think you're crazy. Or old,' she said, still floating in a hazy Drambuie cloud.

'Well, that's very sweet of you.' Hen gave her a comfortable smile. 'I knew I liked the look of you. And you are adopting that dear little cat.'

'My point is,' JM continued, 'is that we're all we have. Rebecca and I never had children. We moved to Little Shaw ten years ago after we sold our art gallery in London, and it was Hen, Alyson and Tuppence who welcomed us without question. And after Rebecca died. Well—' JM's formidable countenance faltered, and she lowered her head.

'JM doesn't like being hugged that much,' Hen explained in a whisper, as they sat there in silence. Then JM blinked, seeming to push away whatever memory had ambushed her.

It was a feeling Ginny knew all too well, and her throat tightened.

'I grew up here but met Taron when I was at university, and we settled back here forty years ago.' Tuppence took over. 'And most of the folk around here thought we were odd. Artists, you see. We would go to schools and teach children how to have fun with paints. And we did many murals all over the country. But Hen never judged us. And after Adam died, then Taron, and then Rebecca, we learned to lean on each other.'

'Which is what we need to do now.' JM shifted to face Ginny. 'Something shady is going on here and we need to get to the bottom of it. Question is, will you help us?'

'You want me to search the library to see if Louisa hid Alyson's letter somewhere?' Ginny tightened her grip on her glass as Tuppence gave her an encouraging smile.

'In a nutshell, yes. It will be ever so much fun... and just think of poor Alyson, and what a weight will be lifted from her shoulders.'

'So, what do you say?' JM pushed.

They were all looking at her: Tuppence with her grey curls bouncing around her face, JM with her straight posture and fearless expression, and the kindly Hen, who seemed to be everyone's self-appointed mother.

'What about Harold Rowe? Even if I did want to look for it, I can hardly do it while he's around. He was in the office for most of the day.'

'Yes, that's a bit annoying.' Hen let out a disappointed sigh. 'And to think he swore he'd never come back. I bet Marigold Bentley almost fell over backwards when he agreed.'

'She did seem surprised,' Ginny admitted, before realising

she was getting sidetracked yet again. 'I wouldn't have a clue where to start.'

'I'm sure you'll think of something. After all, you were the one who noticed that Louisa had been poisoned. Though... if you hadn't, then poor Alyson wouldn't be in such a dreadful mess. Not that you could've known it at the time,' Tuppence quickly assured her.

Ginny closed her eyes. Even when Eric had been alive, they'd lived a quiet life, preferring each other's company rather than going out every night. Which meant that being involved in secret missions wasn't something she'd ever done. Then again, up until this week she'd never found a dead body, adopted a stray cat or drunk Drambuie on a Thursday night.

And I wasn't able to help Mother.

She opened her eyes and let out a decisive breath. 'Okay. I'll look for it tomorrow.'

'Wonderful.' Hen dropped her knitting so she could clap her hands together. Tuppence gave an approving nod and JM's eyes glittered.

'Excellent. And while you search the library, the three of us will start work on figuring out who the real killer is. It's one thing to murder Louisa... but it's another thing entirely to try and frame Alyson for it.'

'You're right. And to think we'd been hoping for a new project. We have the notebooks and everything.' Tuppence fumbled through a large leather backpack and produced a paint-splattered sketchpad. Then she turned to Hen. 'I think we should meet up at your cottage after the library closes tomorrow night. And we can start going over a list of suspects. Do you have a whiteboard?'

Hen wrinkled her nose. 'I don't think so. Though I do have a large piece of plywood that Adam used for his trainsets. We could lean it against the wall. Will it matter if there are a few hedges and farmyard animals still attached to it? The glue he used was very strong.'

'I'm sure we can work around it,' JM assured her, as the alcohol-induced haze that Ginny had been wrapped up in began to fade.

'Yes... but if we do find anything, we will give it to the police, right?'

'Of course we will.' Tuppence gave a casual wave of her hand. 'Like JM said, we're ex-Neighbourhood Watch so are very familiar with following the correct procedures. Isn't that right?'

'Yes,' Hen instantly agreed and then leaned over and took Ginny's hands in her own. Her grip was warm and strong, and her eyes were still bright from crying. But her mouth was curved into a grateful smile. 'And thank you. You have no idea what this means to me and my girl.'

'I'll try my best,' Ginny promised as a rush of heat washed over her, though she couldn't tell if it was because of the alcohol or the fact that for the first time since Eric died, someone needed her help.

SEVEN

'What are you doing here?' Harold Rowe stood in front of the library door the following morning, arms folded, mouth set in a flat line.

'I'm here for work. I-I start at ten.' Ginny gripped her handbag, which was weighed down by the training manual he'd insisted she take home every night. Heat stung her neck at the obstacle in front of her, and there was a dull pounding in her skull thanks to the Drambuie. She'd spent so much time working out the best way to search a building full of books for the missing pages of a diary and a poison letter that she'd failed to consider her temporary manager might not be on board with her plans.

'I'm aware of that. But it's only nine.' His grey eyes had narrowed into two small slits, and he made no effort to stand aside and let her in. 'You're an hour early. Why?'

That was indeed a very good question.

And if only she had an answer.

Unfortunately, lying had never been her forte, and she could hardly tell him she wanted to secretly look for the missing pages of Louisa's diary or a defamatory letter that might be misconstrued as a murder motive.

Harold's mouth twitched in a way that suggested he was waiting for an answer.

The heat that had been travelling up Ginny's neck had now reached her forehead and tiny beads of sweat started to form, under his penetrating glare.

Definitely no more late-night drinking sessions for her. Or even early night ones.

She lowered her gaze, and for the first time she noticed that the sleeves of Harold's dazzling white shirt were rolled up to the elbow, and that the grey wool trousers were smeared with dust. Whoever was responsible for his meticulous wardrobe wouldn't be pleased.

It was the same reason Ginny had decided to wear her jeans, since she hadn't had the chance to set up a cleaning schedule for the library to deal with the obvious neglect, and didn't want to get covered in dirt and grime.

Then she blinked. *Oh. Of course.*

'I want to give this place a thorough scrub. While it's apparent that the cleaners do the floors and bathrooms, there is a lot of dust, which is no good for anyone's health. Or clothing...' She nodded at his trousers.

'My what?'

It was his turn to look flustered as he tried to brush the dirt away. But it only had the effect of rubbing it further in. Which, if he had been the one doing his laundry, he probably would have known.

'There's a clothing brush in the back office. So, is it okay if I make a start? Going forward, we could discuss it with the current cleaners, as well as seeing if any of the volunteers would like to help.'

He gave a curt nod and stepped to one side. 'That's a very sensible idea. Thank you for bringing it to my attention. I suggest you start in the non-fiction area. Now, if you don't mind, I was halfway through cataloguing the botanical drawings of one of our own local luminaries, Reverend Michael... I suspect that's where the dust came from.'

Without another word he disappeared back to the small office, leaving her alone. Ginny had no idea who Reverend Michael was but was pleased Harold had been pulled back to him and his botanical drawings.

In the staffroom, she searched through several cupboards until she found a bucket and cleaning cloths, as well as an ancient vacuum cleaner. It was enough to make a start.

Three hours later Ginny was starting to appreciate just how difficult her self-imposed task was – both the cleaning and the searching. After she'd spent time in the non-fiction section, she'd moved onto the counter and worked her way through the long drawers underneath, which had become a dumping ground for years of rubber bands, random bookmarks, old toys and even a single, bright pink trainer.

In the end she'd filled two large bin bags – one to throw out, and one to donate to charity – and wiped down all the surfaces. But while there was now less clutter and dust, she hadn't found the missing diary pages. She'd also been shocked at all the health and safety hazards she'd come across, and after searching in vain for a current register, she'd ended up making her own spreadsheet so she could discuss them with Harold and come up with a working plan.

The rest of the day had been spent issuing books, talking to the customers, and replying to Tuppence's many text messages. At some stage Ginny would have to ask her not to use all caps.

She'd finally managed to search the office when Harold had announced that he had a doctor's appointment and wouldn't be back. But, as she'd expected, the police had done a thorough job, and there wasn't even any dust.

Which was when Ginny had the good idea to check underneath all the bookshelves.

Armed with a broom, she was crouching down and pushing it underneath the romance section when someone coughed.

It was Connor, leaning against a trolley and looking bored.

'O-oh, hello there. How are you?' she stammered, too late noticing her own jeans had almost identical smudge marks to the ones on Harold's trousers.

'Alive.' His shrug suggested that this was at the top end of his scale. 'I thought you might want to know Cleo is about to strangle someone.'

'She's *what*?' Ginny scrambled to her feet in time to see Cleo step dangerously close to William, who was trying to swat her away with a folded newspaper.

Ginny thrust the broom at Connor and pushed through the gathering crowd, until she was standing between the volunteer and the elderly gentleman. It wasn't the first time she'd had to break up a fight – though usually it was between stressed-out family members who were at loggerheads over how the NHS was supporting them.

'Is there a problem?'

'Yes, there's a problem.' William dragged a handkerchief across his forehead to mop up the sweat. 'All I want is a copy of Monday's paper but apparently that's too much to ask.'

'It is when it's from Monday the eighth of December, 1975!' Cleo retorted, in an Arctic tone. 'You know we can't simply click our fingers and magic it up for you, William.'

'I don't see why not. The manager before Louisa never minded going to the stack for me.'

'The stack?' Ginny knitted her brows together. She knew that libraries referred to their storage areas as 'stacks' but hadn't realised that Little Shaw Community Library had one of their own. Louisa hadn't mentioned anything about them. For that matter, neither had Harold.

'It's at the back of the building,' Cleo reluctantly explained. 'But there's no internal access, which is why it's such a pain to go there at the drop of a hat. You need to walk down the alley to get in. It's beastly when it rains, which is terrible for the books. Louisa said it was impractical and refused to let us go in there.'

'That's only because she didn't want to deal with the padlock,' William retorted. 'She kept complaining that it broke her fingernails. Though why she thought it was a better solution to stop using it than to just get her nails cut, I'll never know.'

Ginny hitched in a breath. Louisa had a broken fingernail on Monday afternoon. Was that how she'd done it? Could it have happened as she hid the pages of her diary in the stack... and Alyson's letter?

It was an hour until closing time, and Harold had already left for the day. This might be the best chance she had to go there on her own.

She turned to Cleo. 'I'd be happy to get the newspaper for William, if you know where the key is kept—?'

'It's under the counter. Would you like Connor to go with you? About time he did some work around here.'

'Pots and kettles,' he called out, from where he was shelving.

'I'm sure I can manage.' Ginny guided Cleo back to the counter before another argument could break out.

'There's a roller door that has a padlock down the bottom – that's the thing that everyone hates because it's quite fiddly. But once it's up, make sure you put the padlock back on at the top, so that no one can roll it down again until you leave,' Cleo instructed, as a customer came up to the counter holding a magazine that was missing half of the pages.

She let out a huffy noise, and Ginny escaped outside and down the narrow alley, to the back of the building.

Discarded crisp packets and drink cans were pressed

against the hedge that separated it from the park next door. At the end was a half-filled skip and a bike rack, as well as a narrow roller door with a large, old-fashioned padlock at the bottom.

She crouched down and slipped her hand underneath it so that she could angle it enough to get the key in. Her own nails were kept short, but she could easily imagine why Louisa had found it difficult. And having a door that could be locked from the outside was far from ideal.

Yet another thing to add to the health and safety register.

The padlock clicked open, and it wasn't long before Ginny stepped inside and fumbled with the switch.

She was in a large room with row upon row of shelves. In the middle was a long workbench covered in piles of books and magazines, many of which had broken spines or pages poking out at unnatural angles. There was a collection of glues and an old-fashioned book press, along with a box of scissors and scalpels, all used no doubt to repair the damaged books.

There was also a microfiche reader and some open-faced shelving piled high with old newspapers. Thankfully, Louisa's predecessor, and perhaps Harold Rowe, had ensured that the older copies were in meticulous order, and it didn't take Ginny long to retrieve the edition William had requested.

Then she put it down and started her search. The air was stale but not damp as she made her way along each shelf, hoping to find the missing diary pages, but after twenty minutes all she'd discovered was more dust.

She stood up and managed to catch sight of her reflection in a small mirror hanging from the wall. There were several smudges on her face... and was that a cobweb in her hair? Using the tips of her fingers, she rubbed away the dirt as best she could and then tried to smooth down her hair, until she looked more like her usual self.

Except her usual self wasn't the kind of person who snuck

around a library looking for hidden letters and the missing pages of a diary. Who had she been kidding?

Even if they were in the library, Ginny clearly wasn't the right person to find them. She wasn't like JM, Tuppence or even Hen. Was that why she had agreed to help? Because she was hoping some of their outgoing personalities might rub off on her?

Then she sighed. No. That wasn't the answer. It was because she couldn't bear to think that Alyson's pain might be used against her, if the hate letter was found by the police.

Not that she'd been much help.

Ginny glanced at her watch. There was no way she could stay there any longer without Cleo or Connor getting into an argument, and it was time to start closing the whole place down for the evening. She just had to hope that wherever Alyson's letter had been hidden, it would stay there.

She picked up William's newspaper and at the same time managed to knock over a pile of books that had been haphazardly piled on the workbench. They toppled sideways in a series of thumps and scattered across the desk. Gritting her teeth, she gathered them up again.

They were mainly non-fiction books with damaged spines, waiting to be repaired, but underneath them was a yellow A4 envelope. It was heavy, and the shape suggested that whatever was inside, it wasn't all the same size. Well, that was a silly place to have put it. Unless... Oh. Was it possible that this is where Louisa had put the letter?

With shaking hands, Ginny eased out a large pile of unbound pages. They all had a row of holes down the side, and looked just like what could be expected to have come out of Louisa's grey ring-binder diary.

Ginny studied the first page just to confirm it was Louisa's.

Haircut 10am.

Go to Gibsons and demand refund on faulty zipper.
Take back champagne and threaten legal action
unless they replace it with something that doesn't
taste like cows' piss.

Adrenaline hummed in Ginny's veins. It definitely sounded like Louisa, which meant she'd done it. She'd found the missing pages of the diary. There was no time to check for the letter... and part of her didn't want to. After all, Alyson had never meant for it to be read by anyone, and Ginny would hate to betray that trust.

Instead, she quickly slipped everything back into the envelope and locked up the stack. She needed to close the library for the evening and go and see Hen, Tuppence and JM... all before the guilt of not handing it straight to the police could take hold of her.

EIGHT

Ginny turned off the car engine and looked up at the two-storey cottage in front of her. She'd almost missed it, set as it was on the bend, without even a footpath between the side of the house and the street.

She climbed out to see three other small, silver cars parked in front of her. They were similar to her own and were what Eric had once dubbed 'one careful lady driver' cars.

She could almost hear his deep, rich laugh.

At least she knew she was at the right place. She patted her handbag to make sure the yellow envelope was still there. The drive over had been spent humming the same Beatles song to stop herself from thinking about the police and what might happen if they found out. She wasn't sure if it had worked, but she'd never enjoy 'Penny Lane' in quite the same way again.

It was almost six at night, but even in the fading light, the pale brown stones and slate roof were charming, as was the cottage garden that wound its way to the front door. Though Ginny wasn't sure how she'd feel living in a place that was quite so close to the road.

'Don't worry, you get used to the noise.' Hen appeared in

the doorway, somehow reading her mind. 'It's why we got the place so cheaply – back when no one wanted to worry about lorries going past or having to duck their heads to get through the front door. Probably lucky that my poor Adam wasn't much taller than I am. Anyway, come in.'

Ginny followed her through the low doorway into a warm sitting room with polished wooden floors, pale blue painted walls and two lovely old sofas – one of which was taken up by a blond labrador with woeful eyes and soft-looking ears.

JM and Tuppence were seated on the other one, and Alyson was by the open fireplace, her eyes red and blotchy.

'Here, sit down.' Hen pointed to a comfortable-looking wingback. 'Brandon doesn't like that chair, so you won't get covered in dog hair. Now, let me get us all a nice cup of tea and then we can see what we've got.'

Hen bustled out of the room, and Ginny peered around. There was a collection of tapestries and paintings dotted around the walls as well as an old school map of Ireland. It was lovely, but considering the circumstances, Ginny wasn't sure it was the right time to talk about home decorating. Then she noticed the large piece of plywood leaning on an artist's easel.

It was half-covered in several pieces of printer paper that had been taped together and were attached at the corners, though there were large bumps there, where some of the model trees, and what looked like a train station, were still visible. There were also several balls of wool, a bright pink marker pen and some thumb tacks, all neatly lined up on an old drinks trolley.

'Did you find it okay?' Tuppence asked. 'First time I came here, I missed it by a mile.'

'Which you would have known if you'd just used a map,' JM reminded her, before turning to Ginny. 'Have you looked at the pages?'

'No. I only had time to feed Edgar and then come straight over.'

'What a sweet name for the cat. At least someone is getting a happy ending.' Alyson, who had been staring into the fire, looked up. Her shoulders were hunched over, as if there was a giant weight on them. 'Sorry I ran out on you all last night. I was a bit overwhelmed.'

'That's okay. How are you feeling?' Ginny put the envelope on the coffee table.

'Not great.' Alyson's eyes brimmed with tears. 'I still can't believe this is happening. The police were in the store again today, asking me more questions. It's like I'm waiting for the other shoe to drop. It's my own silly fault for writing the letter in the first place. I didn't think I was angry about the divorce – just sad. Especially after all this time. No wonder Bernard left me. I don't even know my own feelings.'

'Nonsense. Bernard left you because he is a class A ninny.' Hen had reappeared with a large tray, and puffed out her reply to Alyson over the top of it. She put the tray onto the low table and busied herself with pouring tea and trying to convince Alyson to eat one of the small sandwiches. Then Hen shooed a sleepy Brandon along and settled on the sofa with the envelope that Ginny had brought. 'Now, who wants to do the honours? Alyson?'

'No. I just want this whole thing to go away.' She leaned back and rubbed her thin arms, as if she'd received an electric shock. Then the tears that she'd been holding at bay leaked out. 'I'm so pathetic.'

'Don't be a goose, love. We're all here for you,' Hen said, handing the envelope to JM so as to be able to fish a clean hanky from her sleeve to hand to her daughter.

'Of course we are. But you can't bury your head in the sand forever. Things don't go away just by closing our eyes.' JM briskly eased the thick pile of pages out of the envelope, then tapped the base of the pile against the coffee table to straighten them up. She did that several times then neatly split them into five piles with the ease of a Vegas blackjack dealer.

'That's impressive.' Tuppence whistled.

'Just a little trick I picked up along the way. It will be faster if we each go through a pile.' JM passed one pile to Tuppence, who lifted the pages over her shoulder like a cocktail shaker, and gave them three vigorous thrusts, but all that came out were several business cards and an unpaid parking ticket.

'Well, that's annoying.'

'Maybe we should go back through the appointments?' Hen started on a second pile. 'Goodness, I can barely read this. "Gallop?" Wait, no, I think it's "gallon". Though it still doesn't make sense. "Take gallon red to Barn Clown." Whatever does she mean?'

Ginny leaned over to study the page. '"Tell Graham to do the hedges properly or he won't be paid." And see... there's his phone number.'

'You got all that from this scrawl? How extraordinary. I can't make head or tail of it.'

'It's not that hard once you get the hang of it. See the way she's looped the 'A'? And that tiny dash is an 'I',' Ginny explained, before looking up to where all three women were now staring at her. Heat rose up her neck. 'Eric was a doctor, and I ran the surgery, so it wasn't just his handwriting I had to read – it was all of the locums we had over the years. I suppose I got used to it.'

'New plan.' JM gathered back the piles of the diary. 'It's probably easier if you read them all. It will avoid misdirection.'

'Of course.' She took the piles and settled them in her lap as a single sheet of heavy cream-coloured paper slowly dislodged itself and fell onto the sofa.

It was folded in half but was the perfect match for the envelope that had been in the diary.

'That's my stationery.' Alyson finally joined them.

Hen, who had smoothed it open, quickly held it up, but her fingers were trembling and it was clear she was shocked.

'It can't be a coincidence that it's the same stationery. It looks expensive. Not just the run-of-the-mill stuff you can buy anywhere.'

'It was,' Alyson choked. 'I bought it years ago to write thank-you cards for Bernard to send to his clients. He insisted I buy something classy. I'm not even sure it's still being sold anymore.'

'Which proves that someone has done this on purpose. But who?' Tuppence demanded.

'That's what we must find out. Let's see what it says.' JM fumbled in her pocket for some reading glasses and put them on her nose. She then read the message out loud. '"This is your last warning. I want the files you stole. Give them to me by the end of the week or pay the price."'

There was a short, shocked silence. Then: 'It's blackmail. And I think it's the same handwriting that was on the envelope in Louisa's diary. What do you say, Ginny?' Tuppence passed the note over to where Ginny was sitting. She reached for it, too late remembering about fingerprints. She tried not to imagine Wallace's withering glare if he knew what they were doing.

Instead, she studied the short note carefully and then brought up the photograph on her phone to compare them side by side.

'Yes. See the shape of the 'F'? It's quite distinctive. And judging by the smudge there, the author's left-handed. It's the same person,' she said, then pressed her lips together. 'Are you sure we shouldn't take this to the police? It might be evidence.'

'Yes, but it's evidence that's written on Alyson's stationery,' JM pointed out, which caused Alyson to burst out crying again.

'Hush, love, it's okay,' Hen comforted her while JM tapped her chin, as if considering the matter.

'Knowing Wallace, he'd jump to the wrong conclusion. And it's not like the police have gone back into the library looking for the diary pages. I say we at least try to work out what these files are. Then once we have more evidence, we can take it to them.'

Ginny pushed back her unease, accepting that JM had a point. And if they did give it to the police, only for them to decide Alyson was behind it, they'd be in an even worse mess. 'Okay, let's see what we can find out.'

'Excellent.' Tuppence stood and paced the room. She'd left her shoes at the front door and her white socks were covered in small green frogs, which matched her T-shirt. 'It's all very exciting. So, now we just have to work out what the files are, who would blackmail Louisa, and why they are trying to frame Alyson.'

'Who wouldn't want to blackmail Louisa?' JM snorted. 'Did you see the line of people outside the police station? They were falling over themselves with stories about who Louisa had argued with.'

'That's true.' Tuppence held up her fingers and started counting them off. 'At the library alone there was Esme, William, Rose—'

'Hang on, we need to write this down. I can barely remember what time my doctor's appointment is, so I'll never keep all of this in my head,' Hen said.

JM marched over to the plywood board and picked up the pink marker.

'We could do mind-mapping.' Tuppence joined her, selecting a ball of wool. 'I watched a YouTube show on it. You link everything together with lines.' She held up the wool as if she was on the QVC UK shopping channel. 'So, JM, you write down Louisa's name and then Esme's name, and I'll put a line of wool between them.'

'Wait... no.' Hen put down her knitting and joined them. 'You can't link them up until we write down how they're connected. That's why I have these coloured stickers. See?' She peeled one off and held it up on her fingertip.

Ginny waited until JM had found a spot on the paper to write down the two names and *Library. Armitage/Clarkson DVD mockery. Civil liberties.* Then stepped back for Hen to add her stickers, and Tuppence to pin a line of wool from one name to the other.

'Now... who was next?'

'Maybe we should focus on the letter itself first,' Ginny said, not sure there would be enough space on the board. 'If you can't buy the stationery anymore, someone must have stolen it from Alyson. But how? Did you ever take it to work with you?'

'No. I keep it on the desk in my bedroom. But I suppose they could've stolen it while we were out. We don't always lock the front door.'

'But we will from now on,' Hen said in a comfortable voice that didn't fill Ginny with confidence, as Tuppence added another piece of wool to the board and JM drew a picture of a door.

'Do you think the police will work out that the envelope belonged to me?' Alyson pushed back a strand of unwashed hair.

'I'm sure they won't. How could they? And, if they do, at least we can prove you didn't write it. We have Ginny, who is an expert. You saw how good she is,' Hen told her.

'I wouldn't say I'm an expert,' Ginny protested, which was met by a shuddering sob. 'But I will try my best if it comes to that. Do you recognise the writing?'

'No.' Alyson shook her head a little too quickly and looked relieved when her phone buzzed. She picked it up from the mantelpiece and studied the screen. 'It's my friend. She lives in Newcastle. Would you mind if I slip up to my bedroom and take it? Then I might get a bath... it's been a long day.'

'Good idea.' JM waited until Alyson had left the room before lowering her voice. 'Probably for the best. She's only just holding it together, so I didn't want to say anything in front of her, but her case is not looking good.'

'Janet Marie Rivers, don't you dare say that. We can't give up on her.' Hen's cheeks filled with colour.

'Give up on her? Of course we're not. I'm playing devil's advocate and trying to think like the police.' JM tapped her lip with her finger. 'Between the brutal divorce, the restraining order and the sourdough bread, they're going to build a case. And that's *without* the letters. Which is why our next move is clear.'

'Oh. Well, that's okay then.' Hen's shoulders relaxed, before she wrinkled her nose. 'Out of interest, what is our next move?'

'We have to accept we're not going to find the letter Alyson wrote and focus on who the real killer is.' JM drew four stick figures running after a large, messy circle with T-Rex hands.

Ginny closed her eyes. She wasn't sure that this *was* the next logical step. But she doubted they'd change their minds about taking the note to the police just yet. Still, as soon as they did find enough evidence, then they could hand it over. The worry in her chest lessened, and she sat up a bit straighter as her mind sifted through what little they knew.

The arsenic was in the sourdough.

And the sourdough was in the house.

'We need to start with the bread. Do we know who made it, who delivered it to Collin's... and whereabouts it was stored at Louisa's home?'

'Oh... you *are* smart. I knew you'd be able to help.' Hen put down her knitting to clap her hands together. Brandon opened one eye to see what the fuss was about, then went back to sleep.

'Excellent question. Heather O'Dea is the one who made it.

She only moved to the village a few years ago and is a wonderful baker. I heard she had a business down south, but it fell apart and she lost everything. She was too ashamed to go home to Ireland, and somehow ended up here.'

'Little Shaw has a reputation for being home to waifs and strays,' Tuppence added, before receiving a sharp glare from JM.

'Are you calling me a waif *or* a stray?'

'Of course she's not,' Hen waded into the conversation. 'What she meant to say is that our little village attracts a colourful collection of wonderful souls.'

'Hmmmm.' JM gave Tuppence one final glance and then coughed. 'Let's see, where was I? Oh, yes, Heather lives in the flat above the pub, and when she's not working at the bar, she bakes. At first it was just for The Lost Goat but then she branched out. She does the farmers' market once a month and supplies Collin's Grocery Store.'

'And she has lovely long purple hair,' Hen added.

Ginny recalled seeing a woman behind the bar the other day with purple hair. She seemed to be in her mid-forties and had been softly spoken. 'As for who delivers the bread, I'm sure Alyson can tell us. I'll ask her after she's had her bath.'

'Would Heather have any reason to dislike Louisa?' Ginny asked.

'No more than anyone else.' JM put a question mark next to Heather's name and then drew a large loaf of bread. 'Which leaves us with Louisa's house. Is it possible that someone tampered with it once it was there?'

'Well, we broke in easily enough, so anyone could have done it,' Tuppence said.

When no one else added anything, Ginny swallowed and glanced at the stairs that led to Alyson's room. She lowered her voice. 'Shouldn't we also consider that Bernard might have done it? I-I'm not saying he *is* guilty, but it seems the most sensible place to start.'

Hen visibly paled but Tuppence gave an excited smile. 'They do say it's usually the husband.'

'But why would he blackmail his own wife, and keep the poison in his own home?' Hen said, clearly still not happy.

'Because his hubris wouldn't allow him to think he would get caught. I'll add him to the board. But I'll use code so that Alyson doesn't get upset.' JM wrote a capital F followed by a capital B. 'See, I've put his initials the other way around. Of course, the only problem with Bernard is that he won't let any of us through the door because he knows we're Alyson's friends.'

Like a school of fish changing direction, they all turned to Ginny.

'He doesn't know you.' Tuppence was the first to speak.

'And you were the one to find Louisa,' JM added.

'Plus, you have such a lovely, calm aura.' Hen beamed.

She did?

Ginny's palms prickled in protest. The angry, red-faced man she'd seen at the pub on Thursday night didn't seem like the sort who liked visitors. A soft sob floated down from upstairs, and Ginny wondered how much Alyson had heard.

Plus, there had been something strange about the way Alyson had refused to look too closely at the blackmail note.

Was it because she recognised Bernard's writing and didn't want to admit it? Ginny had read about Stockholm syndrome enough to understand the complicated dynamics that might still exist between Hen's daughter and her ex-husband, regardless of the history.

It could explain why Hen was so worried. Did she think that Alyson might be capable of covering up for him, if Bernard was in fact the killer? Or, worse, let herself take the blame? The idea was terrifying, but it did soothe Ginny's conscience about why they were getting involved. Clearly, they had to help Alyson, even if she couldn't help herself.

'Okay, if you think it would work, I'll go there tomorrow morning. Edgar has a vet appointment at eleven, but I'll visit Bernard first. And I'll take a condolence card.'

'Oh... yes... you're a natural at this,' Tuppence declared.

Ginny wasn't quite sure about that: it was more a case of having an excuse to get through the door. 'Is there anything else I need to know about him?'

'He's a property developer who's never met a corner he didn't want to cut. It means he's not the most popular person around here. But when he was married to Alyson, she managed to smooth out some of his sharp edges. Unfortunately, after four years of marriage to Louisa, they're back in full force.'

'I will need his address. And what about Heather, who baked the bread?'

'I'll go and talk to her tomorrow morning,' JM said, with extra emphasis on the word 'talk'. Maybe it was better that Ginny was going to see Bernard on her own.

'I'll come with you. Heather bakes excellent Eccles cakes and I haven't had one in ages,' Tuppence declared. 'What about you, Hen? Would you like to tag along?'

'I can't. I need to deliver the nests I knit for a bird rescue charity,' Hen explained, holding up her bright pink knitting, which Ginny realised for the first time wasn't a baby bonnet. 'And then, on the way back, I plan to stop at the nursery to buy more bulbs for tomorrow afternoon.'

'Oh, yes, we must get that bank planted out before it gets too cold,' Tuppence agreed, before turning to Ginny. 'We volunteer at the cemetery most Saturdays to try and keep up with the gardening. You should come with us. All you need is a shovel and some gardening clothes. It really is lots of fun. And we can discuss what we've found.'

'Hang on, hang on. Not so fast,' JM broke in, fixing Ginny

with a sharp stare. 'You do know the difference between a weed and a lavender bush, don't you?'

Ginny blinked, not sure what to make of the constant change of pace and topic when she was around the three women. Still, compared to sneaking around the library, agreeing to visit a potential killer, and trying to solve a murder, a bit of gardening was at least well within her wheelhouse.

'I do,' Ginny assured them, as she sank back into the chair, not sure if she'd ever experienced a week quite like this one. Still, at least it wasn't boring.

NINE

Bernard lived on the sort of street Ginny would expect a property developer to live on. Ignoring the charming country-side, it was full of expensive two-storey detached houses with perfectly manicured lawns and hardly any trees. The only way to tell them apart were the different cars that were parked up the driveways. The vehicle at number fifteen was a black Range Rover with a flashy personalised numberplate. She still didn't know much about him, other than he'd been married to Alyson before having his affair with Louisa. And that he was a property developer who owned a business called Allan and Farnsworth Developments.

In her carrier bag was a condolence card, where she'd neatly written out her favourite Percy Shelley poem. It was one of the few she could still bear to look at. She'd also made casse-role for the first time since Eric's death. She hadn't the appetite or inclination to cook big meals lately. She wasn't even sure if Bernard would like simple food, but she couldn't go empty-handed.

She'd assumed that the best way for her to help the widows would be to stay behind the scenes, and perhaps help with the puzzle pieces, rather than doing the more physical aspects. But, here she was.

Her knees knocked together, but Ginny forced herself forward. After all, JM, Tuppence and Hen had come here at nighttime and broken in, armed only with a YouTube video and a lot of resolve. By their standards Ginny's own daytime visit seemed paltry. Unexpected laughter caught in her throat.

She had moved to Little Shaw hoping to find a way through the terrible grief that had been holding her hostage. And while this wasn't quite what she'd had in mind, the trio's easy friend-ship with each other had made Ginny realise what had been missing in her own life.

Feeling braver, she reached the door.

It was ajar, and the sound of Radio Two floated out. At least that meant Bernard was awake. The doorbell let out a raspy metallic buzz, but she resolutely pressed it again and again, until footsteps finally sounded and he appeared.

Oh dear. He looked even worse than he had the night she'd seen him in the pub: the stubble had now turned into a beard, while the stale stench of whisky clung to him. And despite it being nine in the morning, he was clutching a glass of red wine, half of which had spilled down his shirt. But Ginny hadn't been a doctor's wife for thirty-five years without seeing people at their worst. 'Bernard, my name's Ginny and I worked with Louisa. I'm so sorry for your loss, and I wanted to offer some help. I could tidy up, or get groceries, or even do some gardening.'

He blinked several times, as if hoping to remove the map of red lines from his bloodshot eyes. The glass swayed in his hand, and Ginny used her free hand to prise it from his fingers. She half expected him to swear, but instead his face crumpled, and he stepped aside to usher her in.

The wide hallway was impersonal, and if it hadn't been for the large portrait of Louisa – wearing a tight red dress – it might very well have been a display home. The narrow console table and floor were littered with cards and bunches of flowers, much like the ones she had with her. It was clear that he was still in shock.

Feeling a little more in her element, Ginny gave him a firm smile. 'Why don't I make a hot drink then get these flowers into water? It would be a shame for it all to go to waste. When did you last eat?'

He looked down at his shirt, as if hoping the stains would provide a timeline. 'Maybe last night. Not sure.'

'I could make you some toast. Probably best not to have anything too heavy right now.'

The kitchen was even more of a mess, with empty bottles and glasses covering the surfaces. Ginny ignored them and poured the red wine down the sink, before flicking on the kettle. Bernard seemed happy enough for her to clear everything up and load the dishwasher before handwashing the wine glasses. She then gathered the flowers from the hallway and put them into the water-filled sink, while lining up the many cards along the back of the bench.

As she made two mugs of tea, he finally spoke: 'You were the one who found her body, weren't you?'

'I'm afraid so. It was only my second day working at the library.'

'That's right. Louisa came home on Monday night and said you were useless, and that Marigold Bentley must've had rocks in her head,' he said fondly, before his eyes teared up. 'I can't believe she's gone. What am I meant to do now?'

'I wish I could tell you.' She tried not to smart at Louisa's insult, though it wasn't a surprise. The library manager hadn't bothered to hide what she thought of Ginny's suitability for the role. Or as a person. She gritted her teeth. All she had to do was find out what she could, then leave. 'It must have been such a shock to hear the news. Did she seem herself on Monday when she got home from work?'

Suddenly his face darkened, and he let out a bark of laughter. 'You mean was she sitting on her arse drinking wine instead of cooking dinner? Then, yes, she was very much herself. She even remembered to complain about the way I breathe, before telling me I was a tight-fisted so-and-so for not taking her skiing in Tignes. She didn't even like skiing.' Then he took a slug of his tea and coughed. 'This isn't whisky.'

'No, it's not.'

'But that was her all over. Money, money, money. I was just an ATM to her. Sometimes I regret ever marrying her. But what's that saying about having to lie in the bed you made?' It was followed by another manic burst of laughter. 'Man, but she was good in that bed.'

'How about I make that toast for you?' Ginny got to her feet, trying to dredge up sympathy for him. And was he only speaking so frankly because he was drunk? Or was that how he felt? Then she remembered the sourdough and how his wife was poisoned. Should she offer him cereal instead? However, Bernard didn't seem put off by the mention of toast. 'Where do you keep the bread?'

'No idea. The cleaner puts the food away.' He vaguely waved his hand in the direction of a walk-in pantry. Ginny found half a loaf and put two slices in the toaster before venturing in for a better look. As she suspected, most of the contents were gone. Had they been taken away for testing? And who was the cleaner? If she put things away, then she would have had access to the sourdough once it had been delivered.

The toast popped and she spread on some butter and put it in front of him. 'Is your cleaner any good? I was thinking of hiring one. But I'm new to Little Shaw.'

He blinked as if she'd just asked him to recite the periodic table. 'How the hell would I know if she's any good? I have bigger things to worry about than woman's work.'

Ginny's mouth twitched with dislike. But his arrogance made it harder to picture him poisoning his wife. After all, wasn't poison merely 'woman's work', too?

She desperately wanted to leave this house and this man.

On the counter was a pile of unopened bills – and a black leather diary identical to the grey one. *His and Hers?* As much as Ginny wanted to leave, she had to check his handwriting. It was a long shot, and she couldn't see how Alyson wouldn't have recognised it. But since she hadn't managed to find anything else, it would be a shame not to check.

'I need a drink.' Bernard suddenly pushed the toast away and stood up.

'Is that a good idea?'

'It's an exceptional idea.' He burped twice and ignored the wine bottles on the counter as he swayed towards the hallway.

Once the sound of swearing faded, Ginny opened the diary.

His writing was surprisingly neat and pleasing. A compact style with a measured slant and no flourishes. It wasn't a match to the blackmail note.

Which proves you can't judge a chauvinist by his cursive.

Just to be sure he didn't have more than one style, she flipped through the pages, but unlike his erratic temper, it was consistent.

The raspy, metallic buzz of the front doorbell blasted out and Ginny shut the diary with a slam, managing to dislodge an envelope from the pile of letters thrown haphazardly onto the counter beside her. In the corner was the name 'TKL Insurance'. The envelope was thick, as if it was filled with details of the policy.

But what policy?

Did Bernard have life insurance against Louisa? Her fingers itched to open it and find out the answer, but the sound of voices from the hallway was like a bucket of water over her, and she pushed it back into the pile.

'When was the last time you ate?' a familiar voice said. Moments later, Edward Tait, the lawyer, appeared, followed by Bernard, who'd found a bottle of whisky.

'How many Good Samaritans do I need to entertain today? Either have a drink with me or piss off.'

'I'm hardly a Good Samaritan, I'm here to—' Edward broke off, finally noticing Ginny over by the bench. 'What are *you* doing here?'

That was a very good question, since she could hardly pretend to have known Bernard. 'I worked with Louisa at the library. I didn't want to intrude, but I thought Bernard might have questions about—' She broke off, not wanting to say Louisa's name.

Then it hit her. Bernard *hadn't* asked anything about Louisa. Why was that? Because he was grieving?

Or because he'd been waiting for it to happen?

'He doesn't.' Edward's face tightened. 'And my client is in no fit state to be talking to anyone.'

'I understand. Though, if you could get him to eat, it might soak up some of the alcohol. I made a casserole for him,' Ginny said

'Did you just—' Edward broke off as Bernard drained the last dregs from the bottle and stumbled past them, towards the back door. 'Hey, no. That's not a good idea.'

But Bernard didn't answer as he yanked the bifold door back and ran out onto the grass, peeling off his trousers as he went. Edward swore under his breath, and Ginny blinked as a now naked Bernard was running around the lawn, howling like a wolf as he twirled his shirt in the air.

'I can see myself out,' Ginny said, pleased to leave.

Her mind whirled as she drove home to her own house,

where she tried to convince Edgar to get in the travel carrier so she could take him to his appointment.

Ginny was panting by the time she stepped into the Carlyle Vet Clinic, and her jeans were covered in cat fur. Not that she could blame Edgar for shedding so much hair. She wouldn't want to be put in the carrier either.

'I'm only doing it so we can make sure you're well,' she assured him for the hundredth time, once he'd finally climbed in.

'Hi, I'm Pippa. We spoke on the phone. And this must be Edgar.' The receptionist had twinkling eyes that matched her personality, and Ginny felt calmer as she filled out the intake questionnaire and then settled down to wait.

There hadn't been time to call Hen and the others, and despite her dislike of using her phone in public, she reached for it now, wondering whether to make an exception. Except she could hardly say anything in front of a roomful of people. Though she could text.

It wasn't until she had unlocked her handset that she realised the other people in the waiting room were all staring at her eagerly. Her cheeks stung with heat, and she put her phone down and forced a smile.

'You're the new librarian, aren't you?' a woman with a box on her lap said. Ginny wanted to correct her and say she was only an assistant but didn't want to appear rude. Instead, she agreed that she was.

'And you found her? Is it true there was blood everywhere?' A second woman clutched at the collar of a small white dog who was trying to chew the leg of the plastic chair. 'Tut-tut, Miss Florence. Stop it.'

'No. There wasn't any blood.'

The two women let out a disappointed sigh and turned to

each other. 'I heard it was splattered around the place like one of those paintings that don't make any sense.'

'Doesn't change the fact we have a murderer walking amongst us.' A middle-aged man snorted. 'And what are the police doing about it?'

'You can hardly blame them, Bill. They've already interviewed half a dozen people, all with motives. The only problem they'll have is narrowing it down to just one.'

The conversation went on in that fashion, until one by one they were called into various exam rooms. Soon it was Ginny and one other woman. She was only young, maybe in her mid-twenties with ebony hair, dusky skin and exquisite make-up.

'They should add me to that list,' the woman said suddenly to Ginny, before waving a perfectly manicured nail in the direction of the now-empty seats. 'This lot are treating it like a television show, but I'm the one out of pocket over it.'

'Did she owe you money?' Ginny asked, thinking of Elsie Wicks, who also had an outstanding bill with Louisa.

'Oh, yes. Made me cancel two full sets and a pedi, all so I could fix one broken nail – which had clearly been ripped off.'

Ginny's back stiffened in surprise. She hadn't thought to visit the nail technician, despite the fact she'd been right next to Louisa when she'd been arguing on the phone with the poor girl.

'She left work early to go and see you. Are you saying she didn't turn up?'

'She turned up all right.' The woman shuddered. '*And* had enough time to complain about my shoddy workmanship to my other customers. Then her phone rang, and she started yelling at someone before taking off. Didn't even pay me my cancellation fee.'

'Argument? Do you know who she was talking to?'

'No. She didn't know either. She just kept repeating herself:

"Who is this?" and "Tom had the files, not me." Then she swore and ended the call.'

Tom? Ginny opened her mouth but was cut off as a vet nurse appeared.

'Tilda? You're up next.'

'That's us.' The woman got to her feet clutching a carrier cage, where a small cat was shivering. Then she turned to Ginny, her eyes filled with worry. 'Nice to meet you. And apologies for the rant. You probably think I'm a right cow. But things have been tight lately. And with this poor mite here, I can't afford to lose any business.'

'You too, and I'm sorry she forgot to pay.' Ginny always hated seeing the shadows of fear that came from not having enough money. While her own budget was tight, she'd always considered herself lucky that she and Eric had been able to build a life that suited them. Instinctively she pulled out her purse and retrieved two ten-pound notes. 'I-I'm sure it was an oversight. But here, let me do it for her.'

'I couldn't.' The woman's eyes widened, flickering between hope and uncertainty, and Ginny pressed the notes into her free hand, her mind whirling. Who was on the other end of the phone? Who was Tom... and what were the files?

'You can put it towards Tilda's recovery.'

'Thank you, love. I'm Sarah, by the way.' The woman swallowed and followed the vet nurse through to the back, just as a second nurse appeared.

'Edgar Cole?'

A hissing noise came from the cage at her feet, and Ginny quickly stood up. She had a feeling that her new cat was going to be a problem patient.

TEN

Little Shaw's cemetery was tucked away behind a set of wrought-iron gates and twin oak trees that formed an attractive entranceway. However, even in the daylight, the rustle of autumn leaves and musky scent of decay made it look like something from a Hammer House of Horror episode.

Hen's small car was already tucked up against the fence line, and Ginny brought her own vehicle to a halt. It had been a busy morning. The vet had been forced to put on thick leather gloves to handle Edgar who was now at home, curled up on Eric's chair, recovering from the ordeal. But apart from being underweight and in need of some dental hygiene, and his annual boosters, he'd been given a full bill of health. It had left Ginny just enough time to eat a quick lunch and get changed.

The three widows were on the other side of the gate, by a small gardening shed, so Ginny retrieved her two shovels and joined them.

As she made her way over, it was easy to see the neglect: dull, grey, weather-beaten headstones rose out of the ground, leaning at awkward angles, like teeth in need of braces. Weeds were everywhere, as well as wandering willie, which was doing its best to claim back the space for itself. And there were wine bottles and beer cans scattered around, as well as discarded blankets and jackets.

But despite the mess, there were several cleared banks and a corridor of small trees and shrubs that had recently been planted.

'You made it. We were meant to have a group of school students coming to help us, but they bowed out.' JM piled litter bags and weed mats into a wheelbarrow. 'And nice to see you use a Spear and Jackson. By far the best ones on the market.'

'And you won't have any fear of the neck breaking.' Tuppence picked up two buckets of water. 'It's probably better that we don't have anyone else with us. Otherwise, we'll spend the whole time making sure they don't pull out the new saplings instead of weeds.'

'That only happened once. And they were ever so sorry,' Hen said, as they headed towards an overgrown rosemary bush that was half covering a gravestone. 'I think we got up to here last time. Though it's a bit like painting a bridge. We go from one end to the other and by the time we're finished, we need to start again.'

'How long has it been like this?' Ginny asked, as Tuppence began to cut back the rosemary. Nearby, JM dropped to the ground and attacked the weeds, and Hen planted herself by a headstone and used the water and a soft brush to clean it. There was a collection of litter that had gathered around the sides, so Ginny took one of the bags and got to work.

'Seems like forever, but probably about five years. They did have a groundsman, but then the funding ran out and since then it's just been volunteers. We do get help from time to time, but it's never enough.'

'Apart from Mitch. He works Saturdays so tends to come here on his days off. He does a lot of the mowing, and of course the West Wing, as we like to call it.' Hen nodded to a neat row on the other side, which was weed-free, with green grass and gleaming headstones. It was quite the contrast.

'Is that the same Mitch from the pub? He's coming around tomorrow to put in the cat door.' Ginny picked up a soggy newspaper that held the remains of a fish supper, pleased to be wearing gardening gloves.

'He'll do a lovely job for you. As you can see, he's very dedicated.' Tuppence dragged several branches into the wheelbarrow, the pungent scent trailing behind. 'His fiancée died four years ago and that's where she's buried. He went a bit off the rails after it happened, but he's been getting his life back together.'

'It's been a terrible time for him. But I think the gardening helps keep him grounded.' Hen sloshed water on the headstone while JM moved onto the next grave, digging out the weeds in an efficient manner.

Ginny joined her and fell into an easy rhythm. She wasn't surprised that Mitch found it helped him – she'd always felt the same. Yet it had never occurred to her to volunteer her time at a community garden before. Or a cemetery. She felt another surge of gratitude that these three women had so easily extended their friendship to her. Even if it was in such an unusual circumstance.

'Yes, well, it's all very well talking about poor Mitch, but we have a case to crack.' JM checked her watch, as if deciding there had been quite enough casual conversation.

Hen gave her a guilty look. 'You're right. Tell us how you got on with Heather. What did you find out?'

'Not much,' JM admitted. 'The police had already been there and thoroughly searched her flat and the pub kitchen, where she made all the bread. They didn't find anything to link her to the crime, but she's taken it badly and declared she'll never bake again.'

'Including Eccles cakes. There's going to be a lot of

unhappy people. And what about Christmas without her fruit-cakes... oh, and no hot cross buns at Easter? This is a bad business.' Tuppence shook her wild curls.

'Poor Heather. Just when things were picking up for her.' Hen continued to scrub. 'Alyson always uses Eugenie to deliver the local orders, but the police have already interviewed her. Apparently, she has a small video camera in her van, because she was tired of people stealing from her. It shows that no one tampered with the bread.'

'So that's Heather and Eugenie off the list. How did you go, Ginny? Did Bernard let you in? How drunk was he?'

'He did seem a little under the influence,' Ginny admitted, but only gave them an edited version of his behaviour, not wanting to judge him too harshly considering his grief. 'His handwriting wasn't a match, but I did find a letter from TKL Insurance. I looked them up on the internet and they specialise in life insurance. Unfortunately, Edward Tait arrived before I could read it. He didn't look happy to see me.'

'Ho! So Edward's making Saturday house calls, is he? Well, I think we need to pay him a visit on Monday. Because if there's a life insurance policy for Louisa, that's motive.' There was a feral gleam in JM's eye that suggested it might not be a peaceful conversation.

'Why don't I come with you?' Tuppence quickly said.

'Very wise. We don't want a repeat of last year.' Hen finished scrubbing and used the rest of the water to rinse the gravestone, before standing up.

'It was just a small misunderstanding.' JM dismissed it with a shrug. 'And what a nuisance about Bernard's handwriting. That man is a constant disappointment.'

'He could have an accomplice,' Hen suggested. 'What if it's Edward Tait?'

JM brightened up. 'Good point. I'll make sure I look at his

handwriting when I pay him a visit. Who else could be working with them?'

Ginny remembered her conversation with the nail technician, and the argument that she'd overheard, and quickly told her friends what had happened.

'Louisa kept saying that Tom had the files. Does the name mean anything to you?'

'She must have been talking about Bernard's business partner. He was the Allan in the Allan and Farnsworth Developments.'

'*Was?*'

'That's right. Tom Allan died four months ago.' Tuppence didn't appear at all disappointed that a potential accomplice was dead. Nor did Hen or JM for that matter.

'How did he die? Was he murdered?' There hadn't been any mention of another murder in the miasma of gossip that floated around the library.

'No. He got caught in that terrible flood in Liverpool. He tried to drive through it, not realising how much the road dipped down. He drowned in his car. There were ten deaths in all but most of them weren't discovered until the water receded. It was a tragic accident, and while I couldn't say I liked the man, no one deserves that.' Hen started on the next headstone.

'You should've seen the funeral. A huge white hearse and his name written out in roses.' JM tugged at another weed. 'A bit much, if you ask me. But the catering was jolly good. It was at The Lost Goat and there was an open bar. The irony was that Tom was notoriously tight-fisted and would have hated that.'

'Tom Allan made Bernard look like a choirboy, and together they were unscrupulous – not that we can say as much in front of Alyson. She's convinced Tom was the one who led Bernard astray. Wouldn't even go to his funeral,' Hen admitted. 'And while I understand in principle, it wasn't well received. People noticed her absence.'

'So, if Tom was Bernard's business partner, I guess Louisa knew him well—?'

Tuppence snorted. 'Oh, they knew each other *very well*' – this was accompanied by air quotes – 'if you get my meaning.'

'We're all adults here. You can just say they were having an affair,' JM admonished, in a stern voice. 'But, yes, four years ago there were rumours of an affair between Tom and Louisa. It was scandalous because it wasn't long after Louisa and Bernard's wedding. And it gave Alyson all kinds of hope that Bernard would come to his senses, but then it fizzled out.'

'What about the business? Did they dissolve it?'

'No. They continued together and even managed to convince the parish council to sell them a huge section of land called Wilburton Reserve. It was wildly cheap, but the parish council insisted it was done at market value. That argument fell flat when Allan and Farnsworth sold the land six months later to another developer, and doubled their money. And, as you can see—' JM waved her spade in the air. 'The parish still can't afford to pay for any maintenance.'

'There was a huge public outcry when it was discovered. I guess Bernard and Tom were able to set aside their differences to chase the money,' Hen said.

'But what if Bernard hadn't really put it aside? Listen...' There was an excited gleam in Tuppence's eyes and she began to march around one of the gravestones. 'What if Tom and Louisa were blackmailing Bernard with something on the files? That's why he stayed in the business and the marriage? But for whatever reason, after Tom's death, Bernard finally wanted out of it, so he sent Louisa a blackmail letter. When she didn't respond, he slowly poisoned her. After all, he knew her medical history better than anyone.' Tuppence spread out her arms in a triumphant gesture.

'It's very Machiavellian.' JM rubbed her chin before nodding her head. 'And I could totally see Bernard doing it.'

Hen scrunched up her nose. 'I don't want to put a damp-ener on it, but... if he was the one speaking to Louisa on the phone when she left the nail salon... wouldn't she have recog-nised his voice? And his phone number?'

'Not if he used a different phone, and one of those devices to disguise his voice. I'm sure it would be easy enough to do.' JM walked over to stand near Tuppence, making the pair of them look like they were rehearsing for a play. 'And he did it because he knew the poison would soon kill her. Desperate times and all that.'

'We need Louisa's phone to find the number of the person she was speaking to.' Tuppence started to pace again.

'The police took her phone. I was there when it happened. If they did trace the number, they haven't released the informa-tion,' Ginny reminded them.

'Bother.' Tuppence sighed at the inconvenience. 'That only leaves us with the files. Louisa told the caller that Tom had them... which means we need to search Tom Allan's house. It's a pity Keris has that fancy hair salon out the back of the house. We'll have to lure her away from the property so we can break in.'

'Keris was Tom's wife,' Hen explained, catching Ginny's confused expression. 'And while I wouldn't say it was a happy marriage, she always stood by him. Probably because of the money. Mind you, she's done very well in her own right. She's become a bit of a hairdresser to the stars. Or, to the local WAGs at any rate.'

'Couldn't we just speak to her directly?' Ginny asked, her mind already sifting through the possibility that Tom Allan's wife might be Bernard's accomplice. It would make sense that the two spurned spouses came together. Especially if it was true that Louisa and Tom had an affair so soon after the wedding.

The three women exchanged a glance.

'There was a small incident last year involving a goat. And... let's just say she might not be happy to see us.'

Ginny suspected Keris would be less happy if they broke into her house. More importantly, while her new friends didn't seem to have the least fear of breaking the rules... or the law for that matter... Ginny didn't want to see them get into real trouble. Not to mention that if they were caught, it might make things worse for poor Alyson.

And things were bad enough already.

A prickle of guilt went through her. She was the one who'd noticed the Mees' lines on Louisa's fingernails, and who'd handed in the diary, along with Alyson's stationery. Not that the police had connected the envelope back to Hen's daughter yet, but it was only a matter of time.

Her hand drifted up to her soft grey hair. 'Did you say she was a hairdresser? What if I went to see her? As a client? I haven't had a proper cut since before the funeral. It's just been me and the nail scissors. I can't guarantee I will find anything out, but you never know.'

'I suppose the idea has merit. And if she doesn't start singing, we can still break in next week when she's at Power-hoop,' Tuppence said, in a reassuring voice.

'I'll call for an appointment. I have Monday afternoon off, so hopefully she can fit me in,' Ginny quickly said, before the other women could start planning anything illegal. 'And I thought I'd look through Louisa's diary to get the name of their cleaner. Bernard said she always put away the groceries.'

'Good idea. I don't know who they use. They could never keep people for long because, apparently, they were vile to work for,' Hen said. 'But I'll ask around.'

'And on Monday JM and I will pay Edward Tait a visit. We could have this whole case solved in time for Taco Tuesday at the pub.' Tuppence held up her fingers to show they were crossed.

Ginny finished filling her bag of litter and took it back to the wheelbarrow, hoping that Tuppence was right.

It was almost one in the afternoon by the time Ginny put away her shopping and tidied the house. She'd spent her Sunday morning going through Louisa's diary, making a note of the many appointments it contained. From there she'd compiled a spreadsheet for each name and occupation and then used the internet to get their contact details.

It was calming to do the kind of work she was good at, and it helped her relax after what had been a very strange week.

Not wanting to disturb anyone on a Sunday, she'd simply emailed them separately and had been surprised that several called back within the hour. No one had anything good to say about Louisa, especially not the cleaner. But, unfortunately, nor did they share anything useful. Still, it had been nice to chat to more of the locals, and tomorrow she'd call the rest.

Her luck had been in, though, with Keris Allan, who had been happy to give her an appointment for the following afternoon at three. That had left her just enough time to pick up some things at Collin's Grocery Store. There had been no sign of Alyson, but the young man behind the counter simply said it was her day off. And so she'd hurried home to finish tidying the house before Mitch arrived to install the cat door.

With a curious chirp, Edgar jumped up on the back of Eric's wingback and stared out of the window as a dented white van pulled into the small driveway.

'Ah, here we go,' Ginny said, as a man in his mid-thirties climbed out. He had messy brown curls and blue eyes that suggested he might have been handsome if it wasn't for the general air of neglect that clung to him. Still, from the broad array of jobs people seemed to hire him to do, he must be skilled.

She opened the door before he could knock.

'I'm Mitch. You booked me to install a cat flap,' he said, gaze sweeping from Ginny down to Edgar, who had woven himself around her legs, preventing her from moving. 'I'm a few minutes early. I hope that's okay.'

'Of course. I'm Ginny, and thank you for fitting us in. As you can see, my cat is outraged at having to wait for someone to open the door for him.'

'My ma's cat is just the same. Though she prefers the cat door to be held up for her,' he said. As he smiled at Edgar, some of his weariness seemed to fall away.

'Let's hope Edgar doesn't get any ideas. Come in and I'll show you where I want it. Would you like a cup of tea?'

'Nah. I'm good.' He took off his work boots before following her into the house.

It didn't take long for him to inspect the cat door she'd bought before disappearing out to the van to get his tools and start work.

Edgar was perched on the table, watching him intently while Ginny mixed up a batch of biscuits to take into work with her the next day. She was just taking them out of the oven when he reappeared, tool bag in hand. 'Right, that's all done.'

'Thank you.' Ginny retrieved her purse, took out several twenty-pound notes and passed them over. 'I was at the cemetery yesterday with Hen, JM and Tuppence, and they told me what a huge help you've been.'

'It's no big deal.' He thrust the money into his jeans.

'I wouldn't say that. Are you sure I can't give you a cup of tea before you go? And a biscuit?'

'I'm fine.' He shook his head and walked down the hallway, before coming to a dead stop and pressing himself back into the wall, as if wanting to avoid being seen.

'Is everything alright?' She peered out to where a familiar

electric vehicle had silently pulled in next door. DI Wallace climbed out.

Mitch's face was the colour of her magnolia walls, and his stomach was sucked in, as if he was trying not to breathe.

Clearly, she wasn't the only one who wanted to avoid the bad-tempered detective.

'Um, yes. But I might take you up on that cup of tea after all,' he said, blue eyes wide with alarm.

Ginny's chest tightened. She knew why *she* wanted to avoid Wallace, but had no idea why Mitch was so eager to. Still, there was only one way to find out.

Back in the kitchen, she boiled the kettle and made a pot of tea. And, because he looked on the thin side, she put several biscuits on a plate and halved one of the scones she'd made last night. Then she spooned jam and cream into two little dishes before setting it all out on the table.

'You're probably wondering why I was trying to avoid Wallace—?' He studied the feast in front of him, not looking up.

'It did cross my mind. Is everything okay?'

'Sort of.' His Adam's apple bobbed in his throat. 'Did the widows tell you about my fiancée, Sophie?'

'Only that she died, and that you miss her. I'm so sorry. It must have been awful. Is that what this is about?'

'In a way. She committed suicide four years ago. But she was so smart and beautiful – it was like a glow that came from her, from the inside. I think it was because she always did the right thing.' His fingers twisted around a gold chain that was hanging under his shirt. He tugged it out to reveal a slim gold band with a plain diamond set in the middle. 'We got engaged in the June. I got down on one knee and everything. Still seems surreal that eight months after she made me the happiest man—' He made a choking noise and then quickly put the chain back under his shirt.

'It's terrible to lose someone you love.'

'She wasn't the sort of person to take her own life. And everyone kept trying to tell me it was because her mum had cancer, but that wasn't it at all. It was because Louisa Farnsworth made her life a living hell.'

'Louisa?' Ginny sat up straight. 'Sophie knew Louisa Farnsworth?'

'Oh, she knew her, alright. Soph was the parish clerk and she was the best thing that ever happened to that place. Then Louisa claimed that Sophie had gone to some special part of the library, where the parish records and documents were kept. She accused her of shredding a whole lot of them. Money had been missing as well, and Louisa implied that Sophie had stolen it and was covering her tracks.'

'What happened?'

'That's the thing. There was no proof that Sophie did anything. Then, her mum took a turn for the worse, and Sophie needed to go back to London. I'd already planned to drive to Cornwall on the Friday for a mate's bachelor weekend, so I dropped her off. I was meant to collect her on the Monday. But for some reason she caught the train back on Sunday night... and the next morning they found her body at the bottom of Bluehead Quarry. It's been disused for years, and—' He buried his face in his hands.

'Mitch, I'm so sorry.' Ginny's chest tightened as he took a shuddering breath.

His eyes were bright with tears when he looked up. 'It's hard not to feel guilty. And after it happened, I was a mess. I'm the first to admit I went off the rails. Was drinking way too much and fighting anyone who could swing a punch. I got arrested a few times for property damage and drunk and disorderly.' He ran a hand through his messy hair. 'And I had a stand-up shouting match with Louisa, right in the middle of the pub.'

The penny dropped. 'That's why you're avoiding Wallace?'

'At the time I wanted him to investigate more. To prove Louisa bullied Sophie. He reckons he did, but I don't know, why wouldn't he have arrested her if so? He's already had me down at the station once to give a statement, and Rita says I just need to keep my head down and stay off his radar. Don't give him a reason to look at me.'

'That's good advice,' Ginny agreed. 'How long have you worked at the pub?'

'About a year. She got so sick of kicking me out that she gave me an ultimatum. Told me to not bother coming back unless I was sober. And that if I could manage it for a month, she'd give me a job. I owe her a lot.'

'Sounds like she did a similar thing for Heather,' Ginny noted, and for the first time he grinned.

'Yeah, she has a soft spot for loners.' Mitch suddenly noticed the scone and smeared one side with jam and then cream, and the other side with cream first. Was he hedging his bets? However, he then pressed them together and took a giant mouthful.

Once he had finished it, he drained his tea and his pallor improved. 'Thanks. I didn't realise how hungry I was.'

'You're welcome. Probably not as good as Heather's, from what I've heard.' She looked at him. 'Can I ask you something? Who do you think killed Louisa Farnsworth? Did Sophie have any family who might still be angry about what happened?'

'No. She was an only child, and both her parents died within a year of Soph's funeral. That's why I make sure her grave is kept in good order, because I'm the only one left.' He pulled out his wallet and carefully unfolded an old newspaper clipping. The poor quality of the print made her think it was from a local paper. It was a death notice.

Sophie Janine Hudson, beloved daughter of Mark and Moira Hudson. Taken too soon, but never forgotten.

Then he produced an equally crumpled photograph of Sophie's grave.

In the background were many faces she knew: Hen, Tuppence and JM, as well as Cleo, Andrea and Marigold Bentley. Even Harold was there. But it was the three figures in the foreground that her focus kept going back to.

The people who loved Sophie best.

Mitch was in the middle. He was younger then, but the bleak expression and black, ill-fitting suit made Ginny guess it was the day of the funeral. On the left was a frail woman, though her gaunt frame was at odds with her bloated face. Ginny had seen it enough times to recognise the ravages of chemotherapy. There was a black scarf wrapped around her skull and her shoulders were slumped. On the other side was a man, equally frail, who was leaning heavily on a cane.

They all looked broken.

She turned the photograph over to where a single line was written in capital letters: *ALWAYS WITH ME. NEVER ALONE...*

'It's beautiful,' she said, as he brushed a finger along it then folded everything back up. When he looked up his eyes were dark. 'In answer to your question about who I think killed Louisa...? My money would be on either Bernard or Keris. About seven months ago all four of them were in the pub together and there was a big fight. Bernard and Keris both stormed off, but Louisa and Tom stayed and kept drinking.'

'Do you know what the fight was about?'

'No idea. Though a few of the regulars were speculating that they'd started having an affair again. Apparently, they had one a few years ago. Which was news to me, though I'm not much one for gossip.'

This was the first time Ginny had heard that Tom and Louisa might have resumed their affair, and it lent credence to the idea that Bernard was behind the murder.

'Have you told the police?' Ginny asked, trying to ignore the hypocrisy considering everything she and her new friends had been doing.

Mitch shook his head. 'No. Like Rita said – best for me to keep my head down and stay off their radar. Plus, there were plenty of other people in the pub that night. I'm sure someone would've told them.' He picked up his mug and finished the tea it contained. 'Anyway, I'd better get going. But thanks for the scone. And for listening... Usually it's just me having silly one-sided conversations with her when I'm alone in the flat. It's nice to speak about her out loud.'

Ginny walked him to the door, trying not to shiver at the cooling weather. Despite his wild past and scruffy appearance, it seemed she had more in common with Mitch Reeves than she'd realised.

ELEVEN

Ginny tapped her pen against her chin. She was meant to be doing a crossword, but she kept getting distracted by all the things swirling around in her head. If only they would settle into some kind of logical order. None of her friends had been answering their phones, so after Mitch left, she'd spent the early evening going over what she'd discovered.

He thought the murderer was either Bernard or Keris.

They certainly both had a reason, given Louisa and Tom's affair. And now she'd spent time with Bernard, it seemed plausible. As for Keris, Ginny didn't want to think too much about that, since she would soon be receiving a haircut from her. And what about Louisa's fight with Sophie Hudson about destroying parish records and money going missing? Was it simply a coincidence, or was it tied to the murder? Though it was hard to see how, considering it happened four years ago.

Still, it would be worth looking into. She opened her laptop but was interrupted by the doorbell.

The three widows were standing in front of Ginny's pink door, but none of them had their usual sparkle. Hen's large eyes were downcast. Tuppence was shifting from foot to foot and

JM's mouth was set in an uncertain expression. Next door there was no sign of the electric vehicle and none of Wallace's lights were on.

Ginny ushered them inside and through to the sitting room and they all sat down. 'What's going on? Has something happened?'

'Not yet. But I'm worried that it won't be long. The police collected Alyson this morning and took her to the station.' Hen's voice shook and she wrung her hands.

'Did they arrest her?' Ginny hitched a breath.

'No. They. Did. Not.' JM folded her arms and made a huffing sound. 'I made sure of that. But they did tell her not to leave town. The poor thing's convinced she'll be thrown in jail for the rest of her life.'

'But why were they questioning her? Has something happened?'

There was a beat of silence before Hen finally spoke. 'They received an anonymous parcel yesterday. It was the therapy letter that Alyson wrote to Louisa.'

Ginny's shoulders sagged as the weight of the situation suddenly made itself real. Up until now it had almost felt like a game, despite the dreadful circumstances. She sat down in one of the chairs and tried to calm her breathing. 'What did Alyson say? What did they ask her?'

'She wouldn't elaborate. Just went up to her room and cried.' JM scooped up Edgar and patted him until he purred. Then he curled up on her lap and went to sleep.

'I called that nice PC Singh to explain it all. From the therapy letter to the fact someone had stolen Alyson's stationery. But she didn't seem to believe me,' Hen said, her face downcast. 'What if I've just made it worse?'

'Of course you haven't.' Ginny squeezed her hand. 'Don't forget I've got my hair appointment with Keris. And I've just had the most extraordinary conversation with Mitch.' She

quickly filled them in on what he'd told her, from the argument
in the pub between the two couples and regulars who thought
Tom and Louisa had started their affair again, to the fight
between Louisa and Sophie over council documents.

'I remember that. But how can it be relevant? Sophie's been
dead for four years.'

'I'm not sure. It might be nothing, but it's worth looking
into. And we need to find out if it's true about Louisa and Tom
starting up their affair again.'

'You're right. And tomorrow I'll be paying my friend
Edward Tait a visit,' JM reminded her. 'We'll get to the bottom
of this, and then they'll see that the letter really was harmless.'

They all nodded, but the mood was subdued, and no one
seemed in a hurry to mention the elephant in the room: that
whoever had murdered Louisa had also managed to get hold of
Alyson's letter, and was doing their best to convince the police
that she was the killer.

The following afternoon, Ginny walked down the side of a large
mock-Tudor mansion to the purpose-built hair salon. Just ahead
of her was Keris Allan, surrounded by a halo of Givenchy
perfume and a jangle of heavy gold bracelets.

She was a small woman in her mid-forties with a wide forehead and a bold streak of red running through her bottle-blonde
hair. She was wearing a leopard-print wrap dress that hugged
her waist, and her nails were even longer than Louisa's.

The studio had bright pink walls that were covered in
photos of models who looked like they were about to marry
Hugh Hefner, complete with feathery lingerie. Ginny
wondered if this was the real reason why JM, Tuppence and
Hen had preferred to break in, rather than get a haircut.

Still, she was grateful Keris could see her so quickly. And
even more grateful to make the five-mile drive and get away

from the library and all the speculation. No one had mentioned the therapy letter the police had been sent, but they'd all heard about Alyson's trip to the station and were making wild guesses as to what had gone on. Most of them were calling it a crime of passion from a thwarted ex-wife, including the local newspapers, which had all run stories.

'Don't worry, I'm not going to turn you into a page three girl,' Keris assured her, in a Cornish burr. 'But thanks to all the footballers who live in Walton-on-Marsh, most of my customers are WAGs, and they're a glamorous mob. It's important to set the mood. Now... what would you like done today?'

'Just a trim, please. It's been a while, I'm afraid, and needs a little neatening up.'

'I see.' Keris guided her to a swivel chair and spun it around to face the mirror.

Ginny's reflection was the same as it had always been: unremarkable blue eyes, small nose and a crooked smile, while her silver hair hung in unpredictable waves that she'd long ago given up trying to tame. Instead, she had simply taken to using a black headband to hold it back off her face.

Keris removed said headband and dropped it onto the mobile cart filled with scissors and brushes. With her fingers, she combed Ginny's hair forward, her mouth set in a thoughtful expression. 'It seems a shame not to thin this out and give you some layers. It would sit better and frame your face.' The fingers continued to prod and pull strands of hair. 'It will take a bit longer, but you know what they say: a change is as good as a holiday.'

Ginny was aware that she was meant to be there to find out information, not change the way she looked. Besides, Eric had liked her hair the way it was. But she didn't want to get off on the wrong foot. And, if she hated the haircut, she could always get out her nail scissors. 'I guess so. If you think you can do something with it.'

Keris just smiled and beckoned her to stand up. The shampoo station was at the back of the room, concealed behind a free-standing room divider, and soon Ginny was settled and leaning back, hot jets of water gushing over her scalp.

'I haven't seen you around here before. Are you new to the village?' Keris massaged in the shampoo as Ginny stared up at the ceiling, trying to ignore the crick in her neck.

'I am. I moved three weeks ago. I live in Middle Cottage.'

'Oh, I know the place—' The hairdresser broke off as footsteps sounded from across the room. Out of habit, Ginny turned to see who it was, but was trapped, and couldn't do more than look at the ceiling.

'Keris Allan? I'm PC Singh.'

'I know who you are. Question is, what do you want?' Keris turned off the water and dried her hands, not unduly bothered the police were on her doorstep.

Unlike Ginny, whose entire body had gone rigid.

Why was Anita here? Did she know about the blackmail note they'd found? Was she going to arrest Ginny for concealing evidence, or obstructing justice, or both? Her heart pounded in her chest. This whole thing was a huge mistake. And Ginny wasn't even sure what she was hoping to find out. Was it that Tom Allan had secret files a blackmailer was after, or that Keris had a motive to kill Louisa?

'I'm here in regard to the report you made about Louisa Farnsworth breaking into your house,' PC Singh said, and Ginny's panic morphed into curiosity.

A break-in?

'Oh, are you just? Well, you're a month too late. And considering what's happened, I can't see you pressing charges against the crazy cow now.'

'I do apologise that we haven't followed up sooner; we're very understaffed. However, I'd like to get a statement from you. Is now a good time?'

'No, constable, it isn't.' Keris dropped her gaze to Ginny, whose head was still held in place by the wash basin. 'I'm with a client. However, I do have a cancellation at five, if you'd like to come back then. You could consider getting those split ends dealt with at the same time.'

There was a beat of silence followed by footsteps, before PC Singh's face hovered above Ginny's own.

The constable's dark eyes widened, and it was clear she hadn't realised the shampoo station was there, or that anyone else was in the salon.

'Mrs Cole, I—' She broke off, as if unsure what to say. Then she shrugged and turned her attention back to Keris. 'I will come back at five.'

Ginny heard retreating footsteps and then the door to the salon banged. 'Talk about shutting the gate after the horse has bolted.' Keris rinsed away the conditioner and nudged Ginny into a sitting position, before wrapping her head in a towel and leading her back to the seat by the mirror. 'Now I know who you are. You're the new librarian, aren't you? The one who found Louisa. No wonder Singh looked so sick to be caught mouthing off about police business in front of you.'

'She's been under a lot of pressure and she does seem good at her job. But it's her first murder,' Ginny explained, her mind still whirling with the new information. 'Did you know Louisa very well? Did you cut her hair?'

'I most certainly did not cut her hair. You couldn't pay me to have gone near that ratty mess. I knew her well enough to dislike her excessively. And don't go telling me that I shouldn't speak ill of the dead when she tried to break up my marriage.' Keris picked up the scissors, her voice placid, as if they were discussing Ginny's last holiday to Portugal.

'Was that while she was married to Bernard?' Ginny said, trying to mimic the same intense but casual tone everyone else in Little Shaw used when it came to local events.

It must have worked, as Keris shrugged. 'Yes. She often complained about marrying the wrong partner. *"You should always go for the first name in the business. After all, if Tom had the balls to put his name ahead of Bernard's, it proves what a man he is."'*

'That's terrible. How could she say that about your husband? And to your face.' Ginny was genuinely shocked, but Keris just laughed.

'That was Louisa all over. I reckon she was missing a sensitivity chip. She had the cheek to complain that Alyson needed to stop making a fool of herself by going after a married man – like she hadn't been the one to steal Alyson's husband in the first place. Or talked about stealing mine.'

'I heard that Alyson didn't take the divorce well.'

'She only has herself to blame. I warned her the lusty librarian was going to make a play for Bernard. Even offered to give her a makeover, but she refused to listen. Like one of those monkeys who shut their eyes, close their ears, and refuse to open their mouths and speak up.'

Ginny thought of Alyson's lank hair and her vehement defence of Bernard even now, and wondered if there was some truth to what Keris was saying. Especially since she'd written the therapy letter and directed her anger at Louisa, rather than her ex-husband, who had cheated on her.

'Do you really think Louisa tried to convince your husband to leave you?'

'Oh, yes. Tom might like to play away, but he always came home to me and the kids. He did love us... in his own selfish, pig-headed way.' For the first time Keris paused and sniffed. 'He told me about the affair and that it ended when he refused to leave me. It was four years ago now.'

'So, if the affair was over, why would she have tried to break into your house? And are you sure it was her?'

'I know because of the CCTV camera Tom insisted on

installing last year. My husband was completely paranoid, and had cameras hidden throughout his study and the office in town. Clearly, she had no idea because she walked in, bold as brass, and virtually ransacked the place.'

Ginny thought of the blackmail note they'd found.

I want the files you stole.

'Do you know what she was looking for?'

'No, but I can take a guess.' Keris snipped and tugged at Ginny's hair, not missing a beat. 'Like I said, Tom was paranoid and always kept a USB flash drive on him. He called it his BP – back-up plan – or, what I dubbed, his bribery portfolio. She couldn't find it, of course, because it isn't here.'

'It isn't? Did you hide it somewhere? That was very clever.' Ginny leaned forward, forgetting her hair was being cut. Keris gently tugged her head back and laughed.

'No. I searched this place from top to bottom after he died – out of curiosity more than anything else – but couldn't find it. I always said he'd probably take his grubby secrets to the grave with him, and he's proved me right.'

'Maybe some things are better forgotten. What do you think was on it that Louisa could have wanted?'

'Who knows. Could be tax evasion, a list of his favourite beers, or the names of all his mistresses. Maybe she didn't want Bernard to find out that they'd started their affair again.'

Ginny sucked in her breath. Mitch had mentioned seeing the two couples together at the pub and that after an argument Bernard and Keris had both walked out. Did this mean it was true? She tried to think of a way to ask about it, without appearing rude.

'You poor thing. That must have been difficult.'

'You'd be surprised.' Keris shrugged. 'Not that he admitted it, but he was sleeping with someone. Tom could never keep it in his pants, and six months ago he went to the Old Regent Hotel in Liverpool and stayed the night. I found the receipt in the back of his car, and room service was for two. On my birth-day, no less. Dirty sod said he'd gone to Scotland to visit his brother.'

'And you think it was Louisa?' Ginny asked. The more Keris revealed, the more motive she seemed to have to be involved in Louisa's death, perhaps even with Bernard. Her shoulders stiffened as the cool steel of the scissors pressed against her skin and her body caught up to the fact that she might be in the presence of a murderer.

Maybe this hadn't been such a good idea.

'I really couldn't say. He didn't tend to go back to the same woman twice, but then he didn't usually try to drive through floods, so there's a first – and last – time for everything. All I know is he stayed there three times, including the night of the floods. Now... relax your shoulders so I can make sure it's straight.'

Ginny tried to imagine what it must have been like to be in a marriage with no trust. But it was so far from her own quiet-but-safe experience she couldn't fathom it. Or fathom what it might make someone do.

'It must have been very hard on you. And on Bernard. Unless he didn't know.'

'Oh, he knew. Most of the town did. And you'd be surprised how easy it is to work and live with someone you can't stand. In a way, it takes away any power they might have to hurt you. But listen to me yammering on.' Keris put down her scissors and picked up a hairdryer.

The next ten minutes were like torture, before she finally stepped away. 'I think we're done. Do you like it?'

Ginny reluctantly studied her reflection, then gasped.

The soft frizz of hair was gone, replaced with a shiny bob that framed her face, and softly covered her forehead. And her blue eyes, which had always seemed so dull against her pale skin, seemed brighter, as if they'd finally been released from prison after a long time inside.

'I had no idea it could look like this.' Instinctively, her hand reached up to the nape of her neck, which was now free of the heaviness that had always been there.

Keris removed the cape before brushing off the last of the stray hairs on her shoulders.

'See... it's never too late. Now, let me show you how to care for it and we'll book you in for another appointment in, say, six weeks.'

Over at the counter Ginny paid for the cut – it cost as much as she usually spent on her hair in a year – and Keris wrote out an appointment card.

'Thank you.' Ginny took the card, not sure whether to be pleased or disappointed that the handwriting was nothing like the one on the blackmail note.

TWELVE

The sun was partially hidden by darkening clouds while a rising wind brushed past the hedgerows as Ginny drove along the narrow A-road back to Little Shaw. There was hardly any traffic, leaving her to contemplate everything she'd discovered.

Louisa had broken in, possibly to find Tom's 'back-up plan'. And even though their original affair had ended four years ago, he'd started up a new one more recently, which could have been with Louisa. It still left Bernard very much in the picture.

But what about Keris?

Before meeting her, Ginny had no problems imagining that she might be guilty of Louisa's murder... or working with Bernard. After all, hell hath no fury like a woman twice scorned by a wayward husband. But Keris had seemed quite accepting of Tom's infidelities, and if she hadn't kicked him out after the last affair, it didn't seem logical that she'd suddenly get into a murderous rage over Louisa this time around.

Especially when the affair was over, and Tom was dead.

Still, it was something she'd need to discuss with the others. And that she had the name of the hotel in Liverpool where Tom had stayed.

Beeeeeeep.

A horn blared out, dragging Ginny back to what she was meant to be doing: driving the car. In the rearview mirror a black Ford hurtled towards her, then crossed over the white line into the other lane. There was a round of cheering from the occupants as they went past, before they crested the hill and disappeared.

Adrenaline flooded her system and she gripped her steering wheel, relieved they were in front of her. However, as she reached the top of the hill, a horn sounded again and Ginny was given a full view as the car slowed to a crawl, allowing the passengers to leer at a woman on the side of the road.

A large 4WD was parked against the hedgerow, and the driver had a phone in her hand. Had she broken down?

As Ginny got closer, the offending car sped up again, tyres screeching as it disappeared down the road. Feeling shaken herself from this aggressive behaviour, Ginny slowed down to see what assistance she could offer, which was when she noticed the shoulder-length brown hair and neat figure.

Marigold Bentley.

Ginny pulled off the road, cut the engine and hurried over, the brisk wind biting into her skin. 'Are you okay? They over-took me on the other side of the hill. I'm surprised they haven't crashed, considering the speed they were going at.'

But Marigold's mouth suggested she was more annoyed than scared. 'Takes a lot more than a group of young fools to rattle me. Unfortunately, I can't say the same for my car. I'd just been to the nursery to buy some wych elm saplings when the engine started smoking. The tow truck can't get here for another two hours, so now I'm waiting for an Uber, which is late. And I have a meeting in an hour.'

The first drops of rain began to fall, and Ginny peered around the empty road and the miles of farming fields. 'What if you cancel the Uber, and let me give you a lift home?'

'Are you sure? I'd hate to put you out.'

'It's no bother. Now, let's get the saplings loaded into my car.'

'Wait... you look different. Have you had a haircut? Yes, that's it. It suits you.'

'Thank you.' Ginny touched the nape of her neck, wondering how long it would take for her to get used to it.

It didn't take long to transfer the saplings and for Marigold to cancel the Uber and contact the towing company to arrange for them to collect the keys from her house.

The rain increased as Ginny followed Marigold's directions through the back of Little Shaw, until they came to a tree-lined road that overlooked the village.

She drove through a large gate and up a gravel drive, to a stunning Georgian stone mansion with sweeping gardens ablaze with gold and russet colours. There was a second car parked on the drive, and a large dog appeared from around the side of the house.

'What a lovely place. I had no idea it was even here.'

Marigold lowered herself down to greet the dog and then glanced up fondly at the house. 'It is rather nice, isn't it? My family's owned it forever. Once upon a time it was a hunting lodge, but it's been the main residence since sometime last century. I can't imagine owning two properties – this one's quite enough work on its own. Doesn't help that my husband is off in Spain for four months on a language intensive. Still, I manage to potter along.'

If the exquisite herbaceous borders and the topiary shrubs were anything to go by, Ginny suspected she did a lot more than just potter. But she was starting to appreciate that Marigold was one of those people who managed to accomplish a lot of work without breaking a sweat.

'Well, I hope you don't try and plant these today.' Ginny

opened the boot and lifted one of the trays. 'Where would you like them?'

'These aren't for here,' Marigold admitted. 'They're for the cemetery. I feel so dreadful at our lack of funding and we rely solely on volunteers. So, I've been doing my bit and buying as many plants as I can.'

'How generous of you. I went along on Saturday to help out and saw all the new plantings.' Ginny carried the tray of saplings over, deciding not to mention that some of them had been unwittingly pulled back out by over-zealous volunteers.

'You did? I knew you would fit into our village life.' Marigold followed behind her. 'It makes me feel like all the hard work is worth it.'

Ginny paused. There hadn't been a chance to pick up her search about the parish council and the documents that Sophie Hudson was accused of destroying. But this was an opportunity to find out first-hand.

'How long have you been chairperson?'

'Seems like an eternity but it's been eight years. It's not a paid position, but then that's not why I do it. I see it as my way of giving back to the village that I love so much. I suppose I've always been civically minded.'

'It must be difficult with limited funds.'

'I'm afraid it's a constant juggle. And probably the hardest part is managing all the competing interests. We have the historical society unhappy that the library got a book budget, while the Friends of the Village Hall want to know why we can't give them new curtains. Though despite all the complaining, not many of them put their hands up to help, or even come along to the meetings. I tell them to read the minutes and they'll see exactly how we've reached our decisions.'

Ginny pressed her lips together. 'Are they stored in the library stack with other parish documents? I heard that Louisa thought some of them had been destroyed. Is that something I need to be aware of? In case it happens again?'

'I was wondering if you'd hear about that.' Marigold's shoulders slumped. 'Louisa accused our previous clerk – lovely girl – of doing it. Though there was never any proof, and I'm afraid I did have to reprimand Louisa over the matter, which is never something I enjoy.'

'That's good to hear. I'm not sure what I would've done if I'd found someone at the shredder,' Ginny said, keeping her voice light.

'Let's hope it doesn't come to that, and if it does, just call me and the police, because it's something we take very seriously. Now, speaking of the council, I'd better get ready for my meeting. And thanks again for the lift. You really are a treasure.'

It was almost six in the evening by the time Ginny parked her car in Hen's driveway. Inside the cottage Tuppence was seated on the sofa, surrounded by a pile of old wool jumpers, which spilled out around her like snakes trying to escape. Brandon was curled up in a basket at her feet but looked up with huge eyes as Ginny sat in the armchair.

'Let me pour you a cuppa. It's freshly brewed.' Hen made herself busy before handing over the cup. 'JM's not here yet and Alyson's having dinner with a friend. Now, here you go. And look at your hair! It's wonderful. There's no denying Keris knows how to cut.'

'I agree. She's done a great job.' Tuppence grinned at her. 'The only thing missing is a bit of colour. Next time I buy pink hair dye, you can have half of it,' she promised, as she unpicked the seam of a bright purple and blue cardigan. 'It's for Hen's birds' nests. The charity collects old jumpers and JM and I unravel them because we're useless at knitting.'

'I'm happy to help.' Ginny picked up an orange cardigan and got to work. 'So, how did it go with Edward Tait?'

'Very well. We even recorded the interview.' Hen proudly tapped the screen on her phone and brought up a video clip.

It was very blurry, and the voices sounded like everyone was swimming underwater. Then there was a crashing noise, and someone swore, before the clip came to an abrupt stop.

'Of course, we might need to iron out a few technical difficulties,' Tuppence admitted. 'But JM was magnificent. She walked through Edward Tait's doors and demanded he tell us everything about Bernard and Louisa's life insurance policy that Ginny saw on the kitchen bench. He refused to answer and told us to go away because it was now a police matter. Then his face turned red... as if he wasn't meant to say that.'

'Do you think that means the police are looking into the insurance angle?' Ginny recalled the peevish solicitor she'd met at The Lost Goat, and then again at Bernard's house. 'And why isn't JM here yet? I hope she didn't try to make him break client confidentiality or do anything illegal.'

'Illegal? Of course not. She only used the law as a weapon. And she did a cracking job,' Tuppence assured her. 'But while there, we noticed what a terrible mess the office was. There were case files everywhere, not to mention discarded takeaway containers and empty whisky bottles. So, JM stayed to do a bit of cleaning. I offered to help, but she thought I'd get in the way. He was quite lost for words.'

Ginny didn't doubt Edward Tait had been lost for words. She was feeling a little that way herself.

However, her concern didn't last long and JM arrived several minutes later holding bags of takeaway curry, looking her usual confident self. 'Sorry to keep you waiting. I hope I haven't missed too much. And Ginny, I love the cut. Very stylish.'

'Isn't it lovely?' Hen placed a stack of plates and cutlery on the coffee table so that everyone could dish up their food. 'We were just telling her about the life insurance. But let's eat first and then hear what Ginny found out.'

The next fifteen minutes were spent on the excellent food before the plates were cleared away and JM and Tuppence each attacked another jumper, while Hen took up her knitting.

It didn't take long for Ginny to tell them about Louisa's break-in, and that Tom and Louisa had possibly started up their affair again. Along with the news that Keris's handwriting wasn't a match, and that she hadn't seemed unduly bothered by either affair.

'Well, that is a disappointment. I really thought Keris would've been Bernard's partner in crime.' JM sighed and got to her feet to cross the name off the murder board, trailing yellow wool behind her.

'It's probably for the best.' Tuppence followed her over to retrieve the wool. 'We all know how hard it is to find a good hairdresser, and now that Ginny has one, it would be a little sad for her to end up in jail.'

'And there's still the possibility that Bernard acted alone and disguised his handwriting,' Hen reminded them. 'Especially now we know about the insurance and that the affair might have started up again. Though why he would frame Alyson for the whole thing is another question.'

'Because he's a rat?' JM drew a picture of a rat next to his name, along with several bags of what looked like money. 'But it would be useful to know if it was true about the affair.'

'If Tom went to the Old Regent Hotel on Keris's birthday, then it means it was the second of March.' Tuppence returned to the sofa and tugged at another seam. 'Remember she always has a champagne soirée in the beer garden? Not that I ever go because it's far too cold to sit outside that time of year.'

'And because Keris is a social climber who likes to show off with her gold jewellery and rich clients, and you don't like being around her,' JM added.

'Well, yes. That, too.'

'I'll call the hotel in the morning and see if they remember Tom being there, and who he was with. He was also there the night of the floods,' Ginny said. 'Oh, and I spoke to Marigold Bentley as well. She denied any council documents were ever destroyed, and that Louisa had been disciplined for suggesting it.'

'Which doesn't leave us with much to go on.' Hen's needles clicked together at a rapid pace. 'Without Tom Allan's flash drive we still don't really know who killed Louisa.'

'Then we need to get it. While Ginny's at work tomorrow, I suggest we have a look around Bernard's office. I did happen to look at Edward's diary while I was tidying, and he's got a twelve o'clock lunch meeting with Bernard at the Richmond wine bar in Walton-on-Marsh. So, it would be the perfect time to search the place. Maybe that's where Tom hid it? I'll also swing by Edward's office later in the day and see what else I can shake out of him.'

Ginny wasn't quite so sure, but Hen gave them all a grateful smile as JM added a picture of what looked like a hair pin and a padlock to the board. Brandon, who had been sleeping by Hen's feet, made a snuffling sound.

'I really think we're getting close. I can feel it.' Tuppence looked at the large board, which now resembled a Picasso painting, and then handed JM the end of a piece of wool so she could start rolling it up.

THIRTEEN

Ginny picked up the teapot and swirled its contents around. She only drank one cup in the morning, but years of habit had made it impossible to stop making enough for the two of them.

This morning she needed to do something to shake away the dreams of Bernard, Louisa and Tom – all caught in a game of cat and mouse that had ended in an accident for one and a murder for another.

And Alyson caught in the middle of it all.

There had been no further contact with the police, and it was clear by Alyson's grey complexion and the weary set of her shoulders when she'd walked in last night that she wasn't holding much hope. It was almost as painful to see the grim despair in Hen's eyes, and the worried looks that Tuppence and JM kept exchanging. It reconfirmed how close the three women were, and how they felt about Hen's only daughter.

And what was at stake if we don't get to the bottom of the mystery.

The fog refused to clear, and Ginny reached for the teapot. 'Sorry, love. I hope you don't mind if I finish this off. I've gone from having nothing on my calendar to being busy day and night,' she explained, as a wave of guilt assailed her. She'd also been too busy to give Eric an update on the case. Had he noticed? Had he been waiting here... or in the ether... or wherever he was... for her to speak to him, only to watch her hurry in and out without so much as a hello?

Pain jabbed in her chest and it wasn't until she'd drunk the second cup of tea that she felt calm enough to fill Eric in on what they'd discovered, as well as telling him about her new friends.

'I knew you'd be happy with that part. You always did worry that I was too solitary,' Ginny finished off. As usual there was no answer but Edgar, who'd been asleep on the chair next to her, opened an eye and yawned. She glared at him. 'You could at least pretend to be interested.'

The cat ignored her, and suddenly the weight of the empty room pressed against her.

Was that what Eric was doing? Yawning at her constant conversations with him? If he was there at all? Ginny wrapped her arms around her waist. Was *that* the real reason she'd thrown herself into this adventure so wholeheartedly? To avoid admitting Eric might not be able to hear her?

The cat yawned a second time and Ginny leaned over to pat him. His fur was warm and soft under her fingers, and he let out a rumbling purr, which helped push away the many questions swirling around in her mind.

Feeling happier, she reached for her notebook. There was just enough time to call the hotel in Liverpool where Keris said Tom had stayed on at least three occasions. Next to it, she'd also written down the date of Keris's birthday, and the date of the floods.

'Old Regent Hotel,' a woman with a thick Liverpudlian accent answered on the second ring.

Ginny sat up straight. 'Hello, I hope you can help me. M-my husband and his... friend stayed at the hotel on the second of

March, and the fifth of May. His name is Tom Allan... but I was hoping someone there might know who his... er... companion was.'

'Your old fella cheating on you, was he?' the woman said casually. Not waiting for an answer, she continued: 'Let's see who was working that night... oh. It's Jimmy, but he's not back in work until Saturday.'

'If I leave you my number, could you get him to call me?' Ginny said, not disappointed, since even if someone did recognise a couple from six months ago, the chances of them telling a stranger weren't high.

'Sure. Can't promise he'll remember. He really needs to knock off the weed.' The woman hung up before Ginny could thank her.

It took five minutes to clear up her breakfast dishes before she put on her coat and slipped her large workbag over one shoulder. Ginny looked into the mirror to apply her lipstick, only to let out a little yelp at the sight of her new haircut. She hadn't washed it in the shower, nor had she put on any make-up yet, so had somehow forgotten all about it.

Now, as she stared at the straight silver hair, it was like looking at a stranger. The only thing she recognised were the dark shadows under her eyes from her restless nights. But even they seemed alien. Was it because they'd come from worrying about Alyson, rather than from the grief of losing her husband?

Then it hit her. She hadn't asked Eric if he'd liked her haircut.

'What must you think of me? Leaving you here while I'm running all over town, and then not even asking what you think about it.'

A wave of pain washed over her once more but before she could let it take her down the familiar path, the alarm on her phone went off, reminding her it was time to leave. She opened the door and pushed back the grief. Later she'd talk to Eric, explain that it didn't mean she'd forgotten him. Reassure him that nothing had changed. But she couldn't do it now because, while she might have a new haircut and other things going on in her life, there was no way she would be late for work.

It was a small comfort to know she hadn't changed *that* much.

By ten-thirty, Ginny was pleased she'd had the second cup of tea when she'd had the chance. The library had been busy with customers and book requests. There had also been several compliments on her hair, which Ginny had found a little unnerving.

However, by the time Andrea returned from her morning break, there was a lull, which meant Ginny could slip away to look at the council documents. 'If you can manage the counter on your own, I'm going to do a health and safety check in the stack.'

It wasn't technically a lie, and she'd already conducted one in the main library – and was still horrified at how many issues she'd found, including two fire extinguishers that needed replacing and a blocked emergency exit, so she didn't feel too bad.

She walked to the shelf for the key, only to find it gone. Cleo, who was standing nearby, turned to Connor. 'Did you move the key?'

'Yeah. I live to move random keys around. So much fun.' Connor didn't look up from the trolley of books he was sorting.

'Well, there's no need to be rude. And if you didn't take it, who did? Andrea's scared of ghosts, so you know she'd never touch it.'

'I took it.' Harold suddenly appeared in front of them, holding an armful of newspapers. 'I discovered mould down there, so am limiting access until I know it's not toxic.'

Mould?

'I was there on Friday, and it smelt fine to me.' Ginny scrutinised his face, but it was a mask.

'Well, isn't that a relief we have a mould expert amongst us. You should be pleased that I'm taking health and safety as seriously as you do. Now, I have work to do.' He swept his gaze over to the line of customers, who were waiting to borrow books. 'And so, it appears, do you, Mrs Cole.'

He disappeared through the front door, clearly going straight to the stack.

What was that about? And if there was mould, why was he going in there? But Ginny didn't have time to ponder as a man in his twenties shyly approached Cleo with a long list of books he needed help finding.

'Let's see, you want *Successfully Identifying Roadkill*, *Great Ideas for Romance on a Budget* and *Taxidermy for Fun and Profit—*' Cleo broke off, clearly about to make a comment on the man's reading choices.

Ginny hurried over. 'Actually, Cleo. This would be a good chance for me to learn a bit more about the layout of the library. Why don't I go and find them and you can mind the counter?'

'Gladly,' the other woman said, as she glared at the man. His colour heightened and Ginny quickly suggested he wait over at the reading table while she found the books.

Once they'd been retrieved, Ginny resumed her cleaning efforts, taking down the dusty posters and old notices that had only made the place feel gloomy. She returned from emptying the vacuum cleaner to find Cleo and William once again arguing, oblivious to a growing crowd.

'I don't think it's going to be fatal.' Connor pushed an empty trolley in the direction of the returns room. 'They're talking about some singing show. Or rich housewives going to prison. Or ex-football players learning how to cook. I zoned out.'

'I take it this has happened before?'

'Unfortunately, yes.' He shrugged. 'I've finished the shelving. Do you want me to do some returns?'

Ginny looked at the long line of borrowers, who were patiently waiting for Cleo and William to finish their conversation. The two self-issue machines in the corner were deserted, mainly because most of the customers preferred to stop at the counter for a chat. But unless the second computer was manned, it could be a slow process.

It was more frustrating that their perfectly capable young volunteer was only allowed to put books on the shelf. She must run it past Harold to see if she could train him properly. But, until then, there was no reason he couldn't show people how to use the machine. It would give him something to do, and hopefully reduce the growing line of people.

'How do you feel about teaching some old dogs new tricks?' She motioned to Connor to follow her as she walked to the machine, which was currently covered in stacks of deserted books and some random items of lost and found.

'You mean, like, talk to people?' His mouth twitched.

'I suspect there would be some talking involved.' Ginny piled the books on his empty trolley. 'But learning new things is good for our neural pathways. In fact, why don't you show me first, and then we'll see who else is interested?'

Connor's mouth was set in a frown, but grudgingly he turned on his phone and brought up what looked like an electronic version of his library card.

Ginny widened her eyes. She had no idea that was even possible.

Without a word, he scanned it across the screen and picked up a book from the trolley. She watched as he slid it onto the tray below the scanner. Moments later a receipt chugged out from a small slot in the side.

Ginny, who had never used the machine herself, was impressed.

'There,' Connor announced, making no effort to elaborate.

'Excellent. Now, let's do it again and this time tell me what you're doing. And maybe slow down.' Ginny gave him a bemused smile.

He sighed before once again holding up the library card on his phone and moving it slowly forward in an exaggerated fashion.

'You. Must. Scan. Your. Card. Like. This,' he monotoned, as he took her through the process, then handed her the book and receipt. 'Better?'

'Much,' she agreed. 'I know you feel silly, but it will help some of our borrowers to understand it. Now, there's Rose. I'm going to ask if she'd like your help. If that's okay?'

'Do I have a choice?' he replied, in a gruff voice.

'Of course. If you want to do more shelf checking, I'm sure I could show people how to use it.'

There was silence as something flashed across Connor's face. Then he let out a pained sigh. 'Nah. It's fine. I don't mind.'

Ginny beelined to where Rose was waiting. After a quick conversation, Ginny led her back, pleased to see several other borrowers gather around with interest. Unsure if Connor would protest, she waited for several minutes. But he just got on with patiently showing the elderly woman how to use the machine and print out her issues ticket.

At least that was one less problem she had to think about.

'I still don't like those machines. They're trying to do us out of a job.' Cleo tapped her fingers on the clean countertop at four in the afternoon. The line to the counter had gone and was snaking in the other direction as each person waited for Connor to teach them. Ginny was certain that she'd seen William borrow books, return them, and then line up with more.

'Just to make sure I've got it all clear in my head...' she'd overheard the old man telling Connor. And Connor hadn't argued or huffed; instead, simply going through it again.

'I'm sure people will still chat, but it means people in a hurry don't need to wait. Plus, it's a pity not to make the most of Connor while he's here.'

'What do you mean? Where's he going?'

'I don't know, but I assume somewhere. He's eighteen and very bright. He must be looking at other options. He has so much potential.'

Cleo opened her mouth and then shut it again, suddenly contrite. 'I hadn't thought of him like that. He comes from Halton Park, you see. And most of them... well... there's a cycle of poverty that's hard to break. I suppose I just assumed the worst. Now I feel terrible.'

'I didn't mean to make you feel bad. I'd just like to support him while he's here. So that he gets something out of it.'

Cleo swallowed. 'You're right. I... I'm pleased Marigold hired you. I wasn't sure to begin with, but she made a good decision. The place already looks so much better with the cushions and the fresh flowers.'

'I liked the waiting room at the surgery to be comfortable and relaxing. So, I thought I'd try the same here.'

'You've done a good job,' Cleo admitted.

Ginny chewed her lip. She'd avoided asking too many direct questions about the murder, especially to Cleo and Andrea, who were happy to gossip for hours on one small detail. But despite several more attempts to get into the stack again, she'd no success, and JM had called earlier to say the office break-in had had to be aborted because Tuppence couldn't find the right YouTube video to pick the lock. All in all, it hadn't been a successful day.

It had to be worth a try.

'Cleo, you've been here a while. Do you remember Sophie Hudson?'

'Of course. Lovely girl, she was. Very bright. Why?'

'I heard that Louisa accused her of destroying documents in the stack. I was just curious if you knew anything about it.'

Cleo didn't blink. 'There was nothing to know. Louisa and Sophie were always at loggerheads over the banking not balancing, and on the budget. And Sophie would come at least once a month to file everything in the stack, but as for her destroying documents. No... I never believed it for a minute.'

Which is exactly what Marigold said.

'So, there was no mention of what the documents might have been?'

'Goodness, I've got no idea. Besides, it was a moot point. Anyway, we've got Harold back now and since the only thing he does seem interested in doing is guarding the stack, I guess we won't have to worry about it ever happening,' she said, as a customer walked up to the counter. 'I'll go, if you are happy to set up for the book group.'

Ginny left Cleo happily having a discussion on historical fight scenes and went to the corner by the window to drag the comfortable chairs out into a semi-circle, before retrieving the tea trolley from the kitchen.

She was just finishing when Esme appeared, unwinding a large scarf from around her neck with one hand, while clutching a book in the other. Her eyes widened at the plate of baking that Ginny had brought for the group. 'Look, Else, homemade biscuits for our book group! We'll have to take a couple home for after our supper.'

'Very nice.' Elsie fumbled for her glasses. 'What a lovely haircut. Doesn't look like something Barbara would do.'

'I went to Keris Allan.' Ginny had no idea who Barbara was, but suspected she must be the woman responsible for the matching bowl-cuts the sisters sported.

At the mention of the name, Esme sucked in a sharp breath. 'Oh, *her.* Well, I won't deny she does a good job, but ever since the whole debacle, Else and I have refused to go there. It's out of principle, you see.'

'Principle,' Elsie echoed, though she didn't sound convinced. 'But it does look nice.'

'No, Else, we can't falter. If we don't have our standards, we don't have anything,' Esme said in a stern voice, before patting Ginny's arm. 'Keris Allan refused to pay an outstanding bill after that husband of hers died a few months ago.'

'You mean Tom?'

'That's right. He was a funny man. Always wanting his dirty photos sewn into the shoulder of his suit. I'd do it and then he'd come back three months later and make me take it out and put different ones in.'

'His what?' Ginny leaned forward, her brain trying to piece together the narrative. She'd been doing well until the part about photos.

'Dirty photos. Though it's probably a video. Takes all types, I suppose. He kept them all on a little stick and paid Elsie to sew them into the shoulder of his suit jacket. I told her years ago not to bother, since he took an age to pay his bill. And it's not like he didn't have the money. But isn't that always the way with the rich ones.'

A shiver went through Ginny. Was it excitement or horror? She couldn't be sure. But what she did know was that they were talking about a USB flash drive.

The one that would surely point to who was behind Louisa's death.

'Do you know what happened to the suit?'

'Do we know what happened to the suit?' Esme chortled, as several other women in the book group appeared, all clutching their copies of Cold Comfort Farm. 'Yes, we do. That's the reason Keris refused to pay. Said there was no proof Elsie had done the work. Which was rude because she was the one who decided to bury him in the suit. If you ask me, she did it on purpose.'

The adrenaline that had been flooding Ginny's veins abruptly stopped.

Keris hadn't been joking that Tom Allan had taken his secrets to the grave with him.

Buried in a suit, six feet underground.

And Ginny had a terrible feeling that her friends would be in total agreement on what they had to do next.

FOURTEEN

Ginny had been right. The conversation had lasted less than five minutes, and the biggest point of contention was what time to meet.

Tuppence had thought midnight, but Hen had protested she couldn't possibly stay awake that long and so they'd settled on nine-thirty that night.

Like the last visit to the Little Shaw cemetery, the three widows were already waiting when Ginny climbed out of her car. Tuppence was wearing a bright orange boilersuit, had three shovels under one arm and several buckets in her other hand; JM was barely visible in black trousers and a turtleneck jumper; and Hen had swapped her Liberty print skirt for corduroy trousers belted at the waist, suggesting they'd once belonged to her husband.

Ginny retrieved her two shovels from the back of the car and joined them.

'I didn't dare tell Alyson what we were doing. The police hauled her in for questioning again, and she's exhausted. And she wouldn't be happy to know that Bernard's at the top of our list.' Hen clutched at a giant picnic basket.

JM retrieved a torch from her belt. 'She'd be a lot less happy in jail for the rest of her life, just because she refuses to accept the truth about that man,' she retorted, as she swung the beam in the direction of the cemetery's waist-high fence.

'They lock the gate each night, and after what happened at Bernard's office, I'm not ready to try unpicking it,' Tuppence admitted. 'Plus, it's not too high.'

One by one they clambered carefully over the fence and stepped into the cemetery proper. The moon was hidden behind a bank of clouds, but the erratic beam of JM's torch helped them navigate the neglected graves.

'The good part about no funding is that they can't afford security cameras.' JM stepped over a large rock and through to one of the newer sections of the cemetery.

'Just lots of dead bodies,' Tuppence said, as they reached a plot with a single wooden cross and several bunches of plastic flowers covering the raised dirt mound. It was clear the ground hadn't settled enough to have the headstone erected.

'It's not like we don't have experience living with the ghosts of the dead. I still think about Adam every day, so I guess we carry them with us,' Hen pointed out, and goosebumps crawled along Ginny's flesh which had nothing to do with the shadowy tree branches that looked like long fingers against the broken headstones.

She'd never thought of it like that before, and wasn't sure what to do with it. Was that what she had been doing? Living with a ghost?

Hen looked over at Ginny. 'I shouldn't have said that. Especially since you're not even through your first year yet. You know... if you don't want to go through with this, we will understand.'

'Nonsense. She can't leave now. Besides, she's already implicated. Look at the mud on her boots.' JM swung the torch down to Ginny's boots, her voice stern.

'I haven't changed my mind.' Ginny shook off the discomfort and lowered herself down to inspect the dirt. 'We're lucky the headstone hasn't been put down yet. The soil is soft thanks to the recent rain. It should make the digging easier, but first we should clear everything on top so we can demarcate the original dig.'

'You sound like this isn't your first time.' Tuppence leaned against her spade.

'I did a masters in archaeology, so have been on a number of digs, though it wasn't graves. Mainly medieval middens, as it turned out,' Ginny reluctantly admitted, not really liking to talk about herself. 'Then when Eric decided to buy the surgery he'd been working in, and the practice manager resigned, it made sense for me to take over. A lot less dirty.'

'A little bit of dirt never hurt anyone,' JM reminded her, taking a step back. 'But since it's clear you know more about this than we do, we'll let you take the lead.'

Five hours later, they stared into the gaping hole where a glossy white coffin lid was now visible. They were all gardeners, but none of them had expected it to take quite so long, or that there'd be so much soil.

Ginny rolled her shoulders and wrapped her hands around the hot cup of tea she'd just been given.

'Are you sure you don't want an egg sandwich?' Hen held up a plate of neatly cut white bread sandwiches, but Ginny shook her head, knowing that the hard part was still to come. Like the logistics of how they would even get the lid off, let alone seeing the body inside.

JM seemed to be following her line of thought and joined her. 'You know, it's a pity we didn't think to hire Mitch to come along. We must remember that for next time.'

'Next time?' Hen, who was just about to take a bite of her own sandwich, coughed.

'It's good to keep an open mind about things. Still, we've done most of the hard work now, so we might as well press on.'

'Actually, there will be no pressing on,' an all-too-familiar voice suddenly called out, and a torch shone into Ginny's eyes.

Squinting from the unexpected brightness, Ginny held up her spare hand to shield her vision. The beam moved from Tuppence to Hen and finally to JM. Then it dropped into the grave that they'd just finished digging out before it clicked off and DI Wallace joined them.

Ginny's limbs turned to stone as she clutched at the mug in her hand.

Oh dear. This was not good.

'Would someone like to explain what the hell's going on? Or should I just arrest you all?' In the dim glow of the moonlight, the police officer's mouth was pinched, and his eyes were two narrowed slits of annoyance.

Despite her heavy limbs, Ginny's heart thumped in her chest.

'Arrest *us*?' JM was the first to find her voice. 'That's rich, when we're the ones doing all the work in this case.'

'Really? And what work is that?' The detective's mouth twitched, as if it was taking all his restraint not to say what he wanted to say.

'I'm exercising my fifth right amendments. And I will be advising my clients to do the same.' JM folded her arms and gave him a defiant glare.

Ginny wasn't sure if JM realised that they lived in the United Kingdom and weren't covered by the American constitution. Still, it didn't seem like a good time to mention it.

Wallace let out an irritated sigh.

Not good. Not good at all.

'I am cold. I am tired. It's been a very long day. So could someone give me a good reason not to throw you all in jail?'

At the mention of jail, Ginny's heart pumped faster and sweat prickled her collarbone. What had they all been thinking? It was one thing to look for the flash drive to find out who was really behind Louisa's murder, but it was quite another thing to lie about it. Like the old saying went, when you found yourself in a hole, the first thing to do was to stop digging.

And they had dug a very big hole.

She opened her mouth to explain. To apologise and swear never to do it again. But her tongue had turned to cotton, and she couldn't remember how to speak.

'Well?' Wallace continued to glare, but still no words would come.

Panic gripped Ginny as Hen – kind, sweet, quiet Hen who broke her heart over anything sad – stepped forward, still holding the plate of sandwiches.

Ginny could only stare.

'Detective Wallace, we're sorry. Please don't blame my friends. This isn't their fault. It's mine. They're only here because they want to help.'

'Help who?' His voice dropped down, cool and deadly. But Hen didn't wilt.

'My daughter. Do you remember the diary that Ginny found the day Louisa was murdered?'

'The one she removed from a crime scene and then contaminated with her DNA?'

'Objection,' JM shouted, before putting her hand over her mouth. 'Sorry,' she said, from between her fingers.

Wallace's mouth twitched again. It was possible he was starting to get a nervous tick.

Ginny shrank back, but Hen just gave him one of her encouraging smiles.

'Correct. Well, after much begging, Ginny agreed to help us

look for the missing pages in the library. She found them, and we also found a blackmail note written to Louisa. It was in the same handwriting as that envelope.'

'Was it just? And you didn't think to give it to the police?'

Hen coloured. 'Of course we planned to. But you weren't very receptive when Ginny gave you the diary, so we wanted more proof first.'

'Is that so? It must just be a coincidence then, that that envelope turned out to be an exact match for the very threatening letter that Alyson Farnsworth sent to Louisa two months before her death.'

'It was a therapy letter.' Hen clutched at the plate, her voice wobbly with emotion. 'I've already explained it to PC Singh. Alyson was expressing her feelings of abandonment and betrayal. It was my fault that it got delivered. She was meant to burn it and release her feelings.'

'"*I hate you. How dare you ruin my life like this? You don't even love him. Not like I do. But you're not going to win. Bernard is mine and if I can't have him, then neither can you.*"' Wallace quoted, his voice devoid of emotion.

Ginny had the terrible feeling it was verbatim from Alyson's letter. Now she understood why the widows had been so determined to find it before the police did.

She also realised that by telling Wallace about the blackmail note, they could have made the case against Alyson worse, not better.

The detective was silent. He clearly wanted to see the diary pages.

Ginny finally convinced her legs to move. It wasn't fair for Hen to take all the responsibility, especially when it was Ginny who'd actually found them. She gingerly stepped forward, pleased her knees didn't give out as she made her way to the bright green and white checked picnic rug Hen had laid out, and retrieved the letter from her handbag. She'd

THE WIDOWS' GUIDE TO MURDER

slipped it into a clear plastic folder to stop it from getting damaged.

'And what are "the files"?' he asked in an icy voice, after he'd scanned it.

'That's what we're trying to find out. According to Keris Allan, Tom always carried a USB flash drive... sorry, that's a device used to store digital files,' Tuppence explained in a patient voice, as if teaching him how to use a computer. 'Louisa broke into their house looking for it after Tom died.'

At the mention of the break-in, Wallace's face morphed from a scowl into an open-mouthed glare. 'How did you know about that? No, wait, just tell me how you went from possible break-in, to... this.' He gestured at the gaping hole where Tom Allan's white coffin was glinting in the pale moonlight.

'Ah, now you're going to be impressed with this part,' Tuppence continued, seemingly oblivious to Wallace's furious countenance. 'Turns out Elsie Wicks has been doing suit repairs for Tom Allan, for years. And it wasn't taking up the legs or expanding the waist band. It was to sew in a flash drive to his suits. She thought it was his porn collection.'

'So, let me get this straight. You decided to come out here and dig up an innocent man's grave on the preposterous notion that you might find proof that someone was blackmailing Louisa Farnsworth.'

'Well done. That's it in one.' Tuppence gave him an encouraging nod. 'We believe whatever is on it will explain the motive of the killer.'

'And solve the crime,' JM chimed in.

Hen, still holding the plate of sandwiches, suddenly stepped forward. 'I know it sounds a little bit odd, but we had to do something to convince the police... er... I mean you, that Alyson's innocent. And you've had a very long day, which is bound to make anyone hangry. Maybe you should have something to eat?' She pushed the plate towards him.

'What we're saying is our case is waterproof, and you can't touch us,' JM corrected, before taking one of the proffered sandwiches and biting into it.

Wallace was saved from answering by the sound of sirens in the distance. 'I am going to say this just once. Leave this case to the police. Now, if there's any other evidence you happened to "find", I suggest you hand it over. Then I want you to take your shovels and picnic basket and go home.'

'Why? So you can bury this case and arrest Alyson?'

He gritted his teeth. 'So I can get a warrant to exhume the body, and to remind myself that I *don't* have the energy to arrest four women who are trying to put me into a grave of my own.'

Without another word he stalked back towards the main gate, where the sound of police officers arriving echoed through the cemetery.

Once he was gone, Ginny leaned forward, not sure whether to be happy they hadn't been arrested, or shocked Wallace believed them. It was several moments before she could finally slow down her hammering pulse. 'I can't believe that just happened,' she whispered.

'I know.' Tuppence frowned. 'Hen was right. He's definitely hangry.'

FIFTEEN

'What's wrong with people?' JM scowled as a group of tourists walked into The Lost Goat the following lunchtime. They were clutching the latest edition of a national newspaper, discussing the case in loud voices. 'They're acting like they're experts who know exactly how to best solve this thing. Now... where were we?'

'We were discussing how we could best solve the case.' Hen's tone was unusually dry. Then she put down her knitting and sighed. 'Sorry. I didn't mean that. We were so close before the police swooped in. What if they find something bad on the flash drive?'

'Yes, but we were always going to hand it over,' Ginny reminded her.

'I suppose you're right.' Hen sighed. The others murmured in agreement, not seeming to realise that if Wallace had caught them looking through Tom's coffin, she doubted they would've only got off with just a warning.

Hysterical laughter suddenly bubbled up in Ginny's throat. All this time she'd feared turning out like her mother... and now... here she was. Making bad decisions and risking getting arrested. Risking everything because of her grief.

'Are you okay?' Hen asked, voice full of concern. It snapped her out of the trip down memory lane and she stammered an assurance.

But when her friends didn't reply, she felt the silence slide under her skin and prickle her nerves. She'd spent a lifetime being reserved, only sharing her true feelings with Eric. And even then it wasn't all the time.

Still no one spoke and Ginny's chest tightened as JM's bright fearless eyes bore into her. Tuppence picked at a fingernail, ragged from last night's adventure, while Hen clutched her glass. All patient and accepting.

Ginny realised she owed them the truth. 'I'm a little shaken from last night,' she admitted, before telling them about her mother. Not all of it, but some. The part about how the breakdown and the arrests had changed her. And left Ginny feeling like her future was in someone else's hands. 'You'll think I'm a terrible coward, but I thought Wallace was going to arrest us. I'm sorry.'

'Oh, your poor mother. That must have been terrible for you both,' Tuppence whispered.

'You have nothing to be sorry for,' Hen agreed.

'And you weren't the only one to be scared. I was terrified,' JM added.

'Really? I wasn't even sure you realised how angry he was,' Ginny said, the space between her shoulders suddenly loosening up, as if a weight had been lifted, just by talking about it.

'Oh, we realised.' JM let out a bitter laugh. 'He was livid. I thought he was going to burst a blood vessel. Thank goodness for Hen. She knew just what to say.'

'I'm pleased you think so.' Hen gave them a wistful smile. 'But I'm not sure I did. In fact, I can't help but think we've made everything worse. We should never have gone there.'

'Hen's right. All everyone's talking about is why the police are exhuming Tom Allan's body. They're already whispering that Alyson must have killed him as well,' Tuppence said, repeating what Ginny had been hearing all morning in the library.

It was one of the reasons she'd been so pleased to slip away during her lunch break and meet with her friends. And now she was relieved she had.

Though they'd joked when she first met them that they didn't talk about their feelings, being able to be honest about how she felt, even in a few words, had been refreshing.

Unfortunately, it didn't solve any of their problems.

'Someone has clearly set Alyson up.' JM lowered her voice, which was more of a concession than she usually made. 'And if the police were doing their job, then we wouldn't have been forced to get involved. So, really, they've only got themselves to blame.'

'Yes, but we're not getting very far,' Hen reminded them. 'We still only have one suspect – Bernard – and then our proof is flimsy. A possible affair and life insurance. But someone else wrote the blackmail letter, so he's clearly got help.'

'Short of making everyone submit a writing sample, it's going to be hard to find out who. But don't forget what Mitch said about Louisa. She made Sophie's life hell and accused her of stealing money and destroying council documents. So why are Marigold and Cleo convinced it didn't happen? Someone isn't telling the truth.'

'But how can we find out? If council documents were destroyed, they won't be anywhere.' Tuppence took a sip of her half-pint of bitter.

'Have you had any luck getting into the stack again, to look at the parish council documents?' Hen asked Ginny.

'No. The library was busy today, with everyone talking about Tom Allan, and the few times I did try looking for the key,

Harold gave me jobs to do.' Ginny stared at her fingers, hating that she didn't have better news. 'But I'll try again this afternoon—'

'This is not good enough. I want my drink, now,' a voice suddenly bellowed out. Everyone in the pub turned to where a tall man was leaning over the bar, glaring at a

trembling Heather. 'I'm sorry, but I can't—'

'Not good enough,' he repeated, in case the punters in the far corner hadn't heard him the first time.

Heather gripped the beer taps, eyes wide. But she was saved from answering when Rita emerged from the kitchen door holding two plates of shepherd's pie. She calmly delivered them to the right table then joined the man at the bar.

'Is there a problem?'

'Yes, there's a problem. Yesterday, the chalkboard outside said, "Free beer, tomorrow." But this incompetent woman seems to have problems understanding that. I want to speak to the manager.'

'Well, you're in luck. I'm the manager, and my advice is that unless you want to embarrass yourself further, it's time to pay for your drink and wait for your lunch order. And you're always welcome to come back tomorrow and try again.'

'But if I come back tomorrow, you'll just give me the same stupid—oh.' The man's eyes widened as he finally got the joke. A sheepish expression formed on his face, and he mumbled an apology.

Rita raised an eyebrow, as if to remind him that she wasn't the one he needed to apologise to.

Turning to Heather, he had a short – much quieter – conversation, handed over some money and slunk to a table in the corner, where two other men, with expensive-looking cameras, were waiting.

Once he was gone, Heather disappeared into the kitchen, head bowed.

'In the old days, Billy would've had that man in a head lock and marched him out of here, spilling drinks and knocking over tables in the process.' Hen resumed her knitting as Rita walked past the table, holding a tray of empty glasses.

'Thirty years of running an East End pub taught me that you win more fights with honey than vinegar,' Rita shot back. 'But I'm sorry for the disruption. I usually catch it sooner.'

'Is Heather okay?' Ginny asked. 'She seemed shaken.'

'I told her to take a break. She doesn't talk about what her life was like before she moved here, but I gather it's been difficult. And guys like that don't help.' Rita continued through the crowd, clearing glasses and reassuring the customers as she went.

Once she was out of earshot, the four women turned back to the miniature murder board Hen had constructed out of a cereal box. Bernard's initials were in the middle and the line going out to Keris Allan had been scribbled out.

'I still think it's funny how many people fall for that sign,' Tuppence said.

'I beg to differ.' JM glared at the man who had been shouting. 'Like I said, these amateur detectives are a nuisance. They're just going to get Wallace's back up and make him more determined to pin it on Alyson. No… sorry, Hen. I don't mean to upset you, but we must face facts. After what Wallace said, the situation is urgent, and all we have is a life insurance policy and a possible affair as a motive.'

'Did Edward tell you anything, when you stayed back, clearing up?' Ginny asked.

'Not really. He did say a few things about trespassing and restraining orders, but there was so much dust for me to vacuum up that it was hard to hear. But I'm going back there this afternoon to tackle the reception area. The man is a slob. Anyway, I will try to find out who else Bernard is friendly with.'

'Excellent. And I'll talk to Alyson again and see if she can think of anyone else who might be behind this.' Tuppence drained the last of her bitter as Ginny's phone alarm beeped, reminding her she had to be back at work in five minutes.

She got to her feet and said her goodbyes before leaving.

Outside, there was a young woman standing next to the chalkboard sign, while her friend filmed her.

'And... viewers... this is the pub where Louisa Farnsworth had her very last drink. But as we will reveal...'

Ginny increased her pace. Is that how Wallace saw them? As nosy civilians with more grey hair than wit? It was an unnerving thought.

The afternoon didn't bring any more success than the morning had, and Ginny was pleased when she reached her own cottage. Edgar was waiting by the pink front door, looking outraged at the fact it wouldn't open automatically for him.

'You know you have a perfectly good door at the back of the house.' She put down her work bag, which seemed to get heavier by the day. The training manual took up most of it, but she'd managed to squeeze in more of the old cushions so she could wash the covers and make some repairs.

She fumbled for her house keys and stepped inside. Edgar pushed past her and darted to the back door, where he once again sat down, as if waiting to be let out. Ginny bit back a retort and simply opened the door. She had no energy to argue with cat logic.

The sound of Wallace's voice drifted over from somewhere behind the fence and Ginny stiffened, her fingers tightening around the handle.

'The coroner's found evidence that Tom Allan was already dead before he drowned. And Alyson Farnsworth was caught on CCTV cameras, driving in Liverpool two hours before the flood, which puts her at the crime scene,' he said in a tight voice, and Ginny's stomach dropped with a sickening thud. She took a wobbly step forward as her mind whirled. The coroner had done an autopsy on Tom Allan's body? There were several moments of silence before Wallace coughed. 'No, I agree the cemetery thing was a... yes... I understand. Thank you, sir.'

The silence stretched out again, but this time it was broken by the sound of boots pacing up and down the back yard. But Ginny could hardly concentrate as the horror of his words rang in her ears. Tom Allan had been murdered... and Alyson was near where it happened.

Did Hen know? How was she? The thoughts galvanised her into action and she took a small step back. She needed to call her friends, and—

Crash.

The noise made her gasp out loud as she turned to where one of her potted plants was lying on the concrete in a mess of broken terracotta and soil, while Edgar studied it from his position on the round patio table. A moment later Wallace's head appeared over the fence. A series of emotions flashed across his dark eyes before he let out an irritated groan.

'I take it you heard that conversation?' There were smudges under his eyes and his hair was in disarray, making Ginny wonder if he'd slept at all.

'It wasn't intentional.' She wrapped her arms around her chest, trying not to think of Hen's despair. 'I-is it true that Tom Allan was murdered?'

His jaw flickered but he eventually nodded. 'We will be announcing it soon enough.'

No. Ginny's stomach plummeted. How could this be happening? And why would Alyson have been in Liverpool the same day that Tom died? It had to be a mistake. This whole thing was a mistake. They'd only gone to the cemetery because of the files.

Of course.

She forced herself to return his gaze. 'What about the flash drive? Did you find it in his suit?'

There was yet more silence as he weighed up whether to answer her or not. Then he shrugged. 'It was blank. We spoke to Elsie Wicks, who confirmed that she'd been paid to put it there many times over the years. But she'd never looked to see what was on it.'

'Are you sure? Can your IT department find out why? Perhaps there are hidden files?'

'This is not one of the books from your library. There are no secret files.' His more familiar mask of irritation reappeared. Edgar chose that moment to jump off the table and pad over to the fence to better inspect the detective. Ginny hurried after him and scooped the cat up into her arms. Purring happily, he settled against her chest as she found herself far too close to Wallace.

The flash drive had been their one hope to prove that Louisa's murder had nothing to do with Alyson. Which left them with nothing. No, worse than nothing, because now Alyson was somehow being linked to Tom Allan's murder as well. Edgar shifted in her arms, making her realise she'd been clutching him. She swallowed, trying to push down her panic.

'But it doesn't mean Alyson did it. What about Bernard? He had far more reason to kill his business partner and wife. Especially if Louisa and Tom had started up their affair again. Oh, and don't forget the life insurance—'

She broke off, too late remembering they weren't meant to know about that.

His expression hardened. 'For the last time, you and your friends need to stay out of this. I suggest you get yourself a safer hobby.'

Her cheeks stung, as if she'd been slapped. What a dreadful man he was, and why was he so determined to ignore perfectly good clues? And then something broke. Like a dam being breached, the walls that usually kept parts of her contained were no more.

All she knew was that she was tired, cranky, and maybe just a little bit hangry.

'I *do* have a hobby. I make jam, though it's difficult when someone won't share their fruit.'

'As far as I can tell, you have more than enough low hanging fruit to make your jam.' His gaze locked on hers, but for once she didn't look away.

'While it's easiest to take the first *fruit* you can reach, that's not always what makes the best jam. It's rewarding to work a bit harder and gather *all* the fruit. Even the pieces that seem out of reach.'

Their eyes locked and he worked his jaw before he finally spoke. 'There's an organisational structure to ensure we're methodical in how we collect and process all *fruit*. Our decisions are driven by knowledge, tactics, logistics and legalities. That way we don't miss anything, and it's why I am close to making an arrest. We're done here, Mrs Cole.'

He turned on his heel and stalked towards his front door, leaving her alone and simmering more than her jam saucepan ever had.

'Where have you been? Ian and I have been worried,' Nancy said the following morning, as Ginny managed to answer the phone and gulp down her cup of tea at the same time.

To think that a week ago she was trying to find ways to fill the space in the day and now she could hardly keep up. After her unwanted conversation with Wallace, she'd called Hen to break the news about the flash drive: no evidence, and another murder – thanks to Tom Allan's body being exhumed. And Alyson was still a suspect.

As for why Alyson had been in Liverpool, Hen explained

that her daughter had received a text message from Bernard, asking to meet her there. And while she'd been able to show the police the message, they hadn't seemed very convinced.

They really had made a muddle of it.

'It's been a busy couple of days, and I keep forgetting to take my phone with me.'

Nancy sighed. 'I've been calling since Monday. What has been so important that you couldn't check your messages?'

Ginny closed her eyes. She could hardly tell her sister-in-law that she'd been busy digging up a grave and almost getting arrested, not to mention trying and failing to find out who had killed Louisa Farnsworth. Then again, she doubted Nancy would believe her. Ginny wasn't sure she believed it herself. 'Sorry you were worried, but you don't need to be. I've met three other women who are all widows. They have a book club and do some volunteer gardening. They seem to have taken me under their wing.'

'I'm pleased you've got new friends,' Nancy said. The wind in the background of her call suggested she was walking around her favourite park. 'But how can I not worry with that murderer still running around? It's made it onto the BBC, you know. A couple of days ago they said they had a solid avenue they were investigating. If they have a person of interest, they should just arrest them before anyone is murdered in their sleep.'

Ginny stiffened. 'The fact that they *haven't* arrested anyone means they don't have enough evidence. And whoever did kill Louisa was motivated by something personal and specific. I don't think they're going to start killing random people.'

'Wait... do you know who it is?' The background wind faded away, which meant Nancy had stopped.

Too late Ginny realised her mistake. She never raised her voice or got emotional about things that didn't concern her. And maybe if she hadn't met JM, Tuppence and Hen, and felt their passion for exonerating Alyson, that might still be so.

But it was hard to be neutral now.

They just needed more time to untangle all the separate pieces.

'It's only speculation. I don't want to add to the gossip,' she said, quickly. 'But try not to worry. I'll get better at keeping my phone in my handbag.'

'Thank you. And we still need to talk about when you are coming to see us.'

In the distance the wail of police sirens filled the air, and Ginny rushed to the window. There was no sign of Wallace's car, though it had been there when she'd gone to bed the previous night.

Her breath hitched as several of her neighbours appeared from their houses and then huddled together, deep in conversation.

Oh, no.

'Nancy... I must go. I don't want to be late for work.'

'Okay, but call me later.'

'Will do,' Ginny promised, as she opened her door and stepped onto the front path.

The woman on the other side of Wallace's house beckoned her over to join them. She was in her thirties, and was usually too busy trying to herd around four young boys to stop and chat. But now her eyes were bright with gossip.

'Has something happened?' Ginny asked, trying to control her erratic heartbeat.

'I'll say it has. Wallace got a call-out at five in the morning, didn't he? My little one is teething, so I was already up and saw him go. Face like a thundercloud.'

'Hannah, you can hardly blame him.' The woman four houses down chimed in. 'I heard they were digging up half the bodies in the cemetery, and now this.'

'Now what?'

'Now we have a serial killer on our hands. No doubt about

it.' The old man from across the road made a tutting noise, as if he'd just discovered aphids on his rose bushes. 'It's always the quiet ones.'

'Stop it, Henry. Clearly, she doesn't know what's happened yet,' the other woman scolded him, then turned back to Ginny. 'They found Bernard Farnsworth dead in his house. His throat was slit, and his ex-wife was standing over him, holding the knife.'

'Alyson? A-are you sure?'

'That's the one. As soon as they started talking about anonymous letters, I knew it was going to be her. I've been saying it all week,' the old man assured them.

Ginny ignored him and focused on the second woman, who seemed to be the most informed of the group. 'How do you know?'

'My sister's a paramedic, so I heard it straight from the proverbial horse.'

No. It couldn't be right. Alyson would never kill Bernard. She loved him. It was a mistake. It had to be.

Ginny's knees locked together, but her neighbours didn't seem to notice, and when her phone buzzed she gave them an apologetic smile and retreated back to her house.

It was Hen.

'Oh, thank goodness I got through,' her friend said, before breaking into a sob. 'We're too late. The police have arrested Alyson, and they've been pulling the place apart. It's all my fault.'

'Nonsense.' JM's voice came through in the background. 'Quick, put that thing on speaker... No, I wouldn't have a clue what button to press.'

'Oh, I do. I saw a YouTube video on it once,' Tuppence's voice said in a muffled tone before a loud bang echoed out, followed by a sharp static hiss that rattled Ginny's head. 'Now, let's see, which one was... oh, here we go. Ginny, can you hear us?'

Relieved the jarring noise had stopped, she gasped, 'Yes. But I still can't believe that Bernard was murdered. What happened?'

'Someone broke into his house and slit his throat,' Tuppence said, though none of her usual liveliness was there.

'But why was Alyson there?' Ginny swallowed, still not sure how any of it could be possible. 'They said she was holding the knife.'

'It's my fault.' Hen's voice was raw, like pure anguish. 'Apparently, she went around to see him while we were at the cemetery the other night. It ended up in a huge fight that all the neighbours heard. He told her if she ever darkened his door again, he would call the police.'

'She decided to go back early this morning and apologise. But he was dead when she got there,' JM said before her own voice cracked. 'We think the grief got to her, because as far as we can tell, Alyson started hugging him and trying to pretend it wasn't real. She even picked up the knife, which is when the police turned up.'

'I should have tried harder. Hidden her car keys – anything to stop her going back there.' Hen started sobbing again. 'And now they're saying that Bernard never sent Alyson a text message telling her to go to Liverpool. So they think she killed Tom as well.'

Ginny closed her eyes and leaned against the kitchen counter. 'It's a terrible, terrible mess. But JM's right, you can't blame yourself.'

'But I do. After Adam died, it felt like I was stuck on an island quietly waiting for the tide to rise and pull me under. I thought I would drown, and by the time I got myself together, I realised that my poor girl had been going through the same thing. She needed me and I wasn't there for her. Th-that's when she met Bernard, and since he left her, it's been like watching her drown.'

Ginny's chest ached and suddenly she understood just why the three women had asked her to help. Because like attracted like. They'd recognised her own silent grief. And unlike Nancy and Ian – who she loved dearly – the three widows knew perfectly what the cold bleakness was, and how hard it was to fight against the dark void.

And even though Alyson wasn't a widow, she'd been fighting the same overwhelming grief, but without any support, apart from Hen, who could only watch on, helpless to do anything.

'Where are you now, Hen?' she asked.

'Brandon and I are at JM's house. The police won't tell me when I can go back home. It's all such a mess.'

'Which is why we don't have a moment to waste,' Ginny said, in a firm voice. 'I have to go to work, but I'll come around as soon as I've finished. Together we will figure this out. We won't let Alyson go under.'

SIXTEEN

Ginny had never been one to take sick days unless she really was sick, but by the time the end of the day came around, she wished she had done so. The library had been beyond busy, with everyone eager to stand around and talk about Bernard's murder and Alyson's arrest. The resulting noise had forced Harold to come out of his office three times to remind people it was a library, and to be quiet.

It hadn't worked, and by the time the last borrower had left, they were all feeling frazzled. But Ginny's hope of heading straight to JM's house had been pushed back when Marigold Bentley had called a staff meeting.

Which was why Ginny was currently filling the old stainless-steel teapot with tea leaves, and had set out cups and saucers, as well as two jugs of milk.

'Oh, good, you're here. I'm sorry for such late notice, but after everything that's happened, it's important that we take a moment to reflect and come together.' Marigold joined Ginny at the kitchen bench, holding an impressive chocolate cake that was perfectly iced with the words 'Thanks Team' on the top. 'I hope it hasn't been too dreadful in here today.'

'It's been okay.' Ginny finished with the tea and got out a stack of plates and a large knife to cut the cake. Then she thought of the knife that Alyson had found next to the body, and quickly put it down on the kitchen bench. 'Considering the circumstances.'

'It's hard to comprehend. Louisa and Bernard both murdered within two weeks of each other, and now they think Tom Allan was deliberately killed as well. They weren't the most popular people around here but then again, neither was I after the Wilburton Reserve sale, so I understand what it's like to be demonised.'

Ginny swallowed. 'I heard about that. There was mention they got it at a reduced price. Was that for a reason?'

'I'm afraid the reason was very simple. Allan and Farnsworth Developments gave us a cash deal when we needed the money. If we hadn't sold it... well, let's just say it saved us from going under.' Marigold leaned against the bench as worry lines gathered around her mouth. 'But people have long memories around here. Including Harold Rowe. It's one of the reasons I was hesitant to bring him back in. He was very against the sale at the time and accused us of mismanagement. Still, desperate times and all that...' She trailed off.

'I hadn't heard that part of the story.'

'It's been hard to convince people there was no conspiracy theory. Just a balance sheet that didn't add up. I suppose that comes with the territory. I probably need to get a thicker skin. And it's hard to believe Alyson Farnsworth is behind it all.'

'It does seem surreal,' Ginny said – much like she'd been doing all day. She'd quickly realised no one expected her to have the answers; they just wanted to discuss it, much like they would last night's episode of *Coronation Street*.

Marigold picked up the knife and sliced into the cake. 'Let's just hope this is the end of it. Two murders in as many weeks, not to mention the revelation about Tom, has caused a lot of media interest, and pressure on some of our other local services. It's hard for people to understand just how difficult it is to keep things afloat. But that's not your concern. I wanted to bring in a treat for everyone. To say thank you for all the hard work.'

'Make sure Harold doesn't get a slice then.' Cleo appeared in the doorway, closely followed by Andrea, Cheryl and three other women that Ginny hadn't been introduced to, with Connor trailing in their wake.

'Now... don't be like that, Cleo,' Marigold chided, not showing any hint of the strain that had been there moments earlier. 'Without Harold we wouldn't have been able to reopen. Speaking of him... where is he? I'd like to get started.'

'Probably still in his office,' Andrea offered up. 'I tried to remind him about the staff meeting, but he threw a book at the door. He's in a foul temper.'

'It's as if a triple homicide is a major inconvenience for him and his precious research,' Cleo chimed in. 'What's he even looking for? On Friday I caught him going through all the old newspapers. He's worse than William.'

'He's concerned about the collection, that's all. I had no idea Louisa neglected it so badly.' Marigold sighed. 'He was adamant that if he came back, his priority would be to restore it to its former glory.'

'We could do with a bit less glory and more helping to shelve the books.' Cleo folded her arms.

'How would you know?' Connor deadpanned.

'I'll get him.' Ginny got to her feet, pleased for a break from the constant bickering.

'Thank you.' Marigold slid the knife under the first slice and lifted the rich, crumbling chocolate cake onto a plate. Then nodded at the steaming teapot. 'Who would like to play mother?'

Ginny slipped out of the room and into the library proper. The main lights were off, and the dull shadows were a relief after the brightness of the staffroom. The door to Louisa's old office was firmly shut, but the light filtering out from under the door told her that Harold was still in there.

She knocked on the door. 'Marigold wanted me to get you.'

'Of course she did,' he grumbled, which Ginny took as an invitation to open the door.

The desk was covered in piles of old books that Ginny suspected had come from the stack. She'd seen him go there several times, always returning with a trolley full of leather-bound books and newspapers. With so much going on, she hadn't paid much attention to it, but Cleo was right. What was he doing?

'If you'd like a hand with anything tomorrow, let me know,' she offered.

'My expertise is in the preservation and evaluation of valu-able texts. It's not something that can be taught in half an hour.' He shut the book he'd been reading and pushed it under a pile of newspapers, before getting to his feet.

His arm brushed against the book trolley and it caught on his sleeve. He instinctively pulled back, only to have his gold cufflink catch more firmly in the wire grid. He tugged it again, but instead of releasing it, he pulled the trolley with him.

'Stop moving or you'll tear the cotton. Just stay still while I untangle you.'

'I always knew that these trolleys were poor quality.' He made a harumphing sound as Ginny tried to release the cuff-link. But it was firmly wedged. She released the pressure and instead carefully twisted the gold bar that held the buttonholes together. Once it was off, it was easy to slip it from between the mesh and free him.

Under the shirt cuff his wrist was covered with tiny scratch marks, several of which had stained the meticulously laundered shirt. A crepe bandage flashed from further up his arm and that, too, was dotted with blood.

'Whatever you did to your arm, needs to be redressed. The sudden movement must have caused it to start bleeding again.'

'It's fine.' Harold pulled his arm away and tugged down his sleeve. Then, in one practised move, he guided the cufflink back into the buttonholes on the cuff.

Ginny frowned, still staring at the tiny dots of blood. 'It doesn't look fine. What happened?'

'Just a silly gardening accident yesterday. Nothing that can't wait until I get home,' he snapped, before he ushered her out of the office, and then followed her, taking time to lock the door first. 'Now, let's get this ridiculous meeting over and done with so that we can all go home.'

Ginny nodded. But it wasn't home she needed to go to. She needed to see her friends.

JM lived in a two-storey cottage perched on the side of the canal, which gurgled and gushed as Ginny parked her car next to JM's. Before she could reach the front door, Brandon, Hen's lovely labrador, appeared from the side of the house, quickly followed by Tuppence. She was wearing a navy jumper and dark pink jeans, and her wild curls were held back with a scarf. She looked ready for business.

'Come in this way.' Tuppence led her around to a small patio that overlooked the water. But it was the back of the house that made Ginny gasp. The cottage was clearly old, judging by the honey-coloured stones, but from this angle, it was entirely modern: the original wall had been replaced by full length sheets of glass, providing views from every window.

'Oh, my.'

'It's extraordinary, isn't it? Before they bought the art gallery, Rebecca was an architect, and she designed it. Sadly, she died not long after the renovations were finished. It's quite a testament to someone's life.'

They moved through to a modern living room with two tufted sofas and a glass coffee table laden with glossy design books.

Installed on one of the sofas, Hen was still managing to look comfortable and homely, with her knitting on her lap and her feet in fluffy slippers.

Ginny sat down next to her and patted her knee. 'How are you? Are the police still at your cottage?'

'They've finished, but I couldn't face going back tonight. Not while Alyson is still in custody.'

'Who could blame you, after the mess they left behind?' Tuppence sat on the other sofa as JM appeared carrying four wineglasses and a bottle of something tucked under one arm.

'Ginny, your timing is impeccable.' She knelt at the coffee table and opened the bottle. 'I think we could all use a drink before getting down to business.'

'Thank goodness I managed to find a new murder board at the charity shop.' Tuppence gestured to a whiteboard propped up on an easel, in front of the huge glass wall.

'What happened to the other one?' Ginny asked, worried she already knew the answer. 'Did the police take it?'

'Yes, which is a gross invasion of our privacy and freedom of speech, as I told them at the time. Still, since Bernard was our prime suspect, it's not much use to us now. Or to them.' JM passed around the drinks. 'Here's to Alyson.'

'They wouldn't even let me give her a food hamper.' Hen took a long gulp of wine then picked up her knitting and rapidly pushed the needle through the loop of wool. At first her hand was unsteady but the soft *click, click, click* soon took on a familiar rhythm.

'We will get her out. We just need to keep digging.' Tuppence wrinkled her nose. 'Sorry for the poor choice of words. So, what do we know?'

'Bernard, Louisa and Tom are dead.' JM crossed to the

whiteboard and wrote down their names, along with a picture of a coffin, a little knife and a bottle with a skull and crossbones on it. 'So, what do they have in common?'

'We know Louisa had an affair with both men at different times.' Tuppence held up her hand to count her fingers. 'My count is three. Once with Bernard when he was still married to Alyson, and twice with Tom if Keris is to be believed.'

'And they were all involved in the land scandal,' Hen added. The knitting seemed to have soothed her more than the wine, and the deep lines around her mouth had faded.

'I might have a new lead about that. Marigold Bentley said the only reason the council sold Wilburton Reserve to Tom and Bernard was because the council needed the cash quickly,' Ginny said.

'That's true. I remember there was a lot of talk a few years ago. It's why the cemetery's in such disrepair.' JM picked up a green whiteboard marker and wrote it down.

'And she has concerns about Harold Rowe. He was upset about losing funding for the local historical society, and about the land sale.'

There was silence apart from the soft rush of water from the canal outside. Then Tuppence let out a soft whoop. 'Why didn't we think of that sooner? He sent so many letters to the editor of the local paper that they refused to keep publishing them. And back when the ground was being broken, he tied himself to the bulldozer. Of course, he only used a skipping rope, so it didn't take long to move him. And while I don't mean to judge, he could have at least done a half-hitch.'

'Harold tied himself to a bulldozer?' Ginny tried and failed to imagine Harold with his pristine shirts and trousers getting anywhere near a building site, let alone tying himself to something. Then she recalled the tiny red dots of blood on his shirt sleeve. 'The police said that whoever killed Bernard broke a window to get in, was that correct?'

'That's right. It was at the back of the house. Why?'

Ginny quickly filled them in about the cut on Harold's arm, the dust on his trousers the day she'd started looking for Louisa's diary inserts, and his refusal to let anyone into the stack. And that Cleo had caught him looking through the old newspapers.

'But what does it all mean? Why has he waited so long? And what is he looking for?' Hen completed another nest and cast on more wool with the energy of someone who didn't dare stop.

'That's the million-dollar question. We know he accused Louisa of destroying books, and he disliked Tom and Bernard intensely.' This time JM selected a bright pink marker and drew a line between the two names. 'But why set Alyson up? She wasn't involved in the scandal. It didn't happen until after the divorce.'

'What if Harold blamed her for not putting up more of a fight when Louisa set her sights on Bernard? Hen, didn't you say that Alyson smoothed out Bernard's rough edges?'

'Yes, sometimes he was almost decent.' Hen put down her knitting and considered. 'You think that if they hadn't broken up, Bernard might not have got involved in the land deal?'

'Not me, but what if that's how Harold sees it.' Ginny ran a finger around her wine glass, willing her mind to work. But something was missing. 'None of it explains why he would go to such extreme lengths, though.'

'Because he's grumpy?' Tuppence began to pace, her socked feet making a soft padding noise. But not even Hen, who was usually so supportive, could agree.

'Oh, dear. It's useless. Wallace was right. We're just making this up as we go along. We don't have any of the skills to do it properly, and poor Alyson will never get out of jail.' A tear trickled down Hen's soft cheek. 'What do we know about tactics and logistics and all of those thingamajigs?'

'Speak for yourself.' JM bristled. 'I know my way around the internet quite well, thank you very much. And I have just spent the last five years researching my family history.' They all swung to look at her. 'What? It's true.'

'We believe you. We're just surprised none of us thought of it sooner. Let's see what we can find out about Harold, and what secrets he might be hiding.'

JM opened her mouth and closed it again before setting up her MacBook on the long dining-room table, while the three of them hovered behind her. True to her word, JM's fingers flew across the keyboard at a speed that put Ginny's own touch-typing skills to shame.

'I think we've just found our answer.' JM clicked from one page to the next, before shifting over so they could all see the screen. It was an old newspaper article, dated 12 June 1958.

The Wilburton Legacy

To honour the death of Adrian Rowe (May 1930–January 1957) his family has announced they will be donating the tract of land known as the Wilburton Reserve to the Little Shaw parish council, to protect the red squirrel population that he spent a lifetime observing. Rowe, who was a respected naturalist, philanthropist, and long-serving parish chairman, inherited the land, along with several other properties, when his uncle, Rufus Wilburton, died without having children of his own.

Rowe's final wish was that the ten miles of woodland should be shared with the community, and provisions have been made to ensure that the land is protected. Mr Rowe leaves behind a wife and young son, who might not grow up with a father, but will always be able to see the legacy he left behind.

'Now *that's* a motive.' Tuppence whistled. 'So, Harold's father was not only a past chairman, but he donated the reserve

to the council. No wonder Harold was furious when Tom and
Bernard bought it cheaply and then sold it off and made a
fortune.'

'Especially if it was meant to be protected,' Ginny said. 'But
how did they get away with it? Wouldn't there have been
records of the donation that prevented the council from selling
it off?'

'Unless something happened to those records? We never
did find out what went on between Louisa and Sophie. Was it
to do with the land sale?' Tuppence pondered.

'It's possible.' JM returned to the whiteboard and began to
write down names. 'So Harold was furious about what
happened and demanded that Louisa, Tom and Bernard
confess their crimes. And when they refused, he killed them, all
without leaving a clue behind.'

'Let's hope not.' Ginny got to her feet, suddenly feeling
exhausted. 'Because unless we can find proof of what he's done,
Wallace will never believe us.'

Not that she could blame him.

So far, all their theories had come up short, and those they
did have were tangled with unanswered questions and vague
ideas that they couldn't articulate. It made her think of the
young doctors who would come through the surgery, their faces
weary with fatigue as they tried to adapt to the reality of the job.

Ginny's own brow was pounding with the start of a
headache. No wonder Wallace always looked so tired. Fighting
crime was exhausting.

SEVENTEEN

'Mrs Cole, is there a reason why you're following me?' Harold twisted around with the ease of a ballerina, which was no mean feat considering his stocky body and the book trolley in his grip. It was currently empty, but she knew by the time he left the stack it would be loaded up. 'And why are you holding a fire extinguisher?'

'William wanted a copy of *An Early History of Little Shaw*, and since you were already here, I said I'd get it for him. As for the extinguisher, it just arrived.' Ginny clutched at the red cylinder in her arms, trying to hide her shaking fingers.

Neither was quite true. William had asked for the book two hours earlier, but Ginny had managed to stall him until Harold had started his next trip. And the fire extinguisher had been delivered first thing in the morning, but she'd kept it out of sight.

She needed to get into the stack, especially after last night's discovery.

'Well, I can take the extinguisher and get the book. Assuming you have the correct Dewey number for it.' Harold's mouth pinched together.

Ginny tightened her grip on the extinguisher, her arms

beginning to ache with the weight. 'I thought since you're going in, I could also have a look around. I'm fascinated about Little Shaw's history.'

He raised an eyebrow. 'You didn't seem fascinated yesterday when William was talking to you about the old iron mine. Are you sure there isn't another reason?'

Does he mean apart from proving he's a serial killer?

Ginny shook her head. 'No, no... I'm just curious about my new home.'

'Then I suggest you start with the local history display that I set up last week. Now, if you would like to give me the book request for William, and that extinguisher...? I would hate for you to be exposed to the mould.'

Their gazes met, but Harold's sharp brown eyes were no match for Ginny, and she passed both items over. So far, she'd had no problems getting Keris, Bernard, Marigold and Mitch to talk to her, but clearly that had been a coincidence rather than any skill on her part. She just had to hope her friends were having better luck.

'Are you sure we don't have a second set of keys for the stack?' Ginny asked Cleo several hours later, as she followed her through to the staffroom. It had been a frustrating afternoon, and any hope she'd had of searching Harold's office for the key had been ruined by the new padlock that he'd added to the door.

So now she needed to find two keys.

It was only the thought of poor Alyson that stopped her from breaking into hysterical laughter.

'Just as sure as last time you asked.' Cleo buttoned up her coat and heaved a large, quilted bag over one shoulder. It was bulging with library books to help give her husband some inspiration with the mosaic garden ornaments he was planning to make. 'I need to catch my bus. Young John is getting out of control. He refused to pick me up yesterday, just because I didn't have time to make it to the Macintosh Road stop.'

'What a criminal. Sticking to the timetable and official route,' Connor retorted, donning a larger black hoodie to go over the one he was already wearing. 'At least you get a bus. Half the ones to Halton Park either don't turn up or are cancelled at the last minute.'

'Probably scared they'll get the tyres stolen,' Andrea, who was stacking the dishwasher, retorted.

'Andrea, please, that's not an appropriate comment to make,' Cleo scolded, then gestured for the other woman to get her coat. 'Come on, or we really will miss our bus.'

Connor's mouth dropped open as the women disappeared in a flurry of scarves and bus passes, bickering about the state of the nation.

Ginny could only assume Cleo's newfound attitude towards the teenager must have come from their discussion the previous day. Then she frowned. Was she any better than Cleo, since she'd never considered how he got to the library every day—?

'Is that true about the bus service?'

'Yeah. At least today they've admitted it. It's worse when you're waiting at the bus stop for ages.' His expression reformed into his usual mask of indifference as he thumbed through his notifications on his phone. 'Night, Mrs Cole. I'll put the recycling out when I go.'

'Night, Connor. Thank you.' Ginny followed him through to the dark library. She'd already done a final check but, out of habit, scanned it before exiting and then locking it up.

The sky was overcast, and the clouds were darkening. Her car was across the road, and she was grateful that she'd driven it in with the intention of going to the supermarket on her way home. By the time she reached the footpath Connor reappeared, pushing the recycling bin so it could be collected.

'How do you get home when the bus is cancelled?' she suddenly asked.

He pushed back a strand of long hair that had fallen over his face and gave his trademark shrug. 'Depends. Sometimes the old man is working out this way. Or, one of my mates will come and get me. Otherwise, I'll see if someone from the estate is at the pub.'

'That seems a bit... unreliable.'

'And yet it works better than the bus service.'

'Let me give you a lift home,' she said, as a shadow fell across his face. Oh. Had she offended him? 'Unless you don't want to. I didn't mean to pry. I was just worried it might rain and I have the car here.'

'Sure you're not worried about your tyres getting nicked?'

'I don't think they'd be too interested.' Ginny nodded to the Ka, which almost raised a smile from him. 'What do you say?'

'You don't even know where I live.'

'I'm sure you could show me,' she said.

This was met with silence before he finally let go of the recycling bin and walked towards her. 'Fine,' he grunted, and followed her over to the small car.

Ginny unlocked it and he opened the door before giving the interior a dubious glare. His limbs were long, like a puppy who hadn't finished growing, but he managed to squeeze himself in and she started the engine.

'Right, where are we off to?'

'Go to the end of this road and turn left.'

Ginny did as she was told, but despite making several attempts at conversation, Connor only gave monotone answers. Still, as raindrops started to blur the windscreen, she was pleased she hadn't left him to make his own way home. She put on her wipers and tried to concentrate on the road. The traffic slowed down, and a set of lights came into view. The right-hand lane was backed up with cars. 'It seems very busy. Is that normal for this time of day?'

'Nope.' Connor monotoned again as she recognised the turn. It was for the estate where Bernard and Louisa Farnsworth lived... *had* lived. 'Probably want to see the murder house.'

Murder house? Was that what it was being called now? Her skin tingled and she longed to ask more, but considering his mood, she didn't bother to push. Could all those cars really be going to see the place where a man had been killed? But what were they hoping to see? Maybe she could go back that way once she dropped him off. The lights changed and she drove past the long line of cars.

Connor shifted in his seat and made a low scoffing noise. 'My nan said people have been driving past since yesterday.'

What? Ginny's hands gripped the wheels, and it took all of her willpower to keep her eyes on the road. But her chest was heaving as she slowed down to let a car overtake her. Once she'd collected herself, she dared look over to him. 'Y-your grand-mother was Bernard and Louisa's neighbour?'

Connor's mouth twisted with his scowl. 'Yeah, well, I'm guessing it's not something they went around telling people. When she first moved, I reckon they almost had a heart attack. Tried everything they could to get her out of there, including calling Wallace a few times. But he couldn't do anything. My uncle, Joey, bought the house for her, back when he was, well... in the mood-altering trade. Which is why my old girl won't have anything to do with Joey or Nan. Not that Joey's around anymore. He did a runner and set up shop in Spain. Hasn't been back in years, but he made sure Nan was set up properly before he went.'

Ginny's eyes were wide by the time he'd finished. It was the most she'd ever heard him speak and the effort seemed to wipe him out, because he leaned back and dropped his gaze.

'Did your nan see anything that happened on the day
Bernard was murdered? What did she tell the police?' she
asked, as a large sign for Halton Park announced they were
almost there. Someone had changed the A to an I, making it
Hilton Park. Windblown litter was wrapped around the base of
the sign, flapping like a plastic scarf.

The fields gave way to a rundown set of shops and a pub
that looked more like a war bunker than an alehouse.

'You think anyone in my family would talk to the police?' he
snorted. 'You can take the person out of Halton Park, but you
can't make them play nice with the coppers. Turn here. It's at
the end, on the right.'

Ginny followed his directions, and suddenly she understood Andrea's remark.

Unlike the quaintness of Little Shaw, the small estate was a
collection of post-war terrace houses that had seen better days.
Once upon a time they'd probably been built to solve a housing
problem, but now they were coated in a layer of grime from the
nearby motorway, and the few front yards that weren't filled
with cars and discarded furniture were overgrown with weeds.
Litter was everywhere and several of the houses were boarded
up to prevent vandals or squatters from getting in.

Connor's house was in a slightly better state. The fence and
gate were intact, and a girl in her twenties was standing in the
front door, glaring at a group of kids walking past. She nodded
at Connor then disappeared inside.

'That's my sister.' Connor unbuckled the belt. 'Thanks for
the lift.'

'You're welcome,' she said, still thinking about his nan.
Considering her lack of progress with Harold, this might help
them move forward. Apart from the small problem that his
grandmother didn't speak to the police.

How would she feel about sixty-year-old library assistants?

Imposing on people wasn't something Ginny was used to

doing, but if she didn't ask, then poor Alyson would be punished for a crime she didn't commit. She just needed to channel JM.

Well, maybe just five per cent of JM.

'I would like to talk to your nan, if that's possible. I wish I could tell you the real reason, but—'

Connor turned, one eyebrow quirked. 'You mean you have another reason besides trying to prove that the first Mrs Farnsworth didn't knock off her ex-husband and his wife?'

'Is it that obvious?' She swallowed, feeling silly at thinking she was a top-secret agent, and for underestimating just how much the teenager noticed.

'Don't feel bad. The whole town's trying to figure it out. And since you've been hanging out with the widows, it wasn't a brain teaser. But I don't think many of them are looking at Mr Rowe. I hadn't thought of him either, until you asked Cleo about a spare key for the stack. Not a bad idea.'

'I'm not setting a very good example for you, am I?'

'No skin off my nose. Mr Rowe isn't that terrible, but it doesn't mean he couldn't take out a couple of people if he wanted. None of my business really.' His expression went blank again, as if he'd been forced into a boring conversation with Cleo and was pleased it was over.

'So, you don't think she'll see me?'

'No,' he agreed, before turning back to face her. 'Not if you went on your own. But... if you really want to meet her, I suppose I could take you.'

Something caught in her throat. And it wasn't just at finally getting a step closer to finding out who was behind the murders, but because she suspected he didn't often offer to help anyone.

'Th-thank you, Connor. That would be marvellous. Could we go now?'

He shook his head and opened the passenger door. 'It's

bingo night. But I'll see what I can rig up. You'd better give me your phone number.'

'Yes. Now, let's see. The area code is—'

'You have a landline?'

'Well, yes. It's very useful. Especially if there's a power cut or the cell towers are down.'

'*And* you're at home,' he said in a dry voice, before looking around the car. 'I'm also guessing you don't know your own mobile number and don't have it with you.'

'No... but I do know exactly where it is at home.' Ginny felt like she was being scolded and gave him a sheepish glance.

'Right next to that landline, no doubt.' He pulled out a crumpled piece of paper from his pocket and scrawled down a number. 'Text me when you get home. And, Mrs Cole, start carrying your phone. I know you're old, but Nan is older, and she takes hers everywhere.'

'I will. I promise. And thank you. I hope you have a nice evening planned.'

He gave her a blank stare, as if she'd just suggested he would be eating caviar and drinking champagne, instead of whatever it was he would be doing in the tiny house. Then without another word, he slouched towards the front door.

Still, at least he'd agreed to arrange the meeting.

EIGHTEEN

'Are you sure you don't want me to stay longer? I'd be happy to help. I could do some more cleaning. Or, if you wanted to go home early, I could lock up.' Ginny stood at the door of Harold's small office. She'd agreed to work on Saturday morning, but after another fruitless attempt trying to get into the stack, she was starting to get frustrated.

And she wasn't the only one.

After she'd dropped Connor off the previous night, she'd headed straight to JM's house. Everyone's mood had been as low as hers. The new parish clerk hadn't been able to tell them anything they didn't already know. Which meant until Ginny could get into the stack, or speak to Connor's grandmother, they were stuck in a holding pattern.

'Very,' Harold said now, unmoved by her offer. 'I'm sure you have a million things to do that don't involve being at the library, so I won't keep you any longer.'

He then walked over and shut the door.

So much for that idea. She retrieved her bag and coat and made her farewells to the volunteers before stepping outside.

Once again, the sky was overcast, and she reached for her umbrella before remembering she hadn't checked her phone.

Connor wasn't due back into the library until Monday, but all morning she'd been slipping into the staffroom to see if he had an update about meeting his nan.

But when she looked at her screen, the only message was from a number she didn't recognise. She quickly listened to it.

'This is Jimmy. From the Old Regent Hotel. I had a message to call you?'

Ginny had almost forgotten about the hotel, since it had been to support their belief that Tom and Louisa had reignited their affair, which was why Bernard killed her. But thanks to his murder, that angle was now irrelevant. Should she call Jimmy back and apologise for wasting his time? Then again, she had the whole afternoon off, and hadn't visited Liverpool since her move.

She returned his call, but it went through to voicemail, so she rang the reception desk instead and was told that Jimmy would be working in the bar until seven that night. She thought about calling her friends, but they would all be on their way to the cemetery to do their regular volunteering shift, and she didn't want to disturb them.

Still, there was no reason she couldn't go on her own. Decision made, Ginny hurried back to Middle Cottage, fed the cat and climbed into her car.

An hour and a half later she arrived in Liverpool city centre and pulled up at a charming boutique hotel tucked into Hope Street, with the Anglican cathedral at one end and the Catholic cathedral at the other.

The Georgian front had been restored to its former glory, while the inside was modern, with a sleek reception desk to the left, and a large bar in the righthand corner. There was a piano to one side, and the bar was half filled with well-dressed customers partaking of lavish afternoon teas, as well as champagne and whisky.

It wasn't the kind of place she would've picked for an out-of-town affair. But maybe that was why Tom had chosen it.

The bar was being worked by a short man in his late thirties, who was chatting to a couple, but he broke off as Ginny approached.

'Afternoon. What can we tempt you with this fine day?' He gave her a dimpled smile, and she had the feeling he did very well when it came to tips.

'A lemon, lime and bitters, please.'

'Perfect choice,' he declared, and made the drink. Once he was happy with it, he slid it over. 'Anything else?'

She took a sip and bolstered her JM-shaped courage. 'I'm hoping you can help me. My name's Ginny Cole. I called last week and you were kind enough to leave a message.'

He leaned forward on the bar, curious. 'That's right. Tina said something about a cheating husband? I'm not sure if I can be any help. My memory isn't what it used to be... and we try not to judge who comes in.'

'Of course. I understand,' she agreed, not entirely comfortable with pretending she was Tom's wife. 'Though I have to be honest with you. He wasn't my husband. I'm... looking into it for a friend.'

'Are you just?' He raised a bemused eyebrow. For whatever reason his interest seemed piqued, so Ginny pulled out her phone and brought up a photograph that Alyson had given her.

'This is him. Tom Allan. He was here on the second of March this year.'

'Like I said, I'm not—' He broke off as he stared at the photo. Then he gave her another of his charming smiles. 'I do remember him. He's been coming here on and off for a couple of years. Never sticking with the same woman for long. If you want to be a good friend, tell his wife to get shot of him.'

'I... I'll do that. Though I was hoping to find out who he was with on this specific night. Do you recognise this woman?' She brought up another photograph, this time of Louisa.

'Nope. Not her. This bird didn't dress to stand out. But I can't really tell you much more about her. I only remember him because he tipped *so* well.'

Ginny, who only had a twenty-pound note and a couple of coins in her purse, wasn't certain what 'tipped well' meant, but all the same she took it out. Was this even ethical? She really wasn't sure.

Still, in for a penny, in for twenty-one pounds fifty.

'Is there anything else you can remember?'

'Not really. Just that the last time they were here they seemed to be fighting.'

'Did you hear what it was about?'

'Sorry.' He shook his head as another customer came up to the bar. 'I hope that was some help. And thanks for this.' He'd folded the money up into a thin line and tucked it between his fingers. 'Come back anytime.'

'I'll do my best,' she promised and left a few minutes later, not wanting to admit to him, or herself, that it had been a wasted trip.

After her return drive from Liverpool, Ginny had spent the next few hours cleaning the house before remembering she still had another basket of windfall plums.

It was almost nine at night. A terrible time to start preserving, but despite her tiredness, she would never be able to sleep. And the idea of settling down for a cup of tea and a crossword made her jittery.

'Sorry, love. I promise we'll do one tomorrow. Right now, I just need to keep busy.'

There was no answer, but she could almost picture Eric nodding his head. He had often said *Busy hands, calm mind*.

She plunged her hands into the cool water in the sink, and hoped he was right.

The plum skins were smooth and soft, and after she had washed and dried them, she pulled out her jam saucepan, her favourite wooden spoon and several lemons.

Now all she needed was sugar.

Except, when she opened the cupboard, the large jar was empty. In the past she would've just accepted it and had an early night. But the idea of facing the bed alone was more than she could bear. Collin's would be closed, but she knew there was a small corner shop on the other side of Little Shaw that stayed open until ten. She threw on her old navy coat and locked up.

For a Saturday night, the village was quiet as she drove down Denistone Street and past the library. The rough brick was grey against the darkness, and long shadows fell across the high-set windows from the nearby trees. A horn honked and, out of habit, Ginny automatically slowed down to a crawl and checked her mirrors, worried she must have done something. But the wail of brakes in the distance told her it had come from several blocks away.

Feeling silly, she was about to speed up when a soft glow illuminated the end of the narrow lane by the library.

Was someone down there? She hadn't seen any signs of bedding to suggest people slept there at night. But maybe they were just very tidy.

The more likely explanation was that someone was in the stack.

She pulled to the side of the road and climbed out before catching sight of a familiar navy Rover.

That was Harold's car. The icy cold sweat that travelled up her skin had nothing to do with the cool evening air. What was he doing there at this time of night? Looking for proof that the council had broken their agreement to preserve his father's legacy?

The wind picked up and she tightened the belt on her coat, suddenly pleased for the thick wool. Then she slung her bag over her shoulder and ventured down the lane.

The dull light continued to glow, and the air was filled with a strange haze. Part of her screamed that this was a bad idea. If Harold really was behind the murders, then going down a lane late at night might not be wise.

She came to a stop but before she could turn back, a long shadow of a person suddenly fell across the end of the lane, and Ginny yelped. The noise must have startled them, and something clattered to the ground followed by the *thump, thump, thump* of shoes on concrete. A figure blurred past her, elbowing her in the ribs as they went.

Ginny fell sideways but managed to grip the wall of the building with her hands. The figure was gone by the time she caught her breath, but her pulse jangled as she listened for the roar of a car engine. Harold? It was hard to imagine that the bad-tempered ex-archivist-cum-library manager could do something like that. But who else could it have been? He was the only one with the key. And it was his car out front. Or... it had been.

Nerves shaken, Ginny walked to the metal door. It was closed, but it was getting harder to see through the dull haze—

Which wasn't haze at all.

It was thin tendrils of smoke threading their way from under the door.

Fire.

Her mind whirled with questions, but Ginny pushed them all to one side. Now wasn't the time. She reached into her bag for her phone. The one she'd promised Connor to start carrying.

She held a handkerchief up to her mouth to avoid breathing in the smoke as she made the call. 'There's a fire at the Little Shaw library on Denistone Street. Down the lane at the side of the park,' she said in a calm voice that didn't quite match the thudding of her heartbeat.

The thudding got louder, and the rhythm changed. Thud-bump, thud-bump, thud—

Bump.

It wasn't coming from her chest. A muffled cry called out from somewhere behind the door. She gripped the phone and moved closer. The cry was fainter this time, but sounded human. Someone was trapped in there. Ice skittered along her veins. What had Harold done?

'Excuse me, are you still there?' the operator cut through her thoughts.

'I think someone's inside, but the door is locked. Please, send an ambulance as well.'

There was a pause and the clatter of computer keys in the background. 'They're on the way,' the operator finally said. 'Please stay on the line and move to a safe place.'

But Ginny didn't answer as her gaze fixed on the smoke that was escaping from under the door. It was getting thicker. How long had the fire been going for?

And how much longer did the person inside have?

The bolt had been pushed through, but the padlock was lying several feet away, as if it had been thrown. Was that what Harold had been doing before she'd interrupted him? Locking the person in? The very idea sent a wave of nausea racing through her.

If the padlock had been fastened, she would've been help-less to do anything. But it wasn't on, and whoever was trapped inside might not have long. Decision made, Ginny put the phone into her pocket and wrapped her scarf around her mouth, before shrugging off her old navy coat and slipping her hands back through the arms, like oversized gauntlets. If the metal was hot, the wool would hopefully protect her.

'Do not panic.' She dropped to her knees. Heat emanated from the door, and the hot metal of the sliding bolt stung her fingers, even with the protection of the coat. She tugged it as sweat beaded on her brow. She tugged again. 'You've done much sillier things. Isn't that right, Eric? Do you remember when you broke a window and cut your hand, and I was so worried I ran over to you, forgetting my feet were bare?'

Eric's lack of answer helped calm her down, and the bolt finally slid back. *There. I've done it.* Unsteadily, she tugged at the roller door, the heat searing through her skin now. Then she dropped back into a crouch.

'If you can hear me, get down. I'm about to open the door.' Her voice was muffled behind the scarf, and heat seared her throat as she reached up to grip the handle.

A thick cloud of smoke billowed out, but there were no flames. A figure crouched against the wall, a fire extinguisher at their feet. They started to cough as Ginny stumbled inside. The blare of sirens broke through the night, letting her know help was on the way.

And then she looked at the person.

It was Harold.

NINETEEN

Trenton Hall was a pale stone Georgian manor that had been turned into a private hospital at some stage in its history. But despite the ornate ceilings and skirting boards, the familiar scents and bustles of medical staff let Ginny know it was very much a modern place.

Her hands were lightly bandaged, and her throat was raw, but other than needing rest, she'd been deemed well enough to go home the same night.

Despite the ordeal, she'd woken early and called the hospital, relieved to hear Harold had spent an excellent night and could receive visitors any time after ten.

She was one minute early when she reached the ward.

Hen, Tuppence and JM had wanted to go with her, after she'd texted them about the previous night's events. But Ginny had refused the company. She needed to see Harold on his own. To apologise properly, and to assure herself he really was going to be okay. But she'd promised her friends that she would visit them later.

She followed the blue arrows along the wall until she reached the ward where Harold was being treated. There was no door to block it off from the corridor, so she glanced inside. The room contained six beds, but Harold, propped up against two pillows, a sheaf of papers in his lap, was the only occupant. His hair was neatly combed, and colour had returned to his cheeks. Like her, his hands were bandaged and there were several cuts and grazes up his arms.

'Mrs Cole, I thought you would be having a lie-in now the library is closed.' His voice was raspy, and he broke into a cough.

She poured him a glass of water from the tray by the bed and held it as he sipped from the straw. 'Please, call me Ginny. And I hope it's okay to visit. I wanted to make sure—'

'—that you hadn't found another corpse in the library?' His voice sounded stronger. 'I have no idea what you were doing down that lane last night, but if you hadn't been there—'

'Nonsense.' It was her turn to cut him off. 'According to the fire service, you'd managed to put out the fire, and there was a very good chance that if I hadn't been there, someone else would've sounded the alarm. But I'm pleased you're recovering. Do you know when you will be released?'

'Hopefully today.' He leaned back against the pillow. 'The police are coming in later for a statement. I was told you saw someone running down the lane. Do you have any idea who it was?'

She shook her head, too embarrassed to admit she'd thought it had been him. 'It all happened so quickly. But what were you doing there so late at night?'

'I was on my way home from the historic society when I saw someone walking down the lane. By the time I parked the car, the stack door was open, and the lights were on. I have no idea how they got a copy of the key. They were wearing a mask and were pulling books out, searching for something. Then' – he broke off to cough – 'I woke up to the crackle of flames and a locked door. They must have knocked me out. I was still groggy but thanks to you, I knew exactly where the fire extinguisher was, *and* that it worked.'

So, it was true. Someone had tried to kill him.

Ginny leaned against the side of the bed, her usual calmness deserting her. Despite her reassurances he would have been okay, she was not so sure. Which would mean there would have been another death in the village.

'What do you think they were looking for?'

'I have no idea. But unless it was mould, I doubt they found it.' He sounded more like himself. 'It's been quite a business getting the archives in order, and I quickly realised we needed a better ventilated storage unit. Unfortunately, Marigold refused to give me a budget for it, so I paid for one myself.'

Ginny's breath caught as the terrible realisation washed over her. 'All this time you really were sorting out the archives. Y-you weren't looking for lost parish council documents?'

In return, Harold blinked, letting her see for the first time that beneath his glasses, his eyelashes were singed. 'Council documents? Of course not. I thought I'd made it clear what I was doing. Why would you think that?'

'Because she doesn't know you as well as I do, my dear.' A tall, well-dressed man walked in and planted a kiss on Harold's forehead. His hair swept across his brow in a dashing manner, and there was a hint of a French accent. 'You have to understand that Harold is very straightforward.'

'I wouldn't say straight, *mon copain*.' Harold leaned into the man's shoulder. 'By the way, this is my husband, Myles Dumas.'

'Nice to meet you, Myles. Oh dear. I'm so sorry. I should never have jumped to conclusions,' Ginny whispered, not able to hide her mortification.

'What conclusions?' Harold demanded.

'She thought you were involved in the murders,' Myles told him fondly. 'It's understandable, considering the state you've been coming home in. The dust alone has given me a mountain of extra laundry to get through.'

'You're the one behind his lovely clothes?' Ginny forced her hands back down to her side and dropped her head.

However, Myles seemed delighted, rather than offended. 'I'm pleased to see my work is appreciated.'

'If you two have finished,' Harold snapped, sounding a lot more like his usual self, 'I would like to get back to why I was considered a murder suspect.'

'I read about Wilburton Reserve. Your family donated it to the parish council on the condition it wasn't developed. But they broke that promise and destroyed the paperwork...' She trailed off.

'That's true. But they'd been threatening to sell it for years. Long before Marigold Bentley was elected chairperson. My lawyer kept stalling them while we tried to prove the original terms of the agreement. I was very angry about what happened, and completely preoccupied, to the point where Myles and I almost broke up. Eventually, Myles made me realise that my actions were only hurting myself.'

'Don't give me all the credit. After what happened to that poor girl, you were the one who decided to walk away from the fight.' Myles pressed another kiss to Harold's forehead and rubbed his arm. 'And it would have been a shame for us to break up, when we'd only been legally married for five years.'

'Sophie Hudson?' Ginny's mouth went dry as she remembered the photograph Mitch had shown her. Harold had been at the funeral. 'How does she fit into it all? Are you saying she destroyed the proof?'

'Destroyed it? No. You've got it all wrong.' Harold shook his head. 'Louisa accused her of it several times, but there was no proof. Poor Sophie didn't take it well. At the time she was under a lot of strain. Both her parents were very ill, and she felt guilty at living so far from London. But she'd just got engaged to

Mitch Reeves and didn't want to leave the area. So, she came to see me. I think she wanted to protect her own reputation.'

It was all starting to make sense in a terrible way.

'What happened?'

Harold's expression went bleak. 'She called to say she'd found something but didn't want to talk over the phone. She was meant to come around that evening for a meal – Myles is a wonderful cook – but she had to cancel because her mother took a turn for the worse. She came back on the Sunday and was found dead the following morning.' He stopped, lifting his glasses to wipe his eyes. 'Seeing such a bright, wonderful girl kill herself made me realise just how petty my own obsession had been. So, I vowed to put it behind me, and I like to think I've done that.'

Ginny bowed her head, the shame of misjudging Harold still stinging her cheeks, combined with Sophie's tragic death.

She finally dared look up. 'I hope we can put this behind us as well. I feel terrible about my assumptions, and don't want to affect our work together. I still have a lot to learn, and you're a very good teacher.'

'There's nothing to forgive.' He met her gaze with under-standing before closing his eyes. 'As for working together... I take it you haven't spoken to Marigold?'

'No. She's left several messages, but I planned to call her later.' Along with the many other calls and texts waiting to be dealt with. 'Has something else happened?'

Myles put a protective arm around his husband's shoulders, as if to say: *I'll deal with this.* 'Marigold paid Harold a visit this morning while I was getting coffee.' Myles's voice hardened and his urbane air fell away. 'Seems she thought it appropriate to come here and fire him.'

'What? But why? Surely she can't think it had anything to do with you?' Ginny's hand flew to her mouth, her fingers shaking with agitation.

'No. Her excuse was that I shouldn't have been moving the archives out of the stack without the council's permission. Even though my concerns about it being mouldy and a fire trap were, as it turned out, valid. She said because the library will be closed for at least a month, it will be a good opportunity for them to advertise for a permanent manager.'

Myles growled, but Harold put a hand on his arm. 'It's not so bad. At least the collection was saved, and I was never going to stay there for long. Actually, Ginny, you should consider applying for the position.'

'Me?' Ginny's jaw dropped. Out of all the things he'd told her, in a way this was the most surprising. And ludicrous. 'I couldn't possibly. I've only worked there for two weeks, as a library assistant. I know next to nothing about how libraries operate.'

'In those two weeks I've yet to see you make a member of the public cry, which puts you leagues ahead of Louisa. And, if I'm being honest... myself,' Harold said, in a dry voice. 'If you think I'm a good teacher, I think you're an equally good student. You're practical and have a knack of getting the volunteers to work together, while keeping everyone happy. And that fire extinguisher might have saved my life. I genuinely think you'd do well in the position.'

A nurse bustled into the room. 'Right... let's see how those dressings are going.'

Ginny glanced at her watch. She'd already stayed longer than she intended and gave both men a smile. 'I'll take my leave but, Harold, I'm very pleased you're okay.'

'So am I.' Myles held her gaze. 'And don't look so guilty. Whatever you thought no longer exists because you know the truth. And what you did for my husband isn't something we'll ever forget. When things settle down, please come for a meal. Harold is right, I'm an excellent cook.'

'And so modest,' Harold retorted before his voice softened. 'But I concur. We'd love to spend an evening with you.'

Ginny wasn't sure she deserved such grace. She'd been so convinced Harold was behind the murders that she hadn't considered his safety. Or that he'd just been in the wrong place at the wrong time. Either way, it didn't reflect well on her.

And now he was no longer the manager. She regretted the lost chance to continue working with him.

As she walked to her car, Ginny's mind began whirring again. Why had he really been fired? Marigold believed the library was a lynchpin in the community. It was why she'd brought Harold in to begin with, and he'd only been trying to protect the archives.

Unless he hadn't fully explained himself properly.

Which of course he hadn't.

She climbed into her car and groaned. 'The pair of them are just as stubborn as each other. Two diplomats who need a translator to help them communicate. If only I could've been there,' she said to the car.

Like Eric and the cat, the car didn't answer.

But it did give her an idea. What if *she* talked to Marigold? After all, it would affect Ginny's future as well. And, considering the library would be closed for the next month, they could also discuss her own future.

Ginny retrieved her phone but then put it down again. Marigold's beautiful old house was virtually on the way home from the hospital. She could drop in and talk to her face to face.

The mid-morning traffic was light, and Ginny had spent the drive going over in her head what she would say to Marigold. She'd never been a great one for giving speeches, but she had to try. And while part of it was to ease her own guilt at misjudging

Harold, most of it was spurred on for the sake of the library and all the people who went there every day.

She might only have been there for two weeks, but she'd already seen how important it was to so many of them. And she could almost set her clock for when the different people would show up. William at 9.30 every day. Rose every second day at two... or earlier, if bridge was cancelled. Even Cleo and Andrea and the host of other volunteers who helped keep it running.

Thinking of them helped keep her nerves at bay as she got closer.

The road curved along the side of the sharp hill, with the village of Little Shaw spreading out below her. It really was lovely here, and Ginny couldn't deny that the gardener in her hoped to see more of Marigold's stunning grounds. And—

Woo, woo, woo! The sharp wail of a police siren sounded out from behind her. It was followed by another one, and Ginny immediately slowed down and pulled to one side of the road as the vehicles sped past.

Pulling out again, her fingers gripped the steering wheel as she slowly turned onto the tree-lined road, only to find it blocked by a series of bright orange traffic cones and a marked police car.

And then she saw it.

The stunning Georgian mansion that had been nestled against a backdrop of ancient trees was now half hidden behind pale grey plumes of smoke and steam, as thick jets of water rained down on the once gleaming stone.

No! How could there be a second fire?

A uniformed officer tapped on her window, and she shakily lowered it as an ambulance pulled out of Marigold's driveway and sped off in the direction Ginny had just come from.

'What's happened? Is Marigold Bentley okay?' Ginny's throat, still raw from the previous night's fire, began to ache.

'I'm afraid I can't answer that,' the officer said, their sharp gaze peering into the car. 'Did you have business with her?'

'Not exactly,' Ginny admitted, then gave a brief description of why she was there. The officer flipped open a notebook and made some notes, including her details.

'If we need any more information we'll be in touch. In the meantime, this road is closed, so you will need to turn around.'

'Of course. Can you at least tell me if she's hurt?' she asked, hoping it might result in more information. It didn't.

'Please turn around,' the officer said, leaving her no choice but to do as he asked. There were several cars behind her, while a news van was setting up a camera across the road.

Ginny's temples pounded with the beginning of a headache, and she drove the short distance back to Little Shaw proper. Had the same person who killed Louisa and Bernard, and tried to kill Harold, also been responsible for this?

And why? *How* did it all fit together?

But no matter how much Ginny's mind tried to shape it all into something solid, there were too many missing pieces. Like a swirling double helix that kept showing different sides of itself rather than the full picture.

And she was getting drawn further and further into the middle of the whole thing.

By seven that evening, Ginny's headache had begun to shift, thanks in part to a long nap. She was now settled at the kitchen table, drinking a cup of strong tea as she went through her messages. There were several from her friends, and one from Nancy, all wanting her to call them back as soon as possible.

Edgar was curled up in her lap. The reassuring warmth of his body combined with the rich aroma of English Breakfast helped push away the cobwebs of sleep, and she was just about to call Nancy back when the doorbell rang.

Ginny carefully deposited the sleeping cat onto another chair and opened the door to find DI Wallace standing there.

Dark shadows hung below his eyes, making him look a lot older than his mid-thirties, but the dark stubble had gone, and he was wearing a pale blue jumper instead of his usual black jacket.

'I wasn't sure if you'd be home. It seems you've had a rather busy couple of days.'

'So have you,' she reminded him, her fingers tightening around the side of the door.

'At least I get paid for it. Part of the perks of being on the force.' His tone was dry, but there wasn't the underlying current of exasperation that usually went with it. Instead, he glanced at her hands. 'And I didn't get injured in a fire last night. I heard you refused treatment.'

'I'm fine. Just a couple of blisters, though my wool coat didn't fare too well. Still, it was probably due for an overhaul.' She held up her hands to show the bandages were already off and that the blisters were few. 'Did you need to get another statement? The officer at Marigold's house said someone might be in touch, though I was expecting PC Singh.'

'I'm afraid you're stuck with me. Can I come in?'

He made it sound like a question, but she was certain he would come in regardless. She was too exhausted to be afraid of what might happen.

She stepped to one side and ushered him across the threshold and through to the kitchen. 'I've just made a fresh pot of tea.' She set out a second cup and saucer and picked up the pot, not waiting for an answer.

He didn't seem to take offence and merely deposited a large carrier bag on the counter. Several plump damsons spilled out onto yesterday's half-read newspapers, but he gathered them up and tied the top over.

'It seems there is far too much fruit on my tree, so I thought you might like some,' he said in a gruff voice as he joined her at the table.

'Is this your way of reminding me to stick to making jam?' Ginny pushed the cup towards him, wondering if a lecture was about to come her way. He would be entirely within his rights considering recent events. She couldn't even blame him.

Instead, he let out a weary sigh and leaned back in the chair. 'No, Mrs Cole, it's my way of being a better neighbour. And you were right about the tree needing pruning. Next time my father is in town, I'll ask him to help me trim it. He's the gardener of the family.'

'I see.' Ginny pushed forward the milk jug and sugar bowl. If he was trying to unnerve her with small talk, it was working. 'How can I help?'

'Your trip to Marigold Bentley's house today – was that the first time you'd been out there?'

'No. I gave her a lift home last Monday on my way back from the hairdresser. Her car had broken down and the lift hadn't shown up.'

'And what was the purpose of your visit today? You told the officer that you'd been with Harold Rowe in the hospital. Was it related?'

Ginny flinched under his shrewd questioning. She'd kept the reason vague when she'd given the statement, though clearly Wallace had seen through it.

Yet another reason to leave the detective work to him.

'I'm sorry I wasn't entirely forthcoming. Harold told me that Marigold had visited him in hospital that morning to fire him. She wasn't happy he'd been moving archives out of the stack without her knowledge. I wanted to see if she would reconsider.'

'Ah, yes, which leads me to my other question. Why *were* you visiting Harold in the hospital? Were you worried about his health, or was it something else?'

She deserved that, and heat stung her cheeks. 'Well, yes, I was worried about him. But I also owed him an apology.'

'Let me guess – he was the next suspect who would have been added to that murder board we found at Hen McArthur's cottage?' Wallace sounded more bemused than exasperated. Somehow it made her feel worse.

She closed her eyes, not quite sure how her life had become such a mess in such a short space of time. 'You were right, I had no business poking my nose into anything. All I've done is think the worst of people. But don't worry, you won't have to deal with me anymore. My unofficial detective days are over. Please, can you tell me if Marigold is okay? What happened to her? Was it an accident, or—'

'For someone who is hanging up their detective hat, you're still asking a lot of questions.' He quirked an eyebrow, and for a moment she thought he wasn't going to answer her. Then he sighed. 'There's going to be a press conference in an hour, so you will find out soon enough. We're treating it as attempted murder. It appears the attacker planned to kill her and set fire to the house, but was disturbed by a neighbour who turned up. The attacker escaped, but not before setting fire to the kitchen. There was no car at the front, and tracks indicate they escaped through the woods at the back.'

'Will she survive?'

'There were several stab wounds. She was operated on earlier, and last I heard her condition was serious but stable.'

Relief helped calm her pounding heart. 'What will happen now? Do you have any idea who's behind it? Did they leave any fingerprints?' she asked. Wallace raised an eyebrow again, as if to remind her that she'd promised to step back from the case. She held her hands up. 'Sorry, I know you can't answer that. Did you have any more questions for me?'

'Not exactly.' He picked up a teaspoon and twirled it in his hand before hitting it softly against the table. *Tap. Tap. Tap.*

Then he let out a breath and twirled the teaspoon around again, his gaze following its progress. 'It seems I owe *you* an apology. I was harsh on you, and my obstinance almost cost two more lives. Not to mention Bernard Farnsworth's death.'

Tap. Tap. Tap.

'I'm not sure I follow.' Ginny took the teaspoon out of his hand and put it back where it belonged, on the table.

He looked up, his eyes sheepish. 'Alyson Farnsworth has been released and all charges have been dropped.'

Relief flooded her. Alyson was free. Oh, how happy Hen would be. How happy they *all* must be. But why? How had it happened?

Then she let out a long groan as some of the pieces fell into place. 'Of course. Why didn't I think of that? Alyson was in custody, which meant she couldn't have broken into the stack and left Harold there to die. Or tried to kill Marigold. But... it also means you're assuming it's the same person who murdered Louisa and Bernard.'

His face tightened. 'And Tom Allan. The coroner has officially confirmed that he was strangled before the flood water got into his lungs.'

'So, we have three murders. One killed by poison, one by a knife, and one—' She broke off as nausea churned in her stomach. 'How *did* they manage to strangle Tom Allan then get him and his car into a flood zone? Is it even possible?'

'We're still trying to work that out.' Wallace rubbed a hand across his brow, suddenly looking tired.

'Of course. I didn't mean to speculate. So, Alyson is no longer a person of interest?'

He shook his head. 'No, she's not. A witness has come forward with CCTV footage which shows a figure entering Bernard's house, several minutes before Alyson Farnsworth drove up. She then sat in the car for two hours before entering the house and finding him dead.'

'I can't believe it.'

'That's what we said when Connor and his grandmother, Maureen West, walked in last night. It would be the first time in living memory that a member of the West family has come into the station of their own volition. That's why I wasn't at the fire, because I was too busy being shown footage from the many security cameras Maureen has set up around her house and garden.'

'Oh, that's wonderful! Connor wasn't convinced his nan would help, even if she did know something. I was sure she would want to do the right thing. And now the pair of them are heroes. They must be so pleased.'

He let out a snort of laughter. 'I take it you haven't met Maureen.'

'No. Connor was going to arrange a meeting, but it didn't happen. From what I gather, she keeps to herself.'

'Let's just say she isn't someone you want on your bad side. However, she seems to have a soft spot for her grandson, and he talked her into it.' He ran a hand through his hair, as if still trying to believe it had happened. 'I'm not sure what you said to Connor, but it must have got through to him.'

'I didn't say anything. Though I do hope this is a lesson to you. He's a smart boy and just because his last name seems to bring out the worst in people, he shouldn't be tarred with the same brush. In fact, he was the one who insisted I always carry my phone. Which is just as well because it meant I could call emergency services so quickly for the fire in the stacks. And as for forcing him to volunteer at the library, well... that has to stop.'

'I agree,' Wallace said, taking the wind out of her sails.

'You do?'

'I only suggested it to stop Louisa Farnsworth from pressing charges and giving him a criminal record that he didn't deserve and wouldn't be able to shake off.'

Maybe she'd misjudged him. Then again, who hadn't she misjudged?

'What happens now?' she asked, as a banging sounded at the front door, followed up by the shrill *brrrring* of the doorbell.

'Ginny, it's us,' JM boomed. 'Henry across the road saw Wallace going in half an hour ago. Blink three times if you need rescuing.'

Wallace drained his tea in one gulp and lumbered to his feet. 'I suspect your friends will want a play-by-play description of your adventures. And they'll no doubt be organising some kind of celebration at The Lost Goat. As for me, I'm back to square one with this case. Would you mind if I slip out the back and climb over the fence? Facing Maureen West was one thing, but I'm not sure I have the energy for your friends right now.'

'Of course. And, DI Wallace, thank you for letting me know about Alyson. And Connor,' she said, trying not to think of the job he had in front of him. The job that was no doubt harder thanks to her interference. The blackmail letter that she and her friends had all touched, the grave they'd dug up, and who knew what else.

'Call me James,' he said, and then disappeared through the conservatory door and out to the back garden.

Ginny patted down her hair and went to let her friends in. They had a lot to catch up on.

TWENTY

'We can't have shots of tequila at twelve o'clock on a Monday,' Hen protested the following day, as they sat at one of the long wooden tables in The Lost Goat's beer garden. The sun had come out but there was a sharp breeze that caused the hanging flower baskets to sway, sending the last of the petals blowing away like confetti into the nearby canal.

'Nonsense.' JM passed around the drinks. 'This is a special occasion to mark Alyson's release. Here's to Alyson.'

Everyone raised their glasses, but Ginny noticed that Alyson's hand was shaking, and her face was still tear-stained.

Hen put an arm around her daughter's shoulder and JM put down her empty glass. 'But no speeches right now.'

The announcement took the spotlight off the recently released woman and the conversation returned to the other topic of interest: the attempted murder of Marigold Bentley. The newspapers had been full of grim details, dubbing it 'Big Murders in Little Shaw'. However, they hadn't given any details on her condition, or what progress the police had made.

Ginny, who hadn't sipped her drink, tried to remember they were there to celebrate Alyson's release. But it was hard to be happy when three people were dead, and Harold and Marigold were in hospital, one seriously injured.

Or was it simply the fact that the pressure of the last few weeks was catching up with her? Maybe a cup of tea would help? She got to her feet and made her way to the front door. Today's sign read: *Wine flies when you're having fun.*

Inside the pub, locals talked loudly about the latest twist in the case, while a handful of journalists were dotted around the place, frantically working on their laptops or having quiet conversations on their phones.

Mitch was at the far end of the bar, busy pouring drinks, but he stopped and nodded in her direction. Before he could serve her, however, Rita appeared from out the back carrying a clipboard in one hand and a large coffee mug in the other.

'Don't tell me you're ready for another round of shots. I told JM to pace herself.' The landlady's navy eyes were rimmed with mascara and gold loops hung from her ears, though her face was grim.

'No. I was hoping to get a pot of tea,' Ginny admitted.

'Tea?' a man from further down the bar barked out. 'Nonsense. Let me buy you a glass of something wet. You're a regular hero from what I heard. Running into a burning building like that.'

Ginny coloured and Rita gave the man in question a sharp glare. 'Maybe it's because she drinks tea that she *can* run into burning buildings. Ever think about that, Stanley?'

'Fair point, Rita. Well, at least let me pay for the cuppa.' The man didn't seem to mind the scolding as he slid a five-pound note across the bar. 'And well done, lass.'

'Thank you.' Ginny forced a smile, already regretting coming inside.

'Don't mind him. He means well. Now just wait here while I get you a pot.' Rita put down the clipboard and mug and disappeared to the other end of the bar. She returned a few minutes later with a laden tray that she placed on the bar, waving away Ginny's attempts to pay. 'Stanley took care of it. So, how are you feeling? That was quite an adventure you had the other night.'

'Anyone would have done the same thing, I just happened to be first on the scene.' Ginny slipped her purse back into her bag, then sighed. 'Sorry, I'm not very good at any of this.'

'Rule number one: don't apologise. You did a good thing and should own it.' Rita patted her arm. 'If it's any consolation, I know how you feel. It's strange for people to be celebrating and talking about these murders as if they're nothing.'

'Especially with what happened to Marigold. Sounds like if the neighbour hadn't turned up when they did, she would've been toast,' another woman leaning against the bar added.

'You might want to rethink your phrasing.' Rita glared, and the woman mumbled an apology and hurried away, spilling her drink as she went. 'People, eh? Still, I try and tell myself it's just their way of processing.'

'You're very astute.'

'In this job I tend to see people at their worst... and their best. And I've pretty much heard it all. I guess I've become philosophical over the years. Though it makes my blood boil that someone has got away with this. They're probably sunning themselves on a beach somewhere, having a fine old time of it.'

'I hope not,' Ginny said, remembering Connor's Uncle Joey who'd done the exact same thing. 'It's terrible to think about it.'

'Which is why it's best not to dwell on what we can't change.' Rita shrugged, just as Heather walked into the pub.

Her long purple hair was coiled at the nape of her neck and some of the sparkle had returned to her eyes as she clutched a large bag of baking supplies. She looked a lot happier than the last time Ginny had seen her.

'How did you go? Find everything?'

'Yes. The rest is in the car, but I'll get Mitch to give me a hand unloading. I just wanted to get my ovens on first.'

'You're baking again?' Ginny said.

The woman gave her a shy smile. 'Yes. When I saw Rita fretting about the funeral on Wednesday it made me realise how selfish I'd been. Plus, considering it started with Louisa, it's a good way to get closure and move on.'

'Funeral?' Ginny looked from Heather to Rita and back again.

'You haven't heard? Louisa's body was released and she's getting buried on Wednesday. She has no family and with Bernard now gone, Edward Tait, who's managing the estate, decided to hold it here.'

'But who will come? From what I could tell, Louisa didn't have many friends at all here in the village.'

'Or in the world, I'd imagine.' Rita gave a sad shake of her head. 'But if you think this lot would miss a free feed, you've got another think coming. Especially once they hear Heather's back. Mark my words, this place will be filled to the rafters.'

Ginny wasn't sure how to answer that, so she excused herself, knowing the two women had a lot of work to do.

She carried her tea tray out to the table, which was now covered in playing cards and poker chips as JM gave an impromptu lesson on how to shuffle the cards like a waterfall.

By the time the six o'clock news came on Ginny had cleaned the house, made several bottles of damson gin with the extra fruit Wallace had given her, and shampooed the upstairs carpet. But still the same heavy, uneasy feeling crept through her every time she stopped.

She understood why Heather had been so pleased to get back to work.

'And now we head back to the little village with a lot of

murders...' the news presenter said, before Ginny turned it off. She'd had enough speculation to last her a lifetime. Especially since most of it had come from her own mind.

The crossword book was sitting on a side table, no longer covered in cat hair – Edgar having lost interest in sleeping on it in favour of *Pride and Prejudice*.

Ginny picked it up and turned to a fresh page, not quite able to look at Eric's chair.

'Maybe we could do an extra one tonight. To make up for the last few days,' she suggested, not sure who she was trying to appease. But before she could even get to the first clue her phone rang and Nancy's name flashed up.

Ginny had only spoken with her sister-in-law briefly the previous evening but knew it hadn't been enough to alleviate her worry.

'How was the pub? Did you hear any news?' Nancy said, by way of greeting.

'Not really,' she said, figuring the local gossip didn't really count. 'But Alyson's happy to be out of custody, if a little teary. And... they're having Louisa's funeral on Wednesday. I don't think I'll go.'

'Of course you will.'

'How do you know that?'

Nancy laughed. 'Because I've met you. You always do the right thing, even when you don't want to. *Especially* when you don't want to. Which is a nice segue into—' Nancy broke off as Ian's voice sounded from somewhere in the background: 'Is that Ginny? Tell her she's going to love it. Great sun, and no garden to maintain.'

Nancy let out a little growl and then it went quiet, as if she'd covered the phone with her hand.

'Sorry about that. Ian thought—'

'—that you'd already told me about whatever plan you're

both scheming?' Ginny sighed, not having to work hard to guess what they were talking about.

'Not scheming exactly,' Nancy said, unusually meek. 'But we bumped into the Radcliffes yesterday. They're selling their place but haven't put it on the market yet. You remember it, don't you? A darling terrace with all the hard work done. And it's so close to us... and Em and the girls. They're very interested in a private sale and have agreed to hold it for us for a week. So, what do you say?'

Oh. Ginny closed her eyes. She'd been to several of the Radcliffes' famous New Year's Eve parties and loved the small but elegant house. But did she really want to move back to Bristol?

Wouldn't that be like giving up?

'I'm not—'

'Don't give me an answer tonight. I know you're tired. Just promise to think about it.'

'Okay,' she agreed, and Nancy let out a slow breath.

'Good, good. I'm just worried you'll retreat into your shell now the library is shut for the foreseeable future. Whereas if you move back, you'll easily get a part-time job. Or help me with the babysitting. I love my granddaughters, but I won't lie, I'm starting to feel my age. We could take them out together. Think of how much fun we'd have. And no murders.'

A scuffling noise came from the hallway and Edgar darted into the sitting room, triumphantly pawing at what had once been Eric's *London A–Z*.

'What's that noise?' Nancy demanded.

'It's the cat. He's just playing,' she said, not wanting to go into details of the current crime. Though she was starting to understand why Louisa hadn't wanted him in the library: he wasn't exactly a bibliophile.

'The cat?' Nancy snorted, as if she was presenting her final argument to a jury.

They chatted for several more minutes before ending the call. The crossword book was still in her lap and the mangled A–Z was scattered across the room. She glanced over to the blue wingback chair. 'Hear that, Eric? Your sister's worried about me.'

The room was silent apart from Edgar who – now his work was done – padded back to his Jane Austen. Ginny closed her eyes, as her sister-in-law's question went around in her mind.

What *was* she going to do now?

Talk to her dead husband? Let her cat destroy all her books?

There was the gardening at the cemetery and Hen's birds' nests she could knit. And no doubt she could find some other charities to help, but there would still be endless hours of time to fill in.

All she'd ever been good at was being Mrs Eric Cole, which was a pity because that position was no longer available.

It was a perfect day to be outside, and Ginny wiped her brow and surveyed her work. The overgrown vegetable garden was now cleared, and she had a list of things to buy from the nursery. She still needed to get a greenhouse to germinate her own seeds without worrying about the frost but until then she'd just use seedlings.

It had also helped push some of the brain fog away and given her an appetite. A cup of tea and a scone would be nice and then she'd get a shower. She left her work boots by the conservatory door and stepped into the kitchen just in time to see Edgar looking very pleased with himself as he sat on the large training manual that Harold had given her.

The fact that it was on the floor also suggested he'd knocked it off the kitchen bench.

Again? She quickly scooped him up into her arms and sat down at a kitchen chair. His black fur was soft and warm under her fingers and was so much shinier now that he was having regular meals.

'We really need to talk about this habit of yours. Is it because I hid your scratching post in the spare room? I suppose we can move it somewhere else. In fact, I will do you a deal. No more playing with books and I will buy you a new toy mouse.'

Edgar pushed his nose into the air and gave her an unblinking stare through his amber eyes; the look that told her he wasn't a child who could be fobbed off with such things.

'Okay, but I'm serious about the books. You can't keep doing this.'

In answer Edgar wriggled out of her arms and swiped the upended training manual. One of his claws caught on the vinyl cover, slashing through the printed cover sheet that had been glued over it, exposing the cardboard underneath.

Harold would be furious.

She closed her eyes. No, he wouldn't, because he was no longer the library manager. And who knew when it would open again? Yet it didn't lessen her guilt. She wasn't the kind of person to wilfully destroy property. And even though Harold doubted Louisa or anyone else ever used it, she couldn't return it in such a damaged state.

Eric had a collection of glues that he'd used for making model planes, and it would be easy enough to type up a new cover sheet once the rip was repaired.

Shooing the cat to one side, Ginny inspected the damage. The blue vinyl had the name of the conference the folder was originally from splashed across the front of it, though some of the letters were faded with age, while at the top was an extra patch of blue vinyl that had been glued down like a plaster, suggesting she wasn't the first person to do a running repair on it.

'This thing must have more lives than you do,' she informed the cat, while smoothing down the vinyl to stop the puckering.

As she pressed, her fingers glided over a bump. She tried again. The slight rise felt like someone had inserted a coin between the cardboard and the vinyl cover.

Was that why the extra patch of blue vinyl had been added? To hide the incision mark? It seemed like a lot of trouble to go to just for a—

Ginny let out a gasp. What were Harold's exact words?

Then again, Louisa wasn't known for her love of learning. In other words, a training manual would be the last place anyone would expect her to hide something.

Ginny thought again of the damaged fingernail. That's what had led her into the stack in her search for the missing diary pages.

But had Louisa hidden something else there that day?

Heart pounding, she carefully pulled back the vinyl cover. And there it was. Pressed against the exposed cardboard of the ring binder was a tiny flash drive, not much bigger than a thumbnail.

Was this the missing file that so many people had died for?

And how had her cat known it was there?

She turned to Edgar, who merely licked his paw then padded to his cat door and disappeared outside. She would have to discuss it with him later. But now she had to see what was on there.

Her brother-in-law had helped Ginny upgrade her laptop before she moved, and she was grateful when the drive fitted into one of the slots along the side.

The file manager appeared on the screen.

There was only one folder: *Random Recipes.*

Ginny's finger hovered over the mouse. Would it really be recipes, or was that just a ruse? More concerning was whether there would be a password – which would surely be a safer way to protect it than just giving it a strange name. Or it could be blank, just like the one in Tom Allan's suit.

Only one way to find out.

Ginny clicked, almost surprised when the folder opened instantly, to reveal two items.

A spreadsheet and a video.

She opened the spreadsheet first, and she scanned the cells. There were multiple dates and names like Lewis Ryder Trust, Monkwell Grants, and Stevenson Family Charitable Foundation, along with significant sums of money. Next to them were short notes about the cemetery, historical society, and library renovations.

It took several moments for Ginny to realise she was looking at some of the parish council's previous funding applications, which included if they were successful and the dates money was received.

Altogether the amount came to almost two hundred thousand pounds. It was a lot of money, but she had no context for what it meant. Was this the money that Louisa had accused Sophie Hudson of stealing? Or was it what Sophie had found out while trying to clear her reputation?

Ginny opened the video and expanded the size, then pressed 'play'.

The screen was entirely black, but slowly the darkness began to break up into a grey-scaled flatness, accompanied by erratic moans and the faint hum and skitter of insects. The moans turned into grunts and lasted for several seconds before being replaced by muffled voices.

What was this?

She couldn't understand what was being said and the gloomy greys and blacks on the screen gave no indication as to what she was meant to be watching. Then there was a heavy plod of footsteps as the image altered and a thicket of glowing trees came into view.

'Damn thing was facing the wrong way,' a man's voice suddenly thundered through the speakers, making Ginny jump.

'Stop snorting like a little pig and come and help me get this bra back on,' a second person snapped. The voice was familiar, and Ginny frowned as the camera angle changed, and shakily swung around to show the half-dressed figure of a woman.

Louisa Farnsworth.

No.

Ginny's hand flew to her mouth as Louisa turned to the camera and gave the person holding it a cruel smile. Ginny longed to look away, to turn the computer off and try to decipher what it meant, but the other part of her brain refused to avoid the truth. She sucked in a breath as the video suddenly panned away from Louisa's face and returned to a blur of grayscales and shadows. It was quickly followed by a string of expletives and the sound of something hitting the ground.

Whoever had been holding the device had clearly dropped it. It was followed by a burst of rustling and muffled chatter until someone once again picked it up. And this time it panned back until it revealed the male speaker.

He was tall, with a thick neck and broad shoulders, and while she'd never met him, Ginny had seen enough photographs lately to know it was Tom Allan.

'Why are you in such a hurry?' Tom slurred, sounding drunk as he stood next to a tripod. 'Since we didn't manage to capture it properly the first time, I thought we could—'

'—try again? Because if that's what you think, you have rocks in your head,' Louisa's acid reply sounded from close by, making Ginny guess that she was now controlling the video. 'And next time you want to meet, you can damn well fork out for a four-star hotel.'

'I thought you liked being adventurous.' Tom flashed his teeth, white against the grainy darkness. 'Remember that—'

'Shhhhh!' Louisa cut him off with a hiss, and the camera abruptly shifted away from Tom's face and tilted upwards, displaying the dull half-light of a waxing gibbous moon hanging in the dark sky. It stayed in shot for several moments before panning over to a tangle of branches swaying in the wind. 'I heard something.'

'It was probably just a fox,' Tom muttered, though he'd lowered his voice. Judging by the moon, it must have been late at night, or even early in the morning, and they were clearly in a field or forest.

'Do you think I'm an idiot?' Louisa's voice dropped to a whisper, just as a beam of light appeared in the distance. The video angle changed again and it was clear Louisa was still holding the device. 'Look. Over there. Who was that?'

'Are you crazy? I'm not walking through this place at two in the bloody morning just to find out who's out here.'

'Yes, you are,' Louisa corrected him in a sarcastic undertone. 'Because if they parked in the same place we did, then they'll recognise your ostentatious car and registration plate.'

There was no answer, and the next few minutes were a soundscape of crunching leaves and soft footsteps, the video a blur of ground and sky as they walked. Then it stopped, and a faint outline of a person filled the screen.

The new arrival was lost beneath a long coat, with a hood pulled over their head. The video tracked them as they moved through the darkness, pulling a large lump behind them.

'What the hell? They're almost at the old quarry face. It's a thirty-foot drop.' Louisa hissed, as the camera clumsily zoomed into focus, showing the lump was, in fact, a rolled-up rug tied to a camping trolley. 'Why would anyone be dragging a piece of carpet around at this time of the morning? Don't tell me they're fly dumping.'

'Whatever they're dumping, they don't want to get caught.' Tom no longer sounded drunk as the person tilted the trolley forward, and the rolled-up rug slid off. As it disappeared into the darkness, the video did a sudden pan to where a pale hand was hanging out from one side of the rug.

Louisa's muffled expletive, caught on camera, confirmed Ginny's worst suspicions.

A glint of light suddenly gleamed in the image, revealing that on one finger was a delicate gold engagement ring. And then it was gone, followed moments later by a thud.

Ginny took a shuddering breath as she thought of the engagement ring Mitch wore on a chain around his neck. The one he'd given to Sophie just months before she committed suicide. And the quarry Louisa had been talking about must be Bluehead. The place where Sophie's body had been found.

A tear slid down Ginny's cheek as the cloaked figure came to a sudden stop and pushed back their hood. The camera tracked it all and as the face came into focus, Louisa and Tom both let out shocked gasps.

Ginny didn't blame them as she stared into the face of the Little Shaw Parish Council chairperson.

Marigold Bentley.

TWENTY-ONE

Bright sunlight stung her eyes as Ginny stepped out of Middle Cottage.

She'd watched the terrible video three more times, and it seemed so real that she'd almost forgotten it was ten o'clock in the morning. The tiny flash drive was in an envelope. Too late she'd realised it was yet more evidence that would be covered with her fingerprints, but that couldn't be helped.

It was the content that Wallace needed to see: proof that the death of Sophie Hudson had been at the hands of Marigold Bentley.

Marigold.

Ginny didn't want it to be true.

The chairperson had always been so lovely to her. She'd given her a job despite her age and lack of qualifications. And yet, the video was stark proof that there was a different side to her.

It's hard for people to understand just how difficult it is to keep things afloat.

Ginny assumed Marigold had been talking about the council, but that wasn't it at all. She'd been referring to the financial strain of maintaining her family home, and just how far she'd gone to do it.

Was that what Sophie had wanted to show Harold, before being called away to London instead?

And then what?

All Ginny could conclude was that Sophie had decided to confront Marigold about it first. Maybe to give her a chance to explain. It's what Ginny would've done – never thinking for a moment it would end in murder. But then came the next betrayal.

Tom and Louisa had caught it on video but hadn't turned it over to the police. Instead, they'd hidden it away. She could only think of one reason why.

It was the leverage used to convince Marigold and the council to sell Wilburton Reserve at a cut-rate price. And Bernard must have known about it as well.

Is that what this was all about? Revenge for Sophie Hudson's murder?

It made terrible sense. The three people who had known the truth about how Sophie died were now dead. And Marigold was lying in a hospital bed fighting for her life. It couldn't be a coincidence that they'd saved her until last. That's how revenge went, wasn't it? Cold. Clinical. Calculated.

But there were still so many unanswered questions.

None of which I'm capable of answering.

A brisk breeze danced down the street, sending a chill through Ginny's thin trousers and whipping her hair onto her cheeks as she pulled open Wallace's front gate.

'Good luck. He's in a foul mood.' The neighbour on Wallace's other side leaned over the privet separating the two properties. It was Hannah, the mother with four young boys, and next to her were several more people she recognised. 'Poor Billy was playing on the field behind the houses and kicked his football over Wallace's back wall. He nearly bit my head off when we knocked.'

'Well, he didn't get home until after two,' the woman from four doors down added. 'Looks like you've had a rough night and all.'

Ginny dropped her gaze. She was still wearing her dirty gardening clothes and hadn't even washed her face. Then again, she was sixty years old. What did it matter if she had a few smears of dirt on her jeans and no make-up to conceal the dark smudges under her eyes?

Without answering, she pressed the doorbell three times.

'If he does tell you anything, do let us know,' Hannah said, as the front door cracked open.

Wallace stood in the doorway. They'd been right about his mood.

His face was set into a fierce scowl and his eyes were hooded, due to lack of sleep. It was clear that he didn't think their new understanding included morning house calls. She couldn't blame him.

'What is it?' He glanced over at the neighbours, who'd suddenly become very interested in Hannah's rose bush.

'I'm sorry to disturb you, but it's important,' she said, aware they still had an audience.

'I can't discuss the case.' The last part was directed towards Hannah's house. But he stepped to one side and ushered her in.

It had a similar layout to her own, but while hers had been modernised, there were still remnants of old wallpaper, and dull floorboards that needed to be sanded and polished.

The sitting room was in a similar condition, with several paint pots lying around, along with plastic sheeting. It explained why he didn't have much time to garden if he was working on the inside.

'What's this about?' Wallace pulled back one of the plastic sheets to offer her a seat.

Ginny unsealed the envelope and passed it over, so he could see the tiny flash drive. 'You need to look at this. It's the missing digital files that the blackmailer was looking for. And what's behind the murders.' She half expected him to protest or demand to know more, but instead he just stared at it. 'What's wrong?'

'It's identical to the blank drive we found in Tom Allan's suit.'

Ginny swallowed. So, Louisa and Tom had both kept a copy as an insurance policy. It still didn't explain why Tom's copy had been wiped clean, but like everything else, she now accepted it wasn't her job to find the answers. She waited as Wallace reached for a laptop on the coffee table. He put it into the USB reader and pressed 'play'.

Ginny closed her eyes as Louisa and Tom's voices dragged her back through the terrible night yet again. It seemed to go on forever, and the hairs on her arm stood up. Next to her, Wallace was silent as the video finished. He watched it two more times before a soft thud told her he'd closed his screen. Swallowing deeply, she dared look at him.

His eyes were clouded with silent anger. It was clear he'd found it as deeply disturbing as she had. Though there was a flicker of relief as well. Because he knew it was the key to decoding the puzzle they'd all been trying to solve.

'Let's start at the beginning. Tell me where you found this.'

She walked him through the events, giving as much detail as she could remember. Once she'd finished, he fixed her with a hard stare.

'Who else knows about it?'

'No one. Only you. Trust me, I've learnt my lesson.'

'Good. And you do understand why you can't tell *anyone* about this until after we've started our enquiries.'

She nodded. He hadn't mentioned names, or told her what he was thinking, but it wasn't hard to guess.

Mitch Reeves. The one person she'd never considered, even though he'd admitted how much he blamed Louisa for what happened to Sophie. It was hard to imagine the same devastated man who'd sat in her kitchen with Edgar on his lap, killing so many people.

'How would he have found out about it?'

'My bet would be at the pub. You know the old saying, 'Loose lips sink ships.' Tom Allan wasn't always discreet when he'd had a few drinks. It's possible he drunkenly mentioned the flash drive... or something about Sophie.' Wallace rubbed his hand across his tired eyes.

'The fight.' Ginny let out a soft gasp as her conversation with Mitch came back to her. She shifted to face Wallace. 'Mitch told me that seven months ago Tom, Keris, Louisa and Bernard had all been at the pub together. But there had been an argument and Bernard and Keris had both walked out.'

'What about Louisa and Tom?'

'They stayed and kept drinking,' Ginny said, her mind all too easily picturing the scene. Tom and Louisa drunkenly talking and somehow mentioning what they'd seen that night, all while Mitch leaned over the bar, taking it all in. What then? Had he started to follow them both, determined to get proof?

Wallace must have been thinking along the same lines and he rubbed his chin. 'So Mitch decided to start following Tom Allan. Maybe that's how he found out about the flash drive? And after he viewed it, he began plotting revenge.'

Ginny grimly nodded. 'What about Louisa? Did he assume she had a copy as well, because he'd overheard them both talking about it?"

'It explains the blackmail attempts,' Wallace said, clearly too tired to remember he was discussing the case with a civilian. 'Heather bakes the bread in the pub kitchen, so he could easily have tampered with Louisa's order before it was delivered to Collin's Grocery. And Mitch threatened Louisa more than once that first year after Sophie's death. Back when he was drinking.'

A memory pushed at the corners of Ginny's mind, but when she tried to probe it, it dissolved into nothing.

Wallace narrowed his eyes. 'Mrs Cole... Ginny. If you have another theory, now's the time to tell me what it is.'

She pinched the bridge of her nose, but still the memory wouldn't come.

The last two weeks had taught her that her instincts were flawed. She had thought Bernard was guilty, and then Harold. As for Marigold... she'd liked her a lot. Trusted her. And what if she was wrong again? Would more people be hurt?

'No. Nothing that I can back up.' Ginny got to her feet. 'I'd better not keep you. I suppose you won't be painting today.'

He glanced around the half-finished room and shrugged. 'I suppose not. Still, the old man will be here in a few weeks and once he's pruned back that plum tree, I'm sure he'll give me a hand. And thank you for finding this. I know it can't have been easy for you to view, and if you would like some support, let me know. We have a great family liaison officer you can talk to.'

'That's very kind, but I'm okay. Now, I'll leave you to it. Hen, Tuppence and JM will be arriving any minute, and I'd hate for them to break through your front door searching for me.'

'Wouldn't be the first time – they'd broken through a front door, that is. But I meant what I said. Please don't mention this to anyone until I've given you permission. Our best chance of catching the killer is if he doesn't know we're coming.'

TWENTY-TWO

The following morning was warm, with just enough breeze to tug at the black, wide-brimmed hats so many of the women of Little Shaw had elected to wear as part of their funeral ensemble. There was a low hum of voices as familiar and unfamiliar faces slowly made their way past the gaping hole that was Louisa Farnsworth's final resting place.

As Nancy had predicted, Ginny hadn't felt up to the task of staying at home, but also couldn't bear to put on the same black dress and long coat she'd worn to Eric's cremation. Instead, she'd settled on a pair of wide-legged black trousers and a fitted jacket to hide the plain T-shirt underneath. At least she'd be comfortable.

'I'm pleased that's over,' JM said, as the last of the mourners filed away in the direction of the pub. She looked striking, in a man's tuxedo and white sneakers. 'I suppose it's good so many people turned up.'

'I bet half of them only came to see if they could catch Mitch sneaking in to watch her get buried. You know what they say about the killer always being close by.' Tuppence untangled the long fringe of her black shawl that kept getting caught in the heavy amber necklace she'd teamed it with.

'I can't believe our lovely Mitch was behind it all.' Hen's eyes glistened with tears as she fumbled around for a tissue, before realising she didn't have pockets in the black vintage beaded cardigan or taffeta skirt that she was wearing.

Ginny, who'd brought enough to cover them all, passed her one over.

'He's not our lovely Mitch anymore,' JM said in a stern voice, though she didn't look much happier than Hen.

True to her word, Ginny hadn't told her friends about the flash drive until eight o'clock the previous night, after Wallace had called to say it was being released to the media. He hadn't given her much else. Just that they'd searched Mitch's flat and the pub, but he hadn't been sighted since before Marigold's attack on Saturday.

And so, after she'd ended the call, Ginny had made a fresh pot of tea and told them everything.

Hen had burst into tears, Tuppence had started pacing the sitting room so many times that Edgar had taken refuge under the sofa, and JM had instantly asked if there was a copy of the video she could see. Ginny had shaken her head, pleased to spare them at least that.

Once they'd finished talking, they switched on the television to watch the press conference.

Wallace was wearing the same clothes he'd had on earlier in the day and his voice was flat as he announced a manhunt for Mitchell Reeves, who was wanted in connection with the recent murders in Little Shaw.

He then stared directly into the camera. '*He is considered armed and dangerous, and the public is advised not to get near him. We've increased the security at the hospital where Marigold Bentley is still in a serious but stable condition.*'

That had been last night. And by the time Ginny had

arrived at the church earlier, it was clear that news of the manhunt had spread as camera crews and journalists lined the street, which only added to the shocked conversations of onlookers.

'Do you think they'll go ahead with the wake?' Hen blew her nose as the last of the mourners trailed off towards the car park. 'Without Mitch, they'll be short-handed. Poor Rita and Heather – neither of them even came to the church.'

'Can you blame them? They both loved Mitch as much as we did,' JM said.

'They'd better not cancel the wake.' Tuppence looked alarmed. 'I haven't had an Eccles cake in far too long. Speaking of which, we should go soon if we don't want to miss out.'

'It's been two weeks, not two years,' JM reminded her.

'Time is merely a construct,' Tuppence said, as her phone buzzed with a text message. Ginny's began to ding, too, followed by JM's and then Hen's. Further ahead, there was a murmur of voices from the departing mourners, and several of the cameramen who had been camped at the gates began shouting, soon followed by the squealing of tyres.

The four women exchanged glances and JM unlocked her screen. She swore under her breath, then coughed and read the message out loud.

'Breaking news in the hunt for Mitchell Reeves, the man wanted in the recent murders at Little Shaw... blah, blah, blah, boring stuff... Right, here we are. Police received a tip off that Reeves had been spotted in Manchester. He was apprehended ten minutes ago, and it is believed he had the knife used in the attempted murder of Marigold Bentley with him. This is a developing story and will be updated as things unfold.'

The birdsong and rustle of insects formed a chorus as the four women stared at each other, trying to let the news sink in. So, it was over.

It was Tuppence who finally broke the silence. 'Now I *really* need an Eccles cake.'

'And Drambuie.' JM's jaw was tight. 'Maybe at the same time.'

'It's just so horrible.' Hen's eyes brightened with tears and the tiny beads on her cardigan chimed in response. 'Oh, here's Alyson.'

'I didn't think she was coming.' Tuppence frowned. 'She already boycotted Tom Allan's funeral and said she would be doing the same for Louisa and Bernard... whenever his body is released.'

'She's only here to say goodbye.' Hen dabbed at her eyes. 'She's going to visit friends in Newcastle. It might help clear her head. I know it's for the best, but I can't help but wish she'd stay here so I could make sure she's okay.'

Ginny pressed her lips together. Now wasn't the time to admit that she could fully understand Alyson's need to get away and clear her mind. She could use some help with that herself.

She hadn't told her friends about the call with Nancy, and the house that had come up for sale. Nor had she been able to give her sister-in-law an answer about whether Ginny wanted to make an offer on it. How could she, when she didn't know the answer herself?

As Alyson got closer, it was easy to see the difference a couple of nights back in her own bed had made: her brown hair was freshly washed and hung around her shoulders, and there was a faint glow in her cheeks. Most importantly, the despair that had clung to her was gone.

'I take it you heard the news.' Alyson hugged them one by one, then dabbed at her own eyes. 'I know I should be happy, but poor Mitch. We often talked about the pain of losing someone you love – even though, in my case, Bernard hadn't died. He'd just fallen out of love with me. But I hadn't realised just how deep his despair had gone.'

'None of us did, love.' Hen squeezed her daughter's hand. 'And you can't keep blaming yourself.'

'I know, Mum. And I'm not... well... I'm trying not to.'

'We're about to go to the wake. Are you sure you don't want to come for a few minutes?' Tuppence said, her mind still clearly on the Eccles cakes.

'No. I'm only here to say goodbye.' She gave Hen a long hug before doing the same to JM and Tuppence. Then she touched Ginny's hand. 'Would you mind if we talk for a few minutes?'

'Of course.'

'We can wait for you by the car,' Hen said.

Ginny shook her head. 'That's okay. You go on ahead and I'll walk over. It's only ten minutes away.'

'If you're sure,' Hen said, before they disappeared in the same direction as the other mourners.

Alyson silently toed the overgrown grass, before finally speaking. 'You disappeared from the pub on Saturday, and I didn't get a chance to properly thank you. If you hadn't come along, I might still be in jail.'

'It wasn't just me. It was all of us. Hen most of all. She was beside herself with worry. She loves you so much.'

'And I love her.' Alyson bowed her head, dark hair swinging forward. 'That's why I need to get away for a few weeks. I hadn't realised what a burden I'd become on her. I wasted five years hoping Bernard would come back. It's like I've just woken up from a trance. But I'm determined to make the most of this second chance. Who knows, I might even go on a date.'

There was a lightness to her voice, and Ginny had a glimpse of what Alyson had been like before the divorce. *Or, maybe, before her marriage?*

'Whoever you pick will be a very lucky person.' Ginny squeezed her hand and Alyson blushed.

'We'll see. Anyway, I'd better head off. Can I give you a lift to the pub?'

'No, it's fine. The walk will do me good.'

'Okay, well, I'm parked at the other entrance. I figured it wouldn't be as busy. But thank you again for your help.'

After Alyson had disappeared, Ginny slowly made her way to the main gate, the other woman's words jostling in her mind. *I hadn't realised what a burden I'd become.*

Was that what Ginny would become if she stayed?

It was a grim thought, and her chest tightened as she walked past row after row of neglected gravestones. Another reminder of Marigold Bentley's legacy.

Sophie Hudson's headstone came into view.

Much like the last time Ginny had been there, the grass was neat and tidy and there were no marks on the headstone. But the dahlias had been replaced by pink roses and there was a small card tucked down the side. From where she stood, his boyish block print read:

MISS YOU ALWAYS. LOVE MITCH.

There was a poignancy in the simple phrase that brought a lump to Ginny's throat. Had he visited his fiancée one last time before he went on his final mission to kill Marigold Bentley? Did he talk to Sophie like Ginny talked to Eric? Tell her what he planned... and what he'd already done?

There was that niggle again, the one that had been tugging at her subconscious since she'd found the video. But she didn't bother to try to catch it this time: she'd done quite enough interfering for one lifetime.

And it helped her make the decision she'd been wrestling with. When she got home from the pub, she'd call Nancy and ask her to go and view the house.

The wooden tables outside The Lost Goat were full of people, and music was seeping out of the front doors, along with a sea of voices. The wake was clearly still going strong, and her dread of having to go inside to look for her friends was solved when she spied them standing by the door. They waved her over.

'Are you okay? You look pale. Do you need some water?' Hen's eyes were wide as she clutched a water bottle.

'I saved you an Eccles cake.' Tuppence held up a small box.

'Stop fussing. Poor Ginny is out of breath from her walk. She needs to sit down for a moment,' JM announced, before marching over to a table where several young men were drinking. She leaned down and whispered something, and a moment later they were gone. She gave her friends a cherubic smile. 'Oh, look, this one is free.'

'What did you say to them?' Hen settled herself at the table and pushed the towers of empty pint glasses to one side before extracting her knitting needles from her large handbag.

'Nothing you need worry about.' JM opened her tuxedo jacket to reveal a bottle of wine, and Tuppence opened the box containing the Eccles cake, which also had five wine glasses nestled in there.

Despite her heaviness, Ginny had to smile. Her friends really were resourceful.

'We got an extra one for Alyson in case she changed her mind.'

'She wanted to avoid the traffic,' Ginny explained, as JM poured the wine. 'I can't blame her for wanting to miss it, considering everything she's been through.'

'I agree. It's hectic inside,' Tuppence said, as a loud cheer came from the pub. 'Rita and Heather have been running around like they're possessed. Look, they haven't even changed the sign since Monday.'

They all turned to it. *Wine flies when you're having fun.*

'Poor thing. I can't remember ever seeing the same quote twice in a month,' JM said, as Heather appeared in the doorway, clutching a large wire tray to collect the empty glasses. Her purple hair was messily gathered at the top of her head and her brow had a light layer of sweat. JM waved her over.

'Sorry about the mess.' Heather stacked the empty pint glasses the previous occupants had left behind. 'It's been non-stop.'

'I can imagine. Would you like me to do the sign for you?' JM offered. 'I have excellent handwriting.'

Heather's brow puckered as she glanced over to the chalk-board. She groaned. 'So many things keep slipping through the cracks. I almost forgot to order lettuce yesterday, and Rita dropped a whole tray of glasses this morning. Anyway, thanks for the offer, but Rita hates anyone else doing it. Says it adds to the personal charm.'

JM didn't look convinced but waited until Heather had moved to the next table before leaning in. 'Personal charm, my foot. Some days it's barely legible.'

'She is under a lot of stress. Look at the way some of the letters are smudged,' Hen reasoned.

Ginny frowned as the niggle that had been floating around in her head since yesterday suddenly exploded in her head. 'The handwriting!' she gasped, as she stared at the chalkboard. 'That's what was missing!'

'What are you talking about?' Tuppence, who had lifted her glass to her mouth, paused it midway.

'I've seen Mitch's handwriting twice. Once when he installed the cat door, and then earlier today at the cemetery. It's blocky, and he writes in capital letters. But I know this hand-writing.' She jerked her chin at the chalkboard, and then groaned. 'Why didn't I see it before?'

'Wait... you don't think it's the same as the blackmail letter?' Tuppence whispered, as Ginny unlocked her phone and scrolled through her photographs until she found the ones she needed.

She held it up for them. 'The left-handed smudge... and

look at the cursive with the flourish on the 'f'. It's almost identical to the chalkboard.'

'But why? Rita didn't even move here until after Sophie died! Mitch told us that Sophie's parents are dead and she had no other relations.'

'But we didn't check, and we could have so easily.' JM fumbled with her phone and began to stab at the screen. 'I have the genealogy software, remember? Now, let's see, we know Sophie's full name, so let's start there.'

Ginny's heart pounded in her chest as JM worked.

'Okay, here we go. Her mother was Moira Janine Hudson, née Kennedy, born in 1965,' she read out, before looking up at them all, eyes wide. 'There's no death certificate. Sophie's mother isn't dead.'

They all stared at each other.

Rita Kennedy.

Hen gasped. 'She didn't even try and hide her maiden name.'

'But what about the cancer Sophie's mum had?' Tuppence had picked up the Eccles cake but now put it down again.

'She must have recovered and come to Little Shaw to get her revenge. Trying to right the wrongs that had been done. By killing the three people who used her daughter's murder to make money. And the one at the very centre of it,' JM announced.

'Except Marigold isn't dead, and now that Mitch has been caught, they've probably lowered the security at the hospital.' Ginny's voice shook as the missing pieces shifted into place. She got to her feet and scanned the crowd. 'Where is Rita? Has anyone seen her? We need to tell the police.'

JM stood, using her height to look around. 'She's not out here. Tuppence and I will check inside. Hen, you can cover the kitchen and the beer garden at the back. Ginny, you call Wallace. He's most likely to listen to you.'

She waited until her three friends had disappeared into the pub before she brought up his number.

'This is Wallace. Don't leave a message because I don't check them. If it's an emergency call 999.'

His voice mail was abrupt as he was, and Ginny jabbed the keypad, to try PC Singh and the local police station. But each time there was no answer. Her head pounded. Should she call the hospital? But what if that made it worse? They could think she was a hoax, and it might end up being a dangerous distraction. She tried Wallace again and, despite his message, she told him exactly what they'd discovered. She did the same for Anita and then sent them both a text.

Connor had been right about always having her phone with her. *If only he'd told Wallace and Anita the same thing.*

Hen appeared several minutes later, her cheeks red and flushed. Ginny abandoned the table and hurried over.

'She wasn't there. What did JM and Tuppence say?'

'They haven't come back,' Ginny said, as Esme and Elsie shuffled out of the door, a large box of sandwiches and cakes balanced on a shopping trolley. 'Where could they be?'

'Do you mean JM and Tuppence?' Esme asked.

'That's right. Did you see them?'

'Hard to miss them. That JM is so tall and running around like she was. As for Tuppence, she walked straight around the back of the bar and into the office out the back. I think she was looking for Rita,' Esme said. 'Which was when Heather told them Rita was outside. So they went out to find her, and they all drove off together,' Elsie added.

'What?' The colour drained from Hen's face and Esme patted her arm.

'It's okay, duck. I think they were just taking Rita home. She's not dealing with the Mitch thing well.'

'Are you absolutely sure they drove off with her?'

'Oh, yes. Rita had been watching the smorgasbord like a

hawk. Which is why I followed her out. You see, we wanted to take a few treats home. Makes all the difference on the pension.'

'Th-thank you. We'd better not keep you,' Ginny managed to say, before tucking her arm through Hen's and moving away. There was a sick feeling in her stomach as she pictured what Rita must have seen. JM and Tuppence had clearly been looking for something... or someone. She had probably watched them the whole time as they searched the pub before deciding to act.

'Why would they go with her like that?' Hen's voice was hoarse.

'I don't think they did it willingly. Maybe they followed her to the car, and she overpowered them. She's very strong from all the beer kegs.' Ginny tried not to panic.

'But why? D-do you think she'll hurt them?'

'I'm sure they're safe. Her focus will be on Marigold.' Ginny pushed down her wayward thoughts, but it wasn't easy. Rita had proved that she was willing to turn on anyone who she thought had betrayed her daughter. Did the four of them fall into that category?

And Ginny most of all. After all, she was the one who'd first pointed out the Mees' lines on Louisa's nails. Thereby arguably setting off this whole chain of events.

And what about Marigold? She was still in hospital, recovering from stab wounds. If Rita was to try and kill her again—

'You're right. But what should we do?' Hen's eyes were huge in her face.

'We need to go to the hospital. Will you be okay to drive?'

'The hospital, of course. That's what I'd do if I was an enraged killer.' Hen took a shuddering breath. 'Yes, I'm quite a good driver, as it goes. Adam used to tease me I could've been a getaway driver if I'd wanted to have a life of crime. Usually, I try not to go too fast. It's the speeding tickets, you understand?'

Ginny did.

Like Hen, she'd never done anything to get in trouble or break the rules. She was only ever in the background, going about her business with the minimum of fuss and bother. Yet, since she'd moved to Little Shaw, she'd found a dead body, dug up a grave, saved a man from burning to death, and now here she was trying to stop a not-so-innocent woman from being murdered.

'I think we're going to need to speed,' she said, as they climbed into Hen's little car. In the backseat were several boxes of knitted bird nests, and a dog blanket for Brandon.

Hen slipped on some leather driving gloves, before revving the engine. 'Well then, buckle up.'

TWENTY-THREE

True to her word, Hen proved to be an excellent driver, even if Ginny's knuckles were white by the time the hospital came into sight. She'd continued to leave messages for Wallace and Anita, and at the local police station, but there was still no answer.

Hen pulled up outside the front entrance of Trenton Hall Hospital, engine idling as patients came and went.

'Do you know what Rita's car looks like?' Ginny asked, not sure if she wanted to see it or not. If it was there, it meant they were in the right place. But if it wasn't, it meant Rita had taken their friends somewhere else.

'It's a yellow Transit van.' Hen peered around from behind the driver's wheel. She then let out an agonised sigh. 'Look, I see it. There's no sign of Rita, but if she did kidnap JM and Tuppence, they might be in the back. Should we go there first?' Indecision danced in her large eyes.

Ginny leaned over and wrapped an arm around her shoulder. 'You go and check on them. They might need medical help and, if so, we're in the perfect place. I'll go inside. I know what Marigold did was terrible, but we can't let anyone else die.'

'Of course not.' Hen returned the embrace and then wiped

away her tears. 'But how will you get into ICU? They usually only let family through.'

'I'm sure I'll figure out something.' Ginny climbed out of the car and Hen drove into the main car park at a more sedate speed, leaving Ginny alone.

She stepped into the foyer and looked around. A security guard manned the elevator door, and there was a second one at the far end of the reception desk, a bank of screens in front of him. Should she go over to them? But what if they didn't believe her? The thought kept her frozen to the spot. She couldn't risk it.

So, what then?

A group of nurses drifted towards the elevator, and a porter with tired eyes pushed an empty wheelchair across the floor. The *click, click, click* of the wheels and the light chatter created a rhythmic beat that melted through the tension in her shoulders, leaving her calm and almost relaxed. She wasn't a doctor or even a nurse, but she'd spent over half her life quietly helping people. And that's all she was doing now. Helping someone.

She walked to the lifts and stepped into the first one. Two doctors were already in there and she gave them a placid smile, before scanning the directory. They ignored her and carried on with their conversation as the doors slid shut.

ICU was on the third floor and Ginny's heart pounded as the lift slowly rose up through the levels. Finally, the doors opened at the third floor.

The doctors stepped out first and she followed them calmly, not trying to increase her step or look like she was lost. And she wasn't. Unlike Harold's ward, the arrows on this one were red and she simply followed them until a small reception counter came into view.

There were two women there, but they were lost in conversation, so Ginny continued to walk until she was out of view.

She'd done it. But now she had to find which room Marigold was in and hope that she wasn't too—

A clatter of wheels rang out from down the corridor as a nurse, who was pushing a trolley, came to a stop outside one of the rooms. She was wearing a mask over her mouth, and her hair was caught in a hairnet. Even her hands were covered in plastic gloves, but in her earlobes were two large gold hoops.

Rita.

Ginny's chest heaved as the publican turned the door handle and disappeared inside. Trying not to panic, she increased her pace until she reached the trolley. She still had no idea what she was going to do. Probably because she'd kept hoping to hear the police sirens overtaking them on the way to the hospital, or for Wallace or Singh to call her back. But it hadn't happened.

The door handle was cool to touch as she cracked it open and peered inside.

A hospital bed was in the middle of the room and beneath the crumple of sheets and tubes was Marigold Bentley. Her eyes were shut and there were multiple grazes on her face. The nearby monitors flashed and beeped as the machines they were attached to kept her alive.

Rita was standing next to an IV drip, a pillow gripped tightly in one hand as she used the other to claw at Marigold's shoulder, any pretence of being a nurse now gone. 'Wake up, you cow. Wake up. I want you to see my face. I want you to know who I am, and what you took from me.'

Marigold didn't move, but Ginny thought she saw her left arm twitch under the weight of the sheets. Had she regained consciousness before now? The hospital wouldn't give out information like that, which meant Rita wouldn't know either.

Taking a breath, Ginny stepped into the room. 'She's in an induced coma. Though there's research to suggest she might be able to hear,' she said, hoping to shock Rita into stepping away.

It didn't work, and all the landlady did was glance at her before snatching up the medical chart lying on the bed. 'Induced coma? You think I'm an idiot?' Her eyes flashed with darkness and her mouth twisted into a bitter line. 'Cancer. Remember? I can find my way around these medical notes as well as a specialist these days. Then I had to watch my Mark fade away before my eyes as the doctors tried to work out what was wrong with him. But there's no tick box on any of these charts for a broken heart. And as for our good friend, Marigold... well... she was awake and conscious an hour ago according to this thing. So, she can pretend to be asleep as much as she wants, but I'm still going to kill her.'

'It won't bring your daughter back. As hard as this is to hear, Sophie's gone, Moira. This won't change it.'

'Don't you *dare* say her name!' Rita jabbed the air with the pillow and took a step forward. 'You have no right. No right to even be here trying to ruin everything. If you knew what they did to my angel, you would understand.'

Ginny moved to one side, determined to draw her away from the hospital bed. All she had to do was act as a distraction until help arrived. *If it arrived.*

'I do know. And it was terrible. But is this what Sophie would want?'

'I told you not to say her name.' Rita let out a furious snarl that made the hairs on Ginny's arms prickle. 'You don't get to do that. I'm her mother. And *she* has to pay. It's only right.'

'Of course she does. But that's not your job. Please, Moira. The police are on their way, and Marigold will go to jail for what she did.' Ginny edged her way around the wall until she was pressed up against the window.

'Jail? Oh, no... there will be no jail for this one. That was never the plan.'

'What was the plan, then? Why did you wait all this time?'

'Why? Why? You think I wanted to drag it out?' Rita began

to shake but she gritted her teeth, trying to push down whatever rage wanted to come up. It seemed to work, and she stopped moving. She was almost like a statue as the pillow fell from her hand.

Behind her Marigold's shoulders shifted. Ginny stiffened, willing Rita not to turn back around to the bed. 'You tell me. Four years is a long time.'

'It's an eternity. I was ready to rip that village to shreds to find out what happened to my girl. But for the amount of gossiping those people do, I still couldn't find the truth. And the investigators I paid were no better. Told me that as far as they could see it really had been suicide. But it was lies. They were all lying.'

'I'm so sorry,' Ginny sympathised, but Rita just glared at her.

'Sorry? You think I want your pity? Please. I don't want anyone's pity. I just want revenge. And the only way to get it was to move to the place that did this to my daughter. So, I did what I know best. I bought the pub. Had to convince the previous owner to sell it, of course. And then, I waited. You see, the bigger the secret, the more heavily it weighs on the soul. And when people drink...'

'Loose lips sink ships,' Ginny said, and Rita gave a curt nod. So, Wallace had been right.

'It took longer than I'd hoped. But seven months ago, Tom Allan let something spill. He mentioned his back-up plan and how it made him untouchable. Let's just say I made it my business to... touch him.'

'*You* were the one having an affair with him?' Ginny's spine went rigid.

'How the hell do you know about that?' Rita scowled before collecting herself. 'No matter. You'll soon learn that you shouldn't stick your nose into my business. But, yes, I had an affair. It was the only way to find out what I needed to know.

And I did… I found—' She broke off and grief swept across her face.

Ginny couldn't help but feel for her. No parent should have to witness that video. See firsthand what Marigold had done.

'It has to stop, Rita.'

'Oh, I agree. That's why I'm flying out of Manchester this afternoon, straight to Alicante, where I intend to relax and enjoy myself.'

'You won't get away with it.' Ginny stared at her, remembering their conversation at the pub. What had she said?

They're probably sunning themselves on a beach somewhere, having a fine old time of it.

Rita had been talking about herself.

'Won't get away with it?' Rita mocked before breaking into a cool smile and taking another step forward. 'But I already have. I just have a few loose ends to tie up before justice is fully served. Marigold. You. Those friends of yours who are waiting in my van. Once you're all gone, there's nothing standing in my way.'

Ginny's head began to swim at the vision of JM and Tuppence tied up in the back of the black vehicle. She hoped that Hen had managed to get to them.

'Was it justice to set Alyson Farnsworth up? Or Mitch?'

A shadow of doubt crossed the woman's face, but she shook it off. 'Alyson Farnsworth only has herself to blame. It was pathetic the way she moped after Bernard. And all the public fights she had with Louisa… she almost handed herself to me gift-wrapped. *Not* that it was my preferred plan. Louisa was meant to die like Tom Allan. Just a tragedy, thanks to an inherited heart condition. But *you* put a stop to that.' She jabbed a finger at Ginny's chest. 'Just lucky I had plans in place.'

'You stole Alyson's stationery and found the letter she wrote in therapy. Let me guess… you were the one who sent her a text message, pretending to be Bernard wanting to meet her in Liverpool on the same day you killed Tom.'

'What can I say? I'm a details person.'

'What about Mitch? Did he know who you were?'

'Of course he didn't. He was too stupid to even notice. To think Sophie might have married such a spineless sap. She was killed on *his* watch, and all he did was drown his sorrows and wear that bloody ring around his neck. She deserved so much better.'

'So why give him a job then?' Ginny gripped her handbag and held it up as a barrier to stop Rita getting closer. Her legs felt like lead, as if something was freezing her from the inside, stopping her from moving.

'Because I thought he'd be able to *help* me. But it soon became clear he was useless. He couldn't even die when I wanted him to.'

'What?' Ginny gasped. 'You tried to kill him as well?'

'You're not as smart as you think you are. Mitch was meant to die in the fire with Marigold. A tragic murder suicide. But I had to make some last-minute adjustments thanks to the neighbour. I needed to get the police off my back... and away from this place. So, I dumped him in Manchester. You should have seen how fast Wallace sped off in that stupid car of his.'

Ginny's stomach plummeted. There had been part of her that hoped Wallace would be close enough to get to the hospital in time. But Manchester was over thirty miles away, even without the traffic. Rita must have read her expression.

'What? You didn't think he was coming to rescue you, did you?' Spittle flew from her mouth as she stretched out her arm. The ropey muscles from years of changing kegs flexed as her fingers wrapped around Ginny's neck.

'*Eric, what should I do, love?*' The words were a whisper in her head, still part of the habit that she couldn't break. '*I can't move, and I don't know how to fix this.*'

'*Oh, Gin. When was there anything you couldn't fix, when you put your mind to it? That's why I fell in love with you.*'

Eric? Her chest tore open at the sound of his voice. But instead of the familiar pain that lived there, laughter bubbled up like a spring, spreading through her.

Now he answered her.

After all those months of sitting at home staring at his chair, he picked this moment to say something. She laughed harder, as if suddenly remembering how to breathe, and the weights that had been tethering her feet to the ground dissolved.

'You think this is funny?' Rita's face contorted as if she'd been slapped.

It was all the time Ginny needed, and she darted around to the other side of the bed and reached for the medical chart. Her hand tightened on it as Marigold Bentley slowly opened her eyes, her gaze focused on Rita.

'Moira... I'm sorry.' She spoke slowly, painfully, as tears poured down her face. 'I really am. It was an accident. Sh-she came to me and accused me of stealing. I tried to make her understand that I was just borrowing the money. Of course I intended to pay it back. B-but she wouldn't listen, and—'

'You cow,' Rita howled, but before she could lunge, Ginny snatched for the nurse button that had been covered by the medical chart and pressed it repeatedly.

Rita's face froze as the sound of footsteps came from the corridor outside. 'No! I will not let you kill me as well as my daughter!' she screamed and then bolted for the door, where she almost collided with Wallace, closely followed by JM, Tuppence and Hen. 'No! You don't understand. She must pay,' Rita sobbed, as Wallace dragged her arms behind her back and put her in handcuffs. 'Let me go.'

The three women flung their arms around Ginny, all talking at once, and she laughed harder as she was smothered in a hug of scarves and coats and bags... and friendship.

'I think not,' Wallace growled, before turning to Ginny. 'Are you okay? Did she do anything to you or Marigold?'

Ginny managed to detach herself from her friends and shook her head. 'I'm okay... and I think Marigold is unharmed. But how are you here? Shouldn't you be in Manchester? She dumped Mitch there and tipped off the police, to make sure the coast was clear.'

'I was halfway down the M6 when I had a feeling something didn't add up, so I turned around. But it wasn't until I got back to Little Shaw that I saw your messages. The police in Manchester called to say that Mitch Reeves had been drugged and kidnapped and they'd taken him to hospital to recover.'

'Where he is currently in a stable condition.' PC Singh had hurried into the room, closely followed by a barrage of nurses. 'Did we make it in time? Is she still alive?'

'She is, but we should leave the medical team to check her.' Wallace propelled a still struggling Rita outside to the hallway and thrust her down into a chair. 'PC Singh, keep an eye on her while I go through what happened. Mrs Cole, can you please explain why we're here?'

'This is Sophie Hudson's mother, Moira,' Ginny said, the warmth from Eric's voice still with her.

Wallace let out a sharp breath, and she could almost see his quick mind rearranging the puzzle pieces, just like she'd done.

'Are you saying she moved here looking for answers?'

'Yes, and revenge. That's why she bought the pub. You were right about people talking too much when they're drunk. She overheard Tom Allan boast about his back-up plan, so started an affair with him to find out what it was. Then after she saw the video footage...'

'You can't prove anything,' Rita snapped.

'No, but there's a barman in Liverpool who can. He remembers Tom being there with a woman in her mid-fifties. They had a huge fight and checked out separately the next morning. I'm

sure if you go through their CCTV footage you will find
evidence of Moira packing Tom's body into his car and driving
it into the flooding.'

'She's very strong. She managed to drag me and JM into the
back of her van and tie us up.' Tuppence held up her wrists to
show the red, raw skin. Ginny shuddered at what might have
happened to her friends if Moira hadn't been caught.

Wallace pinched the top of his nose. 'Let's assume that
night in Liverpool was when she found the video. And that
after seeing it, she lost her temper and killed Tom instantly.'

'He deserved what he got. So did Louisa and Bernard,' Rita
hissed.

'What about Heather? She was meant to be your friend, yet
you tampered with her baking. Did you even care that she
might have been arrested instead of Alyson? And Harold Rowe.
That's the one thing I can't understand,' JM said.

'I can.' Ginny recalled Rita's broken expression when she
mentioned the video. 'She was looking for the extra flash drive.
That's why she sent the blackmail note to Louisa. Because she
didn't want anyone else to see it.'

'Do you have any idea what it's like to know that people
might watch that? To casually watch my daughter's dead body
being dragged around in a roll of carpet? I searched her house
multiple times and most of the library. But the only place I
couldn't get access to was the back of the library. Then Harold
came into the pub for a historical society meeting. I slipped the
keys out of his jacket and had them all copied. I went in the
next night but was interrupted before I could find the video. I
wasn't sure if Harold recognised me, but I couldn't take the
chance, so I set it on fire. After all, if it was burnt to the ground,
then the film would be destroyed.'

'Along with an innocent man,' Ginny gasped, but Rita just
shrugged.

Wallace rubbed a hand through his hair as he looked from

Ginny to Tuppence, to JM and then Hen. 'It seems I owe you all an apology.'

'Oh, that's rich. Where is *my* apology?' Rita snapped. 'All of this is your fault. My daughter's death happened right under your nose, and you didn't do a thing about it.'

'That's not true.' Ginny straightened her spine. 'His job is a lot harder than it looks, and a lesser detective would never admit if they were wrong.'

PC Singh's mouth twitched with a smile and Wallace let out a pained sigh. 'Yes, well, thank you, Mrs Cole. I think we can take it from here.'

'I told you, call me Ginny.'

TWENTY-FOUR

Two months later

'Take this book and go and read it to them.'

'Read it out loud?' Connor's mouth dropped as he peered past Ginny's shoulder to the group of mothers gathered in the brightly lit corner. Most of them were settled on the new sofas JM had convinced Edward Tait to donate to the library, while the many toddlers were sprawled on the colourful rugs and bean bags, all waiting eagerly for story time. Then he grinned. 'Just joking. I've been practising it all week.'

'Just like I knew you would.' Ginny smiled as Connor made his way over to the blue wingback chair that had once been in her sitting room.

He sat down and leaned forward, his gaze sweeping over the tiny audience. 'Right, you lot. You ready for the greatest adventure tale *ever* told?'

The children let out a loud cheer, as did some of the older listeners, like Esme and her sister Elsie, who had commandeered one of the sofas further back, not wanting to miss out on what was quickly becoming one of the most popular library sessions.

Ginny headed to the counter, hoping to finish installing the new health and safety software they'd started using.

No one had been more surprised than she had been when Harold Rowe – the newly elected Little Shaw Parish Council chairperson – turned up on her doorstep and asked her to become the library manager.

Even more surprising, Ginny had found herself saying yes, but only on the condition her old position was offered to Connor, if he would like it.

And so, here they were, two months later.

'No, Tuppence, it won't fit through like that. Here, let me do it,' JM's disembodied voice sounded out from near the front door. Then she appeared, dragging a large tree trunk along behind her. She was closely followed by Tuppence, who was herding it in like a sheepdog, while Hen made up the rearguard, arms full of knitted bird nests.

Ginny's lips tugged into a smile as she directed them over to the community space so they could set up the new display. She'd already arranged a large circle of chairs for the many sign-ups they'd had, eager to learn how to knit the nests themselves.

'Oh, look, is that Connor reading? How lovely. And you've convinced him to try wearing a different colour. Well done.' Hen beamed.

JM squinted. 'That hoody looks black to me.'

'Nonsense, it's dark navy,' Tuppence corrected. 'Now, let's get this thing set up. And don't forget we're meeting at the pub later to talk about starting up a new Neighbourhood Watch group now that Wallace doesn't see us as a public menace anymore.'

'Menace? We were hardly a menace,' JM corrected. 'We were an integral part of the investigation.'

'He really is very nice,' Hen said, in that comfortable voice of hers. 'I'm sure that next time something crops up, he'll be happy to ask for our help.'

Ginny wasn't sure she'd go that far, but that was okay. She was quite happy with the way her new life had turned out, and that was as much as anyone could ask for.

A LETTER FROM THE AUTHOR

Huge thanks for reading *The Widows' Guide to Murder*. I hope you were hooked on Ginny's journey. If you want to join other readers in hearing all about my new releases and bonus content, you can sign up for my newsletter.

www.stormpublishing.co/amanda-ashby

If you enjoyed this book and could spare a few moments to leave a review that would be hugely appreciated. Even a short review can make all the difference in encouraging a reader to discover my books for the first time. Thank you so much.

I was ten years old when I read Trixie Belden for the first time, and I've been a mystery fan ever since. So, I'm thrilled to finally be writing my own ones. Like Ginny, I have also worked in a library, and been a volunteer manager, so it's been an absolute joy to throw a bit of my own life into the mix. Though unlike Ginny and her friends, Hen, Tuppence and JM, I have sadly never snuck through graveyards in the middle of the night or got myself muddled up in a murder investigation. And since I would hate to deprive them of fun, I'll leave the sleuthing to them while I sit in my pyjamas and cheer them on.

Thanks again for being part of this amazing journey with me and I hope you'll stay in touch – I have so many more stories and ideas to entertain you with!

Amanda xoxo

KEEP IN TOUCH WITH THE AUTHOR

www.amandaashby.com

instagram.com/authoramandaashby

ACKNOWLEDGEMENTS

As always, I need to give a heartfelt thank you to Sally Rigby and Christina Phillips, who have been at my side from the very beginning. And to Rachel Bailey who never fails to untangle the random plots that float around in my mind and help make them fit for human consumption. I also need to give a shout-out to my beautiful friends Juliet, Katherine and Isabelle, who never seem to mind that I spend half my time plotting murder.

I'm also grateful to all the facilitators and flockers at Flown.com. You've all taught me a new way of showing up at my desk – and staying there. This book was written with your support.

And now we get to the team at Storm. I'd like to thank Kathryn Taussig for the utterly brilliant early notes that helped shaped this new series. And to Emily Gowers, who made me smile from the moment we met, and seemed to perfectly understand everything I was trying to do and say. I feel so lucky to have found my way to the perfect editor! Thank you so much to Alexandra Holmes for keeping the wheels turning and Belinda Jones, whose copyediting and all-around brilliance has been a gift. I'd also like to thank Emily Courdelle for the stunning cover, that had the power to leave me speechless. And a big thank you to everyone else at Storm, who has worked so hard to make this book come to life.

To Pam for continuing to tell her book club that I'm an author, and even making them read some of those books. To Nick and Liz for showing me the many ways to navigate a creative life. To my kids... and of course the cat. Sorry for the burnt meals. And finally, to Barry. I've spent years disappearing into my study and living in my head. Thank you for always being there when I come back out.

Printed in Great Britain
by Amazon